THE
SINNER

EMMA SCOTT

PLAYLIST

Voodoo // Godsmack (opening credits)
Scared to Live // The Weeknd
Devil Inside // INXS
Lady in Red // Chris de Burgh
Follow You // Imagine Dragons
Underneath It All // No Doubt (feat. Lady Saw)
Sympathy for the Devil // The Rolling Stones
exile // Taylor Swift (feat. Bon Iver)
all the good girls go to hell // Billie Eilish
Thistles & Weeds // Mumford & Sons
Thinking Out Loud // Ed Sheeran (closing credits)

AUTHOR'S NOTE

The concepts of life, death, and what happens in between, which are described in this novel, are purely my imagination and not intended to be interpreted as advocating for or disproving any existing religion. I don't have that sort of authority anyway; the mysteries of the universe will remain mysteries until the moment we each take our turn stepping into the unknown. This novel is my way of exploring those mysteries to better understand certain events in my life and for the pure pleasure of letting my imagination run wild. This book is also my heartfelt ode to the romance novel and to the dreamers and romantics (romance readers) who understand the value and power of love stories.

CONTENT WARNING

Please note that this book contains content that may be triggering for some sensitive readers such as the death of a family member, graphic violence, and mention of miscarriage (off the page). It is my sincerest hope I have treated these issues with the care they deserve. Intended for readers 18 and up.

GLOSSARY

Angel: A soul who manifests benevolent energy

Anicorpus: The animal form a demon takes to move more freely on This Side. Not to be confused with Familiar. (see: Familiar)

Archduke of Hell: High-ranking demon

Babylonian Empire: An empire that dominated the Mesopotamia region between the 19th and 15th centuries BCE and again between the 7th and 6th centuries BCE

Before Common Era (BCE): Recorded history leading up to Year 0

Brethren, The: Twelve high-ranking demons who serve directly under Archduke Casziel and command his legions

Common Era (CE): Year 0 to present

Crossing Over: Moving between This Side and the Other, usually by dying. Only powerful demons can move back and forth at will, while others will Cross Over when summoned.

Demon: A soul who manifests malevolent energy

Djinn: (Genie) A demon bound in servitude to a certain location, human, or another demon for a set amount of time or until certain criteria are met

Familiar: A demon's animal companion, e.g. fly, snake, goat. Not every demon has a familiar.

Forgetting: The wiping of all memory of the Other Side and all previous lifetimes prior to beginning another cycle on This Side (life) in order to facilitate learning. Memory is restored upon Crossing Over (death).

God: The Benevolent Unknown

Grimoire: A book of spells that may also contain incantations for summoning spirits or demons

Hammurabi: A king of the First Babylonian dynasty, reigning from approximately 1792 BCE to 1750 BCE

Heaven: The collective term for all angels on the Other Side. Not an actual place.

Hell: The collective term for all demons on the Other Side. Not an actual place.

Innana: Sumerian goddess of war

Larsa: Sumerian city-state conquered by the Babylonian king Hammurabi in 1699 BCE

Lesser servitor: The lowest, most base demons, mindless in their hunger for human pain. They serve in the legions of more powerful demons as foot soldiers and resemble starved, stray dogs or hairless rats. Also known as imps.

Mesopotamia: The region between the Tigris and Euphrates rivers, home to ancient civilizations such as the Sumerians and the Babylonians, now modern-day Iraq

Oblivion: Ceasing to exist completely. Ultimate and permanent nonexistence. "Death for the dead." Only very powerful demons can send another to Oblivion and only when that demon is in his/her human form.

Other Side: The realm a soul returns to after death, between lifetimes. The realm of angels and demons. The human mind cannot fully comprehend the Other Side and knowledge or memory of it would defeat the purpose of living. (see: Forgetting)

Rim-Sin I: King of Larsa, reigned from approximately 1758-1699 BCE

Servitor: Any demon in service to a more powerful demon. High-ranking demons might have legions of servitors.

Sumer: Ancient civilization that existed in the region between the Tigris and Euphrates rivers called Mesopotamia, now modern-day Iraq

This Side: Life on Earth

Veil, The: A crude and overly simplistic explanation of the barrier between This Side and the Other Side

Utu: Sumerian god of light

Ziggurat: Mesopotamian temple, architectural precursor to the pyramids

Zu: The "storm-bird." A demon of Sumerian lore.

For Dad, who I like to think is just in the next room.
And for Izzy, my brave girl, who stepped into the unknown first.
All my love to you both.

PART I

1

I DIDN'T THINK my day could get any worse and then I found the dead body.

Work had been terrible for a Friday. The E train was late, which made *me* late, which set my whole day off-balance. At our morning meeting, Guy Baker mistook me for the intern who brings the coffee, despite us working together for nearly two years. Which meant he still didn't know I existed. On the way home, the train was crammed, bodies pressed to bodies. A few feet down from me, a young couple was taking advantage. She clung to him, he held on to her, and they gazed at each other as if there was no one else in the world. Their happiness was beautiful to see but made my loneliness feel sharp by contrast.

To top it off, there was the aforementioned dead body in the empty lot behind my apartment.

Technically, the lot was more like my front walk. My building in Hell's Kitchen had been chopped up in the 1970s to make the most of the New York City real estate boom. My tiny studio was hardly a functioning apartment, but more of an appendage—an elbow chopped off from the body. It stuck out at the edge of the second floor, and the only way in was by walking to the rear of the building, through the trash-littered lot, and climbing a rickety set of stairs. The interior wasn't much more than a shoebox, but it had one large window. Even if the view was mostly the next building, the light was lovely in the morning.

And it was all mine. In *Manhattan*.

Every time I locked my three deadbolts and looped my three chains in at night, I reminded myself I didn't have any roommates keeping me up, or eating my food, or hogging the tiny bathroom…or to chat with in the morning over coffee. Or to huddle with on the tiny couch and watch Netflix while we talked about our hopes and dreams. Like my hope that Guy Baker would finally notice me and take me around the world with him on his fifty-foot sailboat as we continue our work at Ocean Alliance, the nonprofit where we're both employed. We'd fall deeply in love, the kind of love you find in the romance novels I read every night. The kind of love that felt like a promise that's never been fulfilled.

Which was kind of dramatic, I know. I was only twenty-three; I had my whole life to fall in love. But the loneliness that wracked me felt a lot older than twenty-three years.

That late afternoon in April, on my walk from the subway, I tried to erase my crappy day with my favorite daydream. The one where Guy and I are sailing around the Rock of Gibraltar or the coast at Cape Town…doesn't matter where. We're on a mission through Ocean Alliance, both of us passionate and tireless in our work. In this particular fantasy, Guy and I return to his boat after a grueling day on the trawlers and garbage scows, hauling tons of plastic trash from the water. He looks at me across the tiny cabin, tired but happy, and we fall into each other. He kisses me desperately, then holds my face in his huge, rough hands. His light blue eyes are intent on mine, as if it's impossible to look away.

"Lucy," he says gruffly. *"I never want to do this without you."*
I swallow hard, choked with emotion. "You'll never have to."

My favorite exchange. We'd made it a thousand times in my pathetic imaginings. Lines I could've pulled from one of the hundreds of romance novels that crammed my studio. They took up most of one wall where I didn't have room for *one* thing to take up *anything*.

I rounded the corner to my studio. In my mind's eye, Guy and I were falling onto the bed that was just big enough for the two of us, the sea cradling us in a soft sway, when I stopped short, a gasp catching in my throat.

He's dead.

The words popped into my head before my eyes registered what I was seeing—a man's legs, long and lean and sculpted with muscle. Naked of clothing and alabaster white. The white of porcelain or marble. As if Michelangelo's *David* had tipped over on the asphalt.

I glanced around in the dim twilight. All was quiet but for Mrs. Rodriguez on the third floor watching Telemundo with the window open.

I took one step. Then another. My phone was in my hand, ready to call 911. But my fingers wouldn't cooperate, my gaze locked on those legs that were too perfect to be real. Surreal.

Maybe it's a mannequin. Don't go calling the police because a department store dumped their trash in your backyard.

If that got out at work, I'd never hear the end of it. *Silly Lucy*, Abby Taylor would say, shaking her head, her camera's video eye recording everything. Not that word *would* get out. I barely talked to anyone at Ocean Alliance unless it was during meetings, and then it was to agree with what everyone else agreed on. Even if I didn't actually agree. Even if I had ideas of my own.

Now I was close enough to see that it was definitely not a mannequin but a man, his body just as flawless as his legs. Unblemished. No scars, no freckles, no hair except for the thick mop of black curls on his head. Hair as black as his skin was white. He lay on his stomach (I averted my gaze from the perfect, tight roundness of his butt), eyes shut, his head pillowed on one muscular forearm. The other arm—his right—was stretched out on the ground as if he'd been reaching for something when he…

Fell?

I stepped over one of his wings—*Oh my God Oh my God Oh my God*—and stood as near the man as I dared. His face was mesmerizing. Like a Renaissance sculpture with full lips, angular cheekbones, and thick brows as black as ink. He had a Grecian nose and a jawline that was so straight and perfect, it wasn't quite human.

'Not quite human'? Silly Lucy, how about those wings?

I forced my eyes to accept what they were seeing.

The man wasn't partially wrapped in a blanket.

The twilight shadows weren't playing tricks on my eyes.

Two huge wings, covered in long, glossy black feathers, sprouted from between the man's perfect shoulder blades. Each was easily as long as his body—their tips likely brushed his ankles when he walked.

By my calculations, that would give him a wingspan of more than twelve feet.

He has a wingspan.

A little cry escaped me as the man's full lips parted and then he made a sudden, torturous gasp for air, as if he'd been holding his breath for a long time. He moaned on the exhale, a sound that sent a shiver dancing down my spine, equal parts dread and a strange, tantalizing thrill.

Whatever this *creature* was, he was alive. I fumbled for my phone.

Who are you going to call, 911 or Animal Control?

A crazed laugh tried to burst out of me when the man opened his eyes. My laugh morphed into a strangled scream and the phone fell from my shaking hands.

His eyes were pure black. No irises, no whites. The pupils—if he had any—were lost in the inky black spheres. In those few seconds that felt like an eternity, I had the fevered notion that his eyes weren't black at all but *an absence*. An absence of color. Light. Heat. Warmth.

Everything good in the world…

It was impossible to tell if he were looking at me, except I could *feel* that he was. He saw me. Those onyx orbs seared through me like an icy blade. I shivered and swayed, feeling myself pulled into that endless black. An abyss from which there was no return.

The man's outstretched hand lifted off the ground, his long fingers reaching. His breath cut a harsh whisper, "Help me…"

I staggered back. The back of my head hit a brick wall and the blackness swallowed me whole.

T HE TORCH'S FLAME *flickers, sending shadows dancing across the walls. Bloodstained walls. The stones are slick with it. The floor too, and it's so dark. Screams echo through the narrow corridor. His screams, rising from the very bowels of the temple.*

The corridor widens to a chamber. Bodies—four of them—lie on the stony floor, pools of blood beneath their heads, matting their black hair. The fifth of their number, a woman, is still alive. She is bound and gagged and on her knees. She faces the man who's been screaming. He's bound too, his hard, muscled flesh slashed open in a dozen places, his body broken by torture.

Their eyes meet across the blood-soaked stones, the air thick with death and pain. He shakes his head, agony bright and sharp in his dark eyes. A blade glints in the torchlight and is laid to her throat. His screams begin again, hoarse and ragged; he writhes against his bonds like a man possessed. A quick motion and blood flows in torrent, and the woman falls to the stones. They are made of shadow. She falls in, falls away, and the man's screams—tinged with rage now—chase her down.

The screams become a raven's cry, black wings outstretched...

Then a plea, choked with grief.

"Forgive me..."

My eyes flew open with a gasp. I jerked up against the wall in the empty lot. The twilight's shadows had thickened as the sun sank. I'd lost at least an hour to…what?

A dream. It was all a dream…

Whatever it was, it was quickly slipping away from me—I couldn't hold on to it. A temple? And so much blood…

"About time," a deep voice muttered tiredly. "I was about to give up and find someone else."

Another little cry tore out of me, and I pushed myself tighter to the wall. The man was still there, slumped against a wooden moving pallet, his legs drawn up to hide his nakedness.

At least, I thought it was the same man.

He wasn't as tall but built more solidly and packed with lean muscle. The wings were gone, and the black-on-black eyes were now deep amber, watching me. Intense. His skin wasn't a bloodless white but a healthy olive tone…except for the scars that scored his body. So many scars. Slashes across his torso. A gash on one bicep. Another at his neck. And a circle the size of a silver dollar square over the left side of his chest. Over his heart.

I scrambled to my feet. "What's happening?"

"What is happening is the beginning." The man squinted into the sky, toward the setting sun. "And an end."

"I don't understand. How long have I been…?"

"Unconscious? About an hour."

I shuddered at the idea that I'd been passed out for that long with a naked man sitting across from me. He seemed to read my thoughts and put his hand over that terrible scar on his chest.

"*Gek pro'ma-ra-kuungd-eh.* A sacred vow. I will not harm you. Not in this life or any other."

I had no idea what he'd said—or even what language he'd said it in—but the conviction in his deep voice calmed me a little.

I eased a breath. "Who are you?"

"I am Casziel."

Like Caz-EE-ell but with a hiss in the middle. The sound sent half-frightening, half-electric tingles down my spine. I wanted to say it. I wanted to taste it on my tongue…

"What kind of name is…that?"

"An old one," he said. "And what do they call you?"

"Lucy."

"Lucy is from the Latin, meaning 'born of light.'" Casziel smirked. "How fitting."

He looked to be about twenty-five or so but spoke as if he were older. A jaded, sarcastic tint colored his every word, and I couldn't place his faint accent.

"How did you get here?" I asked. "Were you mugged?"

I hoped that was all it was and not what it looked like—that he'd been stripped naked, assaulted, and left for dead.

Casziel cocked his head. "Are you concerned about my welfare already? That bodes well. But save your pity; no one hurt me. Crossing Over is always difficult."

I nodded as if that made sense and inched for the wooden stairs that led to my place. "Okay...well, then I'll just call the police—"

"No police."

"But you've been robbed...haven't you?"

"I have been robbed, yes. But what was taken no longer belongs to me."

"Um, okay." He spoke in riddles, but the pain in his voice was real. "Is there someone else I can call for you? Family—?"

"You're not afraid of me?"

I swallowed. "Should I be?"

"Most humans are."

"Okaaaay," I took a step back. "I really think I should call someone."

The police or maybe mental health services.

Casziel pinned me with his amber gaze. "Do you believe in second chances, Lucy Dennings? For even the worst sinners? For unthinkable crimes?"

The yawning chasm of bloody death and grief from the vision or dream or whatever it was fell on me like a shadow. I went cold all over and nearly missed that he knew my full name.

"I-I never told you—"

Casziel muttered in a language I didn't recognize—something exotic and *old.*

"Forgive me, Lucy Dennings. It's not my intention to frighten you, though I know it can't be helped. But if you insist on calling the authorities, perhaps something to cover me first?"

"You need clothes," I said stupidly. "Right. Okay. Sure. I'll...be right back."

I took the rickety stairs up to my studio and unlocked my door with trembling fingers, nearly dropping the keys twice. Once inside, I shut the door behind me and threw every lock, barricading myself within.

Everything looked the same as when I'd left for work. This morning's coffee cup on the counter. My bed neatly made. My houseplant—Edgar—in the window. All the strangeness of the situation with Casziel seemed more unreal against the ordinary *realness* of my place.

There was a naked man in my back lot. That's all.

And the wings? And black eyes? And bloodless white skin?

"There's a plausible explanation for all of this," I murmured, taking a steadying breath. I hit my head on the wall harder than I thought."

Except I'd discovered Casziel before I hit my head. Did a *version* of him have wings...?

Not going there.

I raised the phone, my finger poised to dial 911. The police would show up and this man would be out of my life. Everything would go back to normal. I could take a hot bath, heat up some ramen, and curl up in bed with my books until the weekend was over and I had someplace to be again.

Same as last weekend. Same as the weekend to come.

Would it be so terrible if I brought Casziel some clothes first?

Yes. Yes, it would.

I dialed nine and stopped again.

The heroines in my favorite romantic fantasies were always finding themselves in dangerous situations. They faced them bravely and wound up learning they had special abilities, or they became queens of fantastical lands. Bringing clothes to a naked man—a beautiful naked man—with scars and exotic eyes wasn't the same as saving a kingdom or stepping into Narnia, but it was *something.*

Ridiculous, scoffed the sneering voice that always seemed to pop up when I wanted to stand up for myself or try something new. *This isn't a book, it's real and you're not special. You're Silly Lucy, living her silly little life.*

I tilted my chin. "Not today."

My nerves didn't magically turn to steel with that declaration, but bravery, I'd read, wasn't doing something because you were unafraid. It was being afraid and doing it anyway.

At my closet, I scanned the simple blouses, sweaters, and dresses for something that would fit Casziel. I was almost 5'5". He was easily six feet and broad in the shoulders...

With or without wings?

"Stop it."

I pushed aside hangers and then grief punched me in the stomach, hard and fast, knocking everything else out.

Dad's trench coat.

He liked to say the coat was a little old school but that it made him feel like Humphrey Bogart in *Casablanca.* He'd always wear it when we went to the Old Vic movie house to watch a classic matinee on Sundays, back in Milford.

I laid the cuff to my cheek and inhaled. He'd been gone for six months but his scent—Old Spice cologne and pipe smoke—was still strong.

This would fit Casziel.

The thought was satisfying and horrifying at the same time.

"No way," I said through gritted teeth. "Absolutely not."

I imagined I heard Dad's voice in my head.

I don't need it anymore, pumpkin. And neither do you. You'll always have me.

"You'll always have me" was one of the last things Dad said to me before the cancer took him.

I had obeyed his last wish and sold most of his things and our house in Connecticut to give me a nest egg after graduating NYU with a bachelor's in bioengineering. But instead of joining a lab or research project for removing plastic particles from the ocean, I took an entry-level job with a nonprofit where no one expected much from the shy girl in the corner who was good with spreadsheets.

"I can't, Daddy," I murmured into the sleeve. "I can't give your coat to some stranger."

But I was doing it again. Playing it safe. Doing what was expected of me: nothing.

I took the coat down from the hanger, buried my face in it one last time, and went back out.

Casziel was where I'd left him, looking weak and helpless.

He's neither weak nor helpless...and you know it.

Except I didn't know what he was. I wouldn't let my imagination go there. I inhaled, ready to scream bloody murder if Casziel planned…well…my bloody murder.

"That should do," he said, eyeing the coat bunched in my hand.

He climbed to his feet, moving stiffly and stumbling. Keeping my eyes averted, I handed over my father's coat, then quickly stepped away. Casziel turned, and I caught a glimpse of more scars slashed across his back. He pulled the coat over his shoulders. It was a tad too tight but covered him well enough.

"Okay, so…I guess that's it. Good luck—"

"Lucy, wait…"

Casziel swayed, his hand outstretched, grabbing at air. Instinctively—and like a crazy person—I rushed toward him instead of away. I gave him my arm to prop him up and almost buckled at his heaviness. Hints of smoke and heated metal filled my nose and a strange scent I couldn't place.

I looked up at Casziel and he looked down at me. His eyes appeared as if a fire burned behind them. Thousands of sunrises and sunsets, rising and falling over thousands of years. They drew me in until I could hear screams…

"What is happening?" I breathed.

"My time grows short, Lucy Dennings," Casziel said, his voice like smoke. "I need your help. In eleven days, it's all over. For better or for worse. Improbable as it seems, I'm aiming for better."

"Better?"

"It might be too late; my sins are many. Countless. But I want to try. I need you to show me how."

My heart was bursting out of my chest, and I should've run but I didn't. "S-show you how to do what?"

"Find my way back into the light."

Because he's been cast out.

A chill came over me as the truth of who—*what*—Casziel was began to solidify from impossible suspicion into reality.

"No. I…I can't." I let go of him and backed away. "I can't do…whatever this is."

"Lucy…"

"*No.* I'm not like the girls in the stories. I want to be, but I'm just not. I can't help you. I'm so sorry…"

I was up three stairs to my place when Casziel's deep voice arrested me.

"This coat belonged to your father."

I turned, my pulse pounding slow and hard. "What did you say?"

"It's his. You kept it and gave the rest away." Casziel frowned, perplexed. "What is a Hum-free Bo-gart?"

The blood drained from my face. "Who told you…?"

"He told me."

"You're talking to my father? Right now?"

"He says you should let me explain." He frowned again, listening. "Not sure what pumpkins have to do with anything…"

"You're lying," I said through trembling lips, even as I desperately scanned the area for my dad. "You're a liar and you're cruel—"

"I am both." Casziel's lips twisted. "But not today."

I breathed hard, the tears in my throat trying to choke me. "I don't know who you are or how you know about us, but to have some stranger toy with my grief is wrong. And terrifying."

"I beg to differ," Casziel snapped. "*Terrifying* is placing the fate of your eternal soul in the hands of a human girl who clearly doesn't have the guts for it."

I shook my head. "You're not well. You need help."

"Have I not been saying so since the beginning?" Casziel scrubbed a hand through his loose, dark curls. "Gods, woman, I don't have time—"

"I don't care," I cried, backing away and hitting my hip on the stair rail. The pain was sharp but didn't wake me from this insanity. "You have my dad's coat. That's already too much, but that's all you'll get from me. Now leave me alone or I *will* call the police."

Casziel muttered a curse, then said louder, "He says to tell you that you'll always have him."

I froze, turned.

"He says it may seem crazy, but I need your help. And you've never been one to—"

"Turn my back on someone who needs help," I finished. "My God." I took another step closer, squaring my shoulders and meeting Casziel's eyes. "Is this real?"

"It is real."

"Why me?"

"Lucy born of light, you can help me be something other than...what I am."

Black wings and black eyes and visions of death swirled all around me. "What you are..."

"Born into darkness."

Reality warped in those short moments. I was stepping into the wardrobe after all, and there was no going back. And I didn't want to. A strange energy radiated off Casziel that was waking up something deep inside me. Some courage I didn't know I had. Turning him away now would put it back to sleep.

I've been sleeping through my own life long enough.

"My father is here? With me?"

"Always."

"He's an angel?"

"In a matter of speaking."

"But you're not."

It wasn't a question.

"No," Casziel said. "I am not."

"What would they call you?"

His amber gaze seemed to pour into mine. "Can't you guess, Lucy Dennings?"

"Tell me."

I need to hear it.

"We have many names," Casziel said. "Hyang. Fravashi. Kami. Djinn. Yaksha. Sylph. Kakodaimon. Daimon..."

The sun had sunk beneath the tall towers, draping the city in long shadows. Casziel looked at me expectantly.

I inhaled, then exhaled the word.

"Demon."

3

NIGHT HAD FALLEN and there was a demon in my kitchen eating cereal.

I sat at the window at my tiny desk, crammed full of second thoughts. I hugged my elbows, not moving or daring to take my eyes off Casziel. He sat slumped at the island that served as my dining table, scarfing down spoonful after spoonful of cornflakes. A light breeze could shove him over, but sooner or later, he was going to regain his full strength. His *powers*, whatever those might be.

Be brave. This is your house.

I uncurled from the chair and forced myself into the kitchen to pour a glass of water. I leaned against the counter, facing my houseguest. Even unceremoniously shoving cereal in his mouth, he was ungodly beautiful.

Ungodly being the operative word.

"How long's it been since you've eaten?" I asked, watching Casziel pile cornflakes on his spoon, spilling milk on the sleeve of Dad's coat.

"Fifty years," he said. "Give or take ten minutes."

"What does that mean?"

No answer. I cleared my throat.

"You must be hungry if it's been fifty years."

"I don't *need* to eat." Casziel scoffed as if the idea were beneath him. "I don't need to drink. I don't need to sleep. There is nothing on This Side that I *need*." He raised his eyes to mine. "Except you."

A shiver danced down my spine and it wasn't unpleasant. No one had ever needed me before. Certainly not a man who looked like Casziel...

A few moments passed where the only sounds were the demon noisily finishing off his bowl of cornflakes and pouring another, his third.

"I feel you watching me, Lucy Dennings," he said, not looking up.

"Well, gee, I only have about a million questions."

Like what had I gotten myself into or if I were being epically duped.

Of course, you are, piped up that sneering voice. *Silly Lucy, you think you're special? Do you actually believe this strange man, who you let into* your home, *is a penitent demon trying to save his soul?*

Casziel lifted his head, eyes narrowing. "Be silent, Deb."

"Deb?"

"One of your demons," Casziel said, going back to his food. "Nasty one, too."

A wave of goosebumps washed over my arms and down my back. "*One* of *my* demons? How many do I have?"

"Just two."

"*Just?*"

"Two is nothing. Had you more, I might not have found you."

He found me.

Somehow, the idea didn't scare me as much as I thought it should. Not as much as having two demons.

"The demon's name is Deb?"

"And the other is K," Casziel said. "Best to leave it at that. Demons love hearing their true names in the mouths of humans and will often come when called."

"Jesus," I shivered. "What do they do to me? I mean...why are they mine?"

"Not yours alone," Casziel said. "They're two of the most powerful in our ranks. Deb is Pestilence. Like an infectious disease. She contaminates humans and keeps them from fulfilling their true potential. K, the Smiter, wracks them with fear if they try anyway."

"That's...horrible."

Casziel shrugged. "That's their job. Sin. Vice. Immorality. Laziness. What you call 'deadly sins' are our stocks-in-trade."

"What is your stock-in-trade?" I asked, not sure I wanted to hear the answer.

"Wrath."

He said it flatly, with no pride or arrogance but no remorse either. My gaze traced his scars that peeked above the collar of the trench coat. The dream whispered of bloody stones and screams, then faded again.

"Have you ever...killed anyone?"

"In life, yes," Casziel said. "I was a warrior."

"You were human? With the feathered wings, I thought maybe you were a...fallen angel."

It sounded just as crazy to say it out loud as it did in my mind.

He shook his head, his eyes darkening. "No, I had a life, once. A long time ago. I was a commander of armies. Now, my armies do not wield swords; we incite battle among humans. We fuel the rage in men's hearts. The *wrath*."

"You don't sound very sad about it."

"I'm here, aren't I?" he said and went back to his cereal, leaving me to glance over my shoulders for "Deb" and "K."

How many times had I heard their whispers? The ones that told me to keep my ideas for removing plastic out of our oceans to myself because surely someone smarter and cleverer than me was already on it. Or how, when Jana Gill asked me to go out with the gang after work, I always declined for fear of embarrassing myself. Or how, when I worked up the courage to talk to Guy Baker, the whispers would start that there was nothing *Silly Lucy* could say he'd want to hear.

"That's what demons do?" I asked after a minute, anger tightening my voice. "Keep humans down? Send us to war or make us feel crappy about ourselves?"

"Demons can't *make* you do anything," Casziel said. "We insinuate. Influence. Cajole. We stoke the fires of your sloth, or wrath, or jealousy, then feed off it. Whether or not you act on our insinuations is entirely up to you, though you rarely believe that. Our greatest victory was convincing humans they have no control over their reaction to adversity." He tapped his chin. "Asmodeus earned himself a promotion for that one."

This is a dream. I'm going to wake up. Any second now...

I took a long pull of cold water. "Are there many demons on This Side?"

"Not many. Perhaps a few thousand at any given moment."

"*Thousand*?"

"We are legion," he said. "And you're out of cornflakes."

"I'll put it on my list," I murmured as Casziel wiped his mouth with the back of his sleeve and slipped off the stool to wander my living area.

He tapped his long fingers on my window. "Does this unlock?"

"Yes, but…"

He pushed it open.

"I only leave it cracked in the summer," I said, reaching to shut it again. "It's not safe—"

"None dare hurt you. Not while I'm here."

The casual menace in his voice sent another tingle down my spine. I'd never had a man—or reasonable facsimile thereof—vow to protect me like that. As if, under his watch, my safety was a forgone conclusion.

It felt good.

Casziel carried his inspection of my tiny studio into the sleeping area, leaning to peer at the photo on my nightstand. My dad and me at Coney Island when I was ten.

"Ah, so he smiles," Casziel muttered. "I was beginning to wonder if he were only capable of disapproving grimaces."

"Dad's here right now?"

"Yes and no. *Here* is a relative term."

"I thought you said—"

Casziel flapped a hand irritably as he perused my bookshelf that was crammed full. "He's always here and he's also somewhere else. Everywhere and nowhere." He cocked his head, listening, then scoffed. "I beg to differ."

"He's talking to you now?"

"He says I'm being vague on purpose. As if it were that easy to explain the nature of the cosmos to a puny human brain for which 'truth' is only that which the senses perceive."

"That's a little harsh," I said. "Plenty of people have faith."

Casziel snorted. "On the surface. On their knees once a week, if that."

"You have a dim view of humanity." I crossed my arms. "It's hardly fair to incite humans to war and hate, to whisper in our ears that we're not good enough or drive us to temptation and then get all judgy about it."

Casziel shrugged. "I'm a demon. I never professed to be *fair*."

I rolled my eyes and picked up the photo of my father and me. Both of us grinning. Both of us carefree and full of joy. No demons there.

"He's an angel now," I murmured, tracing his face.

"Playing a harp whilst gliding past pearly gates on a fluffy white cloud?" Casziel mused. He ran a finger along a row of romance novels on my shelf. "Heaven's gates or the fires of hell. Divine or infernal. Angel or demon. Everything is black and white for you humans when there are a thousand shades of gray." He pulled a book off the shelf, an eyebrow arched. "More than fifty."

"Okay, then what's it like?"

"The Other Side?" He shrugged and dropped the book on the floor and moved on with his inspection of my place. "You can't comprehend it and I'd rather not drive you to insanity trying to explain."

"Gee, thanks," I muttered and returned the book to its home on the shelf as Casziel poked his head into my tiny bathroom.

"I've known monks with more worldly possessions than you, Lucy Dennings."

I lifted one shoulder. "It's all I need."

He gestured at my shelves. "You *need* all those books? Mostly romantic fiction, I notice."

"And poetry. I love poetry and romance." I smiled self-consciously. "I'm a sucker for beautiful words."

Casziel sniffed. "Those *beautiful words* are your substitute for the real thing."

"I...that isn't true."

"Is it not true?" He stretched his long body out on my too-small couch. "One stool at the counter. One chair at the desk. I'm shocked that your bed is large enough for two."

I tugged at the collar of my sweater, my face growing hot. "This place doesn't have room for more furniture. And not that it's any of your business, but I don't have company over all that often."

Or ever, Silly Lucy.

Casziel shrugged and reached for the TV remote on the coffee table and started flipping through channels. "Can we get pizza?"

I snatched the remote out of his hands and shut off the TV.

"Oh sure, let's get pizza. As soon as you tell me what I'm supposed to do. Help you *not* be a demon?"

He fixed his eyes on me. "My redemption lies with you, Lucy Dennings. You're the expert on living for others, always bending over backwards, often at your own expense."

"I don't do that," I said in a small voice.

"You'd give the shirt off your back, as the saying goes, even if you only had one shirt."

"That's…not true."

"Agree to disagree."

I hunched deeper into my sweater, an ugly, nervous feeling coiling in my guts like a snake. The enormity of what I was being asked to do and believe was too much. Demons or not, the voices in my head were right—I was gullible and silly and always willing to see the best in people, even when they were obviously toying with me.

"This conversation is making me ill," I said. "I was crazy to let you in. For all I know this is a lie, and you're here to…hurt me."

Casziel's lazy smirk vanished. "I told you, I would never hurt you."

"You told me but what is the word of a demon? And how am I supposed to help you? You've committed God knows how many atrocities—"

"God knows," Casziel said, his voice low. "To the last drop of blood spilled, God knows."

I shivered. "This was a mistake. I think you should leave."

The demon sat up, head bowed, his hands hanging off his knees. "Forgive me, Lucy born of light. It's been nearly four thousand years since I last put myself at the mercy of a human's generosity." He looked up at me, his expression strangely soft. "I vowed to never…"

"What?"

He looked away. "Nothing."

Pain hung over him, weighing him down like a second coat. Or a suit of armor grown too heavy. Against my will, my heart softened toward him, but he was right. I did bend over backwards for others, and sometimes—most times, if I were being honest—it left me feeling as though I'd been taken advantage of.

I crossed my arms. "How can I trust you?"

"Your own father assured you that you can."

"And if you're lying about him too?"

"You asked earlier if he were here, and my answer was…inadequate." Casziel winced, annoyed. "Fine. It was rude and dismissive. Better?"

Despite everything, I smiled. I could almost see Dad standing over Casziel, hands on his hips, scolding him. Almost. As much as I wanted to believe, there was no one there.

"The hardest part of losing someone is thinking they're gone forever," I said. "You know in your heart that's not true but the little voices of doubt whisper *what if it is?*"

Casziel nodded, then cocked his head, listening. When he spoke, his tone was gentler than I'd ever heard it.

"He asks me to remind you of your youth. How you would do your homework at the dining room table while he cooked dinner in the kitchen in your house in Milfred."

"Milford." Tears filled my eyes. "I remember."

I could see it as if it were yesterday. Dad banging around in the kitchen of our cozy house, the scent of pot roast or spaghetti sauce in the air. Me in pigtails at the table, my papers strewn all over but organized. I was an A student, always striving to do my best. To make Dad proud, even if he never demanded more of me than I could give.

"If you needed help with an equation or had a question," Casziel said, "he'd come in from the kitchen to help, then go back when you didn't need help anymore."

I nodded, my voice a whisper. "Yes. That's what he did."

"It is so now. He's always here, Lucy. He's just in the next room. And if you need him, he will come."

The tears spilled over now. I smiled through them, feeling as if a weight had been lightened. It wasn't gone; it would never lift completely, but for the first time in six months, I felt like I could breathe again.

"Thank you, Casziel."

I hadn't said his name before. Probably my imagination, but it felt as if the air between us had shifted. A shimmer, like the blurred air above a fire, wavered between us, then vanished.

"And I'll help you," I said. "I don't know how or where to even start. But…I'll try."

Casziel's eyes widened as they met mine. "My thanks, Lucy Dennings," he said softly. Then his irritated scowl returned, as if he'd remembered to put it back on. "*Now* can we get pizza?"

I ordered pizza for my demon and curled on my bed while he watched television from the couch. Eventually, my eyes grew heavy; the events of the day and every wild emotion in it had left me drained. I began to doze, listening to Casziel's running commentary on whatever he was watching—he laughed derisively or muttered in that strange language of his. A language that sounded unearthed from a tomb—dusty and guttural and not heard by living ears in centuries.

I drifted to sleep and dreamed of a woman

standing in the field, her back to me, her black hair braided in a thick rope down to her waist. She wears a shapeless wool dress, belted above the hip. Her skin is bronzed, and silver bracelets with blue stones slide down her arm as she shields her eyes from the setting sun. In the distance, a city of low mud-brick buildings sits against the banks of a river.

I follow her line of sight and can just make out a procession of soldiers marching into the city. The faint sounds of cheering crowds emanate from under horns bleating in triumph.

The woman lets out a little cry of joy, and my heart jumps too. She hikes up her skirts and runs toward the city…

A DEMON IN the guise of a human bouncer lounges at the entrance of Idle Hands. The tavern, tucked in a dark alley, is full, judging by the dark laughter, cursing, and noxious odors seeping from behind the heavy oaken door.

The bouncer watches me approach with flat eyes. "*I fell to Earth and here I lie...*"

"*Who will help me up again?*" I finish.

He nods. "You may enter."

I glance around the alley. It's empty, but New York City breathes around us, electric and alive. Even in the deepest part of the night, it teems with life. Light.

Satisfied there are no watching eyes, I transform into my demonic form and nearly sigh with relief to feel it envelop me in strength and power, like putting on a suit of armor. I'm no longer weak from Crossing Over; the black clothes and greatsword I wear on the Other Side reform with me.

The bouncer falls back, averting his eyes. "My Lord Casziel, I had no idea. Please forgive me."

Not long ago, I would've exulted in the terror my presence creates. Now it reminds me of all I've done to earn it.

"Step aside," I snarl.

He does so with another bow, and I enter Idle Hands. The dark, windowless tavern reeks of a dozen foul odors—vile fumes emanate off the twenty or so demons that are congregated here. Each wears his or her demonic body. Idle Hands is a safe haven, invisible to human eyes.

Few take notice of my arrival, but behind the bar, Eistibus is staring. The djinn seems pleased to see me but not surprised.

"Lord Casziel." Eistibus clasps my arm. "How long's it been?"

"Fifty years by human reckoning."

"Too long and yet it seems like yesterday." The djinn glances at a door at the rear of the common room. "Lord Ashtaroth is waiting…"

"I'm aware."

Let him wait.

"If you think it's best," Eistibus says slowly. "What's your poison?"

It's not a figure of speech; skulls and crossbones mark more than one bottle on the shelves.

"Wine, please. Red."

Eistibus sets a glass of wine the color of old blood in front of me. From the waist up, the djinn appears as a rotund, richly dressed human with ropes of jewels around his thick neck and gems glinting on every finger. Below the cloth-of-gold sash at his waist, he's made of mist. It tethers him to a lamp buried somewhere in the foundations of the tavern. Rumor has it, he lost a bet with Aclahayr.

"How long are you on This Side?"

"Not long," I answer and sip my wine. "A few days."

And then there will be an end, one way or another.

"What of you?" I ask. "How's business?"

"T'is crowded these days. Strange, that. Most times, it's just me and that wormy bastard."

He jerks his jowly chin at the demon at the end of the bar, his head resting on the polished mahogany, one scrawny arm curling around a ring of empty shot glasses.

Eistibus pounds a fist. "Oi! Ba-Maguje! Get yer bloody ugly mug off my bar."

"Piss off," Ba-Maguje slurs. "I'm working."

Eistibus chuckles but it fades fast. His gold gaze flickers toward the back door and then to me. "Not to be pressing the point, but Lord Ashtaroth was adamant that you see him immediately."

"Trying to get rid of me already?" I smile. "I thought we were friends."

"We *are* friends," Eistibus says. "Hence the warning. And you'd be a truer friend to go quick and not let'em cut off my balls for not passing on his message."

"You don't have any balls, Eistibus," I say with a grin, then flap my hand. "I'm going, I'm going."

I drain my wine and now dozens of eyes—or what serve as eyes—follow me as I cross the room. I step over tails and around puddles of vileness. At the door, I square my shoulders and knock once.

"Enter."

The room is dark but for a single black candle burning on an ornate table. Lush furniture in fraying velvet and antiques give it the appearance of a parlor in an old mansion. By the meager light, I make out my liege lord, Ashtaroth, Head of the Eighth Order, Prince of Accusers. He lounges on a settee, his black, webbed wings folded tight to him, the hooked tips gleaming behind his head of damp, tangled hair. He looks—and smells—like a corpse dragged out of a bog. It's all I can do not to recoil at his breath that has filled the room like a vapor.

He strokes the head of his immense white serpent that coils around the settee, watching me with black eyes. Lesser servitors scuttle and whimper at the edges of the light like rats.

"Kneel."

I obey and drop to my knees in the middle of the room.

"My demon prince," Ashtaroth drawls, danger suffusing every syllable. "You are so beautiful and perfect in your malevolence…except when it comes to *her*."

She is called Lucy this time…

I bury the tiny flicker of light that burns in my blackened heart. Even after centuries of ravaging the earth with my rage, that flame hasn't yet guttered out. Lucy is just as bright and beautiful in this lifetime as she is in every other, but she's alone. Always so alone. I dare wonder—hope—if somewhere in her soul she mourns me…

"She does not," Ashtaroth snaps, crawling around in my thoughts. "No matter how many of her lifetimes you skulk about her like a mongrel, you are dead to her. Not even a memory. You know this is true."

I know this is true. But I can't leave her to that loneliness. I need to know she has found happiness at last.

Then I can say goodbye…

Ashtaroth sneers, his wings flaring wide, wafting his stench over me in fresh waves. "I see into your heart. I taste your pathetic hope. The lie you've laid at her feet about *your redemption* would amuse me if it weren't so pitiful."

"This time is mine," I say, defiance in the tilt of my chin. "Eleven days. You swore to me…"

What is the word of a demon worth? Lucy asked. The answer, of course, is nothing.

Ashtaroth's black lip curls. "What of *your* word? Your duty? While you waste time on This Side, your legions go without a commander on the Other."

I say nothing. My course is clear, and I will not waver. A commander does not veer from his mission until victory is achieved.

Or until he's dead.

Quickly, I banish the thought from my mind before he knows my intentions. I must've succeeded because Ashtaroth sighs with disappointment and unsheathes the huge sword strapped to his waist. It gleams dully in the flickering light of the candle.

"Come, then."

I know what he expects—I alter myself into my frail human form, the body that had been scarred and broken so many years ago. Ashtaroth will scar me again to remind me of that frailty—remind me that while I wear the human skin, he can destroy me.

I'm counting on it…but not yet.

I approach, my head held high, unflinching. At either side of Ashtaroth, lesser servitors watch me, waiting for me to show weakness. Starved for a scrap of my fear. I show none. I could destroy the imps with a word or one swipe of my sword.

I bare my arm, offering it to Ashtaroth like a piece of sacrificial meat.

"You have spent one day. Ten remain. My gift to you."

He draws his sword across the flesh above my wrist, and I hold my breath, wondering if he'll hack my hand off. But he keeps the wound shallow. Red blood flows, black in the meager light. The pain is bright, but it's nothing compared to the wounds I suffered in life centuries ago, when I was dragged to the bowels of the ziggurat and destroyed, body and soul…

My thoughts are wrenched from the bloodstained memories as Ashtaroth turns the flat of his blade onto the bleeding gash. Flesh sizzles; smoke curls up in tendrils. The pain sinks in deep. Layers of burning agony. The imps slaver and whine. Still, I don't flinch. I hold steady and let Ashtaroth extract his payment.

When it's over, I take my arm back and the pain with it. I relish it. So long as it belongs to me and not Lucy—never Lucy—I can bear it.

Ashtaroth's wings sag with disappointment at my stoicism. His hunger is unsatisfied, but our pact is intact.

"Leave me," he says, turning his back on me. "Go and play. Have your time."

"Thank you, my lord."

I bow my head and walk away, the smell of my own burned flesh hanging in the room. The servitors mewl and cower in the shadows at Ashtaroth's feet like stray dogs, still hungry.

Let them all starve.

"Casziel."

I stop, turn.

"I know you believe her happiness is the only redemption you'll ever know but you will fail. She will hate you before it's all over. Do you know why?"

My human blood runs cold in my human veins. I say nothing; there is no correct answer but his.

"Because you cannot hide your true self from her." Ashtaroth's voice carries the darkness of countless nights within it. "Because your atrocities cannot be forgiven, not even by one who shines as brightly as she. Because you belong to me. Your black heart and your blacker soul, they are *mine*."

He grins, showing rotting teeth.

"And I will never let you go."

5

W HEN I WOKE, sunlight was streaming through the open window, and the dream of the black-haired woman lingered in my thoughts. It reminded me of other dreams I'd had. Extremely lucid dreams set in different—and much older—eras. This latest felt even older. Ancient.

I glanced around. Dad's trench coat was a rumpled heap on the couch and Casziel was nowhere to be seen.

Maybe I dreamed him too.

Despite the mess of cereal at my kitchen counter and the empty pizza box on the coffee table, it was the most plausible explanation. The twinge of disappointment took me by surprise. More than a twinge, honestly. Casziel was rude and arrogant but had his own kind of strange charm. And sex appeal, if I were being *really* honest. He'd been a warrior and it showed in every hard line of his body, in the way he moved, muscles ready to spring to action. Power and danger radiated off of him, but against all logic, I felt safe with him.

But if my mind had created Casziel, it also meant that everything he'd told me about Dad was a figment of my grieving imagination too.

"No," I said softly, picking up the trench coat. "I can still believe you're here. You're just in the next room."

I returned the coat to the closet. The pipe smoke and cologne smells were overpowered by Casziel's exotic scent; maybe it was real after all. But where the hell was he?

Hell. Obviously.

I ignored that and made my bed, every corner tucked, every line smoothed until it looked like no one slept there. No one *had* slept there but me, ever. The last time I'd shared a bed with a guy was my sophomore year at NYU.

Jeff Hastings had been in my study group and a virgin like me. We decided to not be virgins together. The whole experience was clumsy and awkward but not wholly unpleasant. I even wondered if there was something more between Jeff and me, but having sex bolstered his confidence. He thanked me for "doing him a solid" and went on to date Cindy Nguyen for the rest of the year. For all I knew they were married and had three kids by now.

Since then, I'd gone on a few dates that went nowhere. I told myself I was too focused on my studies for a serious boyfriend. Before I knew it, college ended, Dad passed away, and I got a job at Ocean Alliance. I'd tucked myself into a little life—uneventful, quiet, safe. Small.

A purgatory of my own making.

My phone rang, breaking me out of my thoughts. Cole Matheson wanting to FaceTime.

I smiled and hit the green answer button. "Hey, you."

"Did I wake you?" He tossed the light brown hair that fell over his brow. "At ten a.m., your time, on a Saturday?"

"Not quite." I laughed. "Do I look that tired?"

"Actually, no. You look good." Cole pushed up his square, black-framed glasses. "There's something different about you. Your hair is all loose and rumpled. Sexy, even."

I touched my hair self-consciously. "I...had a long night."

"Oh? Please tell me you participated in nocturnal activities of the adult persuasion."

"No, nothing like that. Strange dreams."

"Damn. I was hoping that guy from your work...what's his name?"

"Guy."

"Right. I had hoped that *Guy* had finally pulled his head out of his ass and asked you to dinner. Dinner turned into drinks. Drinks turned into a roll in the hay..."

"I wish." I sat on the couch and smoothed the rumpled dress I'd fallen asleep in. "But Guy does not have his head in his ass. He has plenty of female attention and I've given him no reason to notice me."

"Uh huh. You're amazing, Luce. It's not that hard to notice."

"You have to say that; you're my best friend. How's school?"

I'd met Cole at NYU and my talented friend had gone on to earn himself a coveted spot at the Royal College of Art in London. Even a year later, I was still bubbling with pride for him.

"It's keeping me busy but not too busy for my side-project." Cole left the screen and came back with his sketch pad. "Number fifteen in my series, *My Friend Lucy, A Study*."

He held up a sketch, unmistakably me, done in pencil and so realistic, it was as if he'd worked off a photograph instead of memory. A portrait artist, Cole's job was to capture the inner spirit of his subjects and reflect them back. The sketch captured all of me—my heart-shaped face, smattering of freckles, and shoulder-length brown hair. Every feature plain and strikingly average.

"This is from our last phone convo," Cole said. "Please note the heaviness in your gaze and the beautiful yet sad smile."

"I'd be offended if you weren't so talented."

"I worry, Luce."

"I know you do, and I keep telling you not to."

"Can't help it. The sketches are all starting to look the same." He smiled gently. "I should rename this series *Still Life with Lucy*."

I plucked at a stray thread on my dress. "Things have been hard since Dad."

"I know that, but I also know how you are."

"How am I?"

"You don't go out. You don't have people over. You're too nice for your own good."

"There's no such thing as being too nice."

"You asked if *I* was okay at your own father's funeral." Cole's smile softened. "I'm not greedy; I'm willing to share your awesomeness with *at least* one other person."

My thoughts went to Casziel.

There's nothing on This Side I need. Except you.

"Woah," Cole cried. "What was that? Your whole face lit up."

"What? No. Your imagination…"

My words failed as a large black raven flew into the room through the open window. The one Casziel insisted on leaving open. The bird hovered in midair, then expanded and somehow unfolded itself. In the next instant, Casziel was standing in my living area dressed all in black. Black jeans, black boots, and a black jacket over a faded Metallica T-shirt.

Cole was rummaging excitedly for his pencil and didn't hear my little cry of shock. I blinked hard, as if that would keep my brain from feeling like it had short-circuited.

Did that just happen?

"Cole, I have to go. Someone's uh…at the door."

"Is that so?" Cole was now grinning ear to ear, his eyes darting between me and his sketch pad, his hand working fast. "Do tell."

"Who are you talking to?" Casziel demanded. Loudly.

Cole's eyes widened behind his glasses. "Holy shit, did I just hear—?"

"Gotta go, love you, call you later." I hung up on Cole and glared at Casziel. "Really?"

The demon glared back. "Our situation is a private one, or did I fail to mention that?"

"That was my best friend, and I haven't told him anything. He'd think I lost my mind. I'm not so sure I haven't, actually. Just now, were you…a *bird?*"

"The raven is my anicorpus," Casziel said. "A mode of transportation on This Side."

"Oh, sure. Anicorpus. Because that's totally normal." I frowned. "How do you have clothes?"

"All matter is energy. Once I acquire garments, I manipulate their energy and fuse it with my own. They become a part of me, just as the energies of my various bodies—raven, demon, human—are all within me. I can wear whichever I choose at will."

"Okay. I'll pretend I understand that." I tucked a lock of hair behind my ear. "But you were distinctly lacking in *garments* when I first found you."

"It takes strength to manipulate energy. At that time, I had none."

"Sure." I gave my head a shake. "Wait. I've seen you as a raven before, too. When I first found you. I had a dream or a vision of a chamber in a temple."

Casziel, busy rummaging in my kitchen cabinets, froze. "You saw a temple?" he asked without turning.

"That's the sense I got but I'm not sure. It was pretty dark. There was blood and...grief. Your grief, I think."

The demon was still for another moment, then resumed his hunt through my cabinets. "It's because we became bonded after you spoke my true name. My existence seeped into yours. Nothing more."

"But that vision came before I said your name—"

"Your cupboards are inadequate, Lucy Dennings," Casziel said, his back still to me. "It's surprising you survive off this meager assortment."

He was changing the subject, but I let it go, more absorbed by how Casziel filled my small space with his masculine presence. Finding him naked hadn't been a bad thing, but putting clothes on his lean, sculpted muscles somehow cast them in even sharper detail.

And black is absolutely his color.

I snapped myself out of lusting after a *demon* and cleared my throat. "Wait, exactly where did you acquire clothes?"

"I possessed a man of my general height and build while he was waiting to get into a nightclub," Casziel said, emerging from my cupboard with a box of Pop-Tarts. He tore a package open and let the foil wrapper fall to the floor. "I'm not a monster. I let him keep the underwear."

"You *possessed* him?"

"Why is this shocking? Your films and books get few things correct about my kind, but demon possession is generally accurate." Casziel tilted his head. "It was Uriel who let that slip. All that messy business with the nuns in 1634."

My jaw worked, then I gave myself a shake. "Did you consider how that guy might've felt suddenly finding himself naked in public?"

Casziel stared at me blankly, chewing his Pop-Tart.

I rolled my eyes. "Look, if you're going to be better, you need to learn a little empathy. And you can't be stealing anymore. Or *possessing* people, for God's sake."

"*Better* will not be good enough, Lucy Dennings. Given the scope of my sins, redemption will require an act of grand proportions. Have you given any more thought to my situation?"

"Well...no. I woke up and you were gone. I thought I'd imagined it all."

"While you *imagine*, my time grows short. As of now, I have ten days left."

"If we fail, you'll remain a demon forever?"

He took a little too long to answer. "Yes."

"But what—?"

"*Enough*," he snapped. "I don't have time for your endless interrogations."

I hugged my elbows. "You're in a bad mood."

"I grow restless," Casziel said. "I did not come to This Side to sit in your tiny apartment all day. And neither, I might add, should you."

"What's that supposed to mean?"

"You have the whole of New York City at your disposal, and you keep yourself tucked away here."

My cheeks burned. "That's not true. I take walks and…do things."

"Not that I've observed."

"Well, you shouldn't be *observing* me."

Casziel shrugged, tore into his second Pop-Tart. "Can't be helped. I needed a human who hasn't been plagued with my kind. Your light hasn't been dimmed. *Yet*."

"I have a light?"

He fumed irritably, as if this information were common knowledge instead of completely insane.

"Between the realms of the living and the dead, is the Veil." Casziel held up his Pop-Tart to demonstrate a barrier. "Humans exist on This Side. The dead exist on the Other Side. Demons crowd as close to the Veil as possible in order to do their work on humankind. Like moths drawn to the light, ravenous and desperate to feed."

I imagined winged, writhing bodies slavering in the dark against a gossamer curtain, trying to get at the humans on the other side.

"And angels? Do they ever come to This Side?"

"Some do. If they have unfinished business here."

"My dad…?"

"Has unfinished business. He won't tell me what it is, so don't ask."

I flinched at Casziel's cutting tone, feeling chastised and small. I hated that any communication with my father was up to a demon, when I wanted nothing more than to have Dad to myself and tell him everything I never got to say while he was alive.

A tension, stuffy and hot, filled my small space until Casziel's low, soft voice cut through the silence. "Your father says there is nothing to regret, Lucy. All that was left unsaid between you, he reads in your heart."

Tears pricked my eyes. "He does?"

"He does."

I drew a shaky breath. "Thank you, Casziel."

He nodded; his hard anger had softened to something almost warm. The moment stretched, our eyes locked, and I felt a strange ache of nostalgia, though I couldn't tell if it came from him or me. A current running back and forth between us. Faint messages over a telephone line. I couldn't make them out, but I had the feeling I got when I closed a romance novel—wanting something I didn't have.

Or no longer had.

ELL, I GUESS we should get busy," I said, giving my head a shake. "You need a big, redemptive idea, and I need a dress for a work function this weekend. We can walk over to the Macy's at Herald's Square and brainstorm along the way."

Because who doesn't take their demon shopping?

The surreal nature of this whole situation swooped on me, as if I were trapped in a strange dream. But I was wide awake, sunlight was streaming in through the window, and there was a beautiful man in my kitchen eating Pop-Tarts and asking me to help save his soul.

"I'll just go get showered and dressed." I gathered some clothes to take with me in the bathroom. "You can watch TV or...do that."

Casziel had found a head of iceberg lettuce in my fridge and bit into it, crunching noisily.

I showered, changed into a T-shirt dress with a navy blue top and a patchwork of different patterns along the bottom. It was shapeless and loose—my preferred style—to hide my small pooch of a belly and thighs that definitely touched.

I made Casziel wait while I cleaned up the lettuce bits and Pop-Tart crumbs from my kitchen counter. Apparently, there were no table manners—or roaches—on the Other Side. Then we headed out into the April sunshine on a stunning Saturday morning.

I hated to admit it, but the demon—and Cole—were right. Left to my own devices, I would've probably stayed indoors on this beautiful day, reading and continuing to put off finding something to wear for my boss's wedding that I was nervous about attending in the first place.

Casziel walked beside me looking darkly beautiful. Pedestrians parted around us, giving him a wide berth, as if they unconsciously picked up on the subtle aura of danger emanating off of him. I, on the other hand, couldn't stop staring now that he no longer looked like a subway flasher in a trench coat.

He felt me watching him and glanced down at me. "Yes?"

"You don't sparkle."

"I beg your pardon?"

"I'm teasing." *Or going crazy.* "Just thinking about one of my favorite books, a romance about vampires."

"I am not a vampire."

"I think you meant to say, *There's no such thing as vampires, Lucy.*"

His gaze slid to me then back to the street.

I gaped. "They're real?"

"Do you really want to know?"

"Actually, no. My sanity will last longer if I pace myself. But…"

"You have questions."

"Only one or two…*thousand.*"

"Ask."

"I thought you were sick of my interrogation."

"I may have failed to take into account the novelty of our situation."

I smirked. "You think?"

"You can't blame me. Your entertainment creates a multitude of films and television shows on the subject, yet humanity has such puny capacity for the supernatural."

"We're trying. We even have a show called *Supernatural.*" I grinned. "You wouldn't like it. It's about demon hunters."

Casziel snorted. "A comedy, I presume."

I laughed. "And anyway, I think I'm doing pretty well dealing with our situation. For instance, I haven't freaked out over the whole anicorpus thing."

"There is nothing to *freak out* over. I told you, all demons have an animal form on This Side to facilitate transportation without drawing unwanted attention."

I nodded and wondered—aside from possessing a guy and stealing his clothes—where Casziel had gone last night. It was on the tip of my tongue to ask, but I wasn't so sure I wanted to hear the answer.

"How many times have you been on This Side?"

He glanced down at me, one brow arched. "Are you asking if I come here often?"

My face went hot all over. "You know what I mean."

"Many times, over the centuries."

"Why? What for?"

"Personal business," he said stiffly.

"Have you been to New York City before?"

"I have. Many of my kind are drawn to cities; they're riper for corruption. It helps that in New York everyone's already in a bad mood." He noticed my dubious smirk. "You don't believe me?"

"I don't know what to believe. I'm still half-sure I'm dreaming. Speaking of which, have you ever been to Japan or Russia on your journeys to This Side?"

He kept his eyes on the street. "Why do you ask?"

"It's nothing, I'm sure. It's just that I've had very lucid dreams that feel like…"

"Like what?"

"Real. In one dream, I was in Japan, hundreds of years ago. There was a young woman pulling a heavy wheelbarrow of supplies through the woods toward her village. I watched her from afar, but she was me. Like an out-of-body experience. I'd been warned the way was dangerous and the woods filled with bandits, but I didn't have a choice. My family needed the supplies to make it through the winter. I was nearly home when three bandits attacked me. They were going to *hurt* me…if you know what I mean."

Casziel nodded grimly. "I do."

"But a warrior came out of nowhere, wearing a mask over his face. A samurai, I think. He slaughtered the bandits, cutting them down with his sword, then pulled my cart to the village for me. He never said a word—I think there were rules about men being around unwed women back then. But I felt so safe. When we got to my village, the samurai set down the cart, bowed, and left."

"Rōnin," Casziel said.

"What?"

"A wandering samurai with no lord or master is a rōnin."

"Oh. Okay. How do you know that's what he was?"

Casziel shrugged. "A guess. And the other dream?"

"Okay...well, I lived in a city by the ocean during World War II. Saint Petersburg, Russia, but it had a different name back then."

"Leningrad."

"Right, Leningrad." I smiled. "You're like a walking history book."

He smiled thinly and waited for me to continue.

"I was about the same age I am now, and the bombs were dropping. So many bombs, I could feel the earth shake. Grit and smoke burned my eyes and everywhere there were explosions and people screaming. I ran through streets strewn with rubble, not knowing where I was going. Then a Russian soldier grabbed me and hurried me into a burned-out building just as another explosion rocked the street where I'd been standing a second before. The soldier saved my life. I didn't even know his name, but I clung to him, and he pressed me against the wall, shielding me from the blasts. As if whatever was about to happen, he wanted it to happen to him instead of me."

Casziel nodded, his face expressionless.

"The bombing seemed to go on forever and I was so scared," I continued. "But in that soldier's embrace, I knew I was going to be okay. When the attack was over, he asked if I were hurt—I wasn't, thanks to him—and then he just...left. Ran back into the smoke and disappeared."

"What do you think the dreams mean?"

"I don't know. Romance novels playing out in my subconscious, maybe. The Russian dream for sure. I must've read *The Bronze Horseman* one too many times." I grinned sheepishly. "I even think of the soldier as my Shura."

Casziel wasn't smiling.

"Or maybe they do mean something," I said, slowly. "My romantic heart is yearning for something real and every time I meet that man, he's always just out of reach. He never stays."

The demon inhaled through his nose. "As fascinating as your subconscious emanations are, this is no dream, and I'm still awaiting your plan for my redemption. One that you won't let Deb and K sabotage."

"Why would you say that?" I asked, feeling a little slapped by his sudden derision.

"I hear their chatter. Silly Lucy and her silly little life?"

I hunched my shoulders, letting my hair fall over my face. "You shouldn't be eavesdropping."

"My fate lies in your hands, Lucy Dennings. If you've ever had 'big ideas,' I see no evidence that you took them to fruition."

"I *do* have big ideas," I said. "Notebooks full of them. But I'm already up to my eyeballs in student loan debt—"

"And Deb and K have convinced you it's a waste of time anyway. That you're not good enough. That someone else will do it better…"

I hugged my elbows, wishing I could fold into myself. Or run back home, curl up in bed and dive into a book.

Be brave.

"You know, it's not cool to take someone's worst insecurities and fling them in my—their face."

Casziel shrugged. "Deb and K—"

"I don't care what you call them. That whispering doesn't sound like demons. It sounds like sneering inner voices I've been hearing my whole life."

"That's why we're successful," Casziel said. "Most humans let their brains chatter away all day, every day. A symphony of garbage into which we lace our insinuations so that they become indistinguishable."

I frowned. "It's not just chatter. We all have thoughts—"

"There is *thinking* and then there are *thoughts*," he said. "Deciding what to eat for dinner or working out a mathematical equation is thinking. Most thoughts are just noise and generally useless."

"So how does someone get rid of their demons?"

Casziel glanced down at me, his gaze suddenly intense. His tone commanding. "Stop listening to them, Lucy. Starve them with inattention."

"Easier said than done."

"Deb hungers for your shame. K is ravenous for your fear. They feed on it."

I glanced up at him. "And what do you feed on?"

He looked away. "The pain of having something precious ripped from you. Rage at the injustice of it. Grief for what has been lost."

The hurt weighed his voice down and I again recalled the vision of the temple and the deep, black chasm of anguish that had seemed ready to swallow me whole. A strong urge to take Casziel's hand in mine came over me. I even let the back of my hand brush his, a small, soft touch. Letting him know it was there if he wanted to take hold...

He flinched and shoved his hands into the pockets of his borrowed jeans.

"To the present matter," he said brusquely. "Any plan for my salvation needs to be a good one, Lucy Dennings. Nothing 'little' about it."

He doesn't want your comfort, Silly Lucy. He's here for him. Not you.

God, I was tired of how small those voices made me feel. I swallowed down my anxiety and steeled my courage to do what Casziel suggested—stop feeding my demons.

"If we're going to have a partnership, or whatever this is, then you need to act like a partner," I blurted, as we took a right from 49th Street to 7th Avenue. A few blocks away, the bells of St Patrick's Cathedral tolled noon.

"Partner," Casziel said. "Is that what I am?"

"Not if you keep talking like Deb and K. Not if you keep telling me I hole up in my place too much or that I substitute romance novels for living."

"Don't you?"

"No. I don't go out a lot because I'm introverted," I said. "Which isn't a crime, last I checked. And there is nothing wrong with enjoying those books. They're about love, which is the strongest force on earth. In them, you can experience different kinds of romance: enemies to lovers, second chances... And the men—the heroes—might be billionaires, mafia mobsters, or motorcycle club members, but they all have one thing in common. They would die for their woman."

"And that is what you want, Lucy Dennings? A man who would die for you?"

I thought he was joking but when I glanced up, his gaze was deadly serious.

"I don't need anything that extreme," I said with a small laugh, ignoring how my heart was beating a little bit faster. "But the intensity of that kind of love, the kind of love where you feel *lost* without the other person. Where your strengths bolster each other's weaknesses. Where you grow and are made better by loving them and being loved... Yes, I want that. And now that I'm saying it out loud, I realize I'm drawn to love stories because there's something in them that I recognize or connect to, despite never having been in love myself."

Holy moly, I hadn't spoken that much in a long time...and especially not my innermost feelings. I glanced up, expecting Casziel to be annoyed with my girlish musings, but he was hanging on every word. My pulse thudded even louder.

"My point is, in those books, you feel all the emotions and you fall in love along with the characters. And yes, you hope that kind of soul-deep romance happens to you too. That's part of the fantasy—that anything's possible. But until then, what's wrong with living in someone else's happiness for a little while?"

Casziel had nothing to say to that as we approached the department store. Maybe I'd gotten through to him after all. I inhaled slowly and let it out. My face didn't feel so hot anymore, and my shoulders came down from my ears.

So that's what standing up for myself feels like.

I liked it. I liked it a lot.

"What about you?" Casziel asked after a minute.

"What about me?"

"Where is your happiness, Lucy? Where is your billionaire mobster? The man on the phone this morning? Is he your *hero*?"

"Cole is only a friend. My best friend."

"You told him you loved him," he said stiffly.

"Because I do," I said. "But it's not a romantic kind of love. He's an artist studying on the other side of the world." I shot the demon a hard glance. "And he's gay."

"What is that death glare for?"

"You know what for."

He laid a hand to his chest, affronted. "Don't look at me. Stoking certain prejudices is Nadroc's domain and he's considered a tremendous asshole, even among my kind."

"Good. Because, honestly, I don't think I could help you find redemption if you have a hand in things like homophobia or racism."

He smirked. "But inciting humans to war is forgivable?"

"There are hundreds of reasons humans fight each other," I said. "Are you responsible for all of them?"

"Well…no."

"Sometimes war is necessary to *stop* evil. And besides, it's not up to me if you're worthy of forgiveness," I said as we waited for the light to change at the corner. "But the fact you're here, seeking it in the first place, means something. It means a lot."

A short silence fell, and the current or strange connection running between us hummed louder.

"I find it difficult to believe you have never been in love, Lucy Dennings," Casziel said finally. "Given your obvious capacity for it."

"Not yet." I glanced down at my shoes, my cheeks warming. "But I like to think I have a potential office romance situation, like in the books. There's a guy at my job. I've had a crush on him forever…"

I glanced up and recoiled at Casziel's expression. He was no longer hanging on my every word but looked almost angry.

"Anyway, never mind. We should be focusing on you, not me." I arched a brow at him. "Hate to break it to you, but you need a lot of work."

He sniffed a grudging laugh.

"I don't know where to start," I said, "but it has to be something monumental. Powerful. And there is only one thing powerful enough to redeem you in the ten days you have left."

"And that is?"

"Love. It's the only answer."

Casziel looked grim. "If love is the answer, Lucy Dennings, then we've lost already."

"Why?"

"Because there is no love left in me."

7

THE SUN WAS bright and high, yet it felt like a shadow had dropped over me. We'd arrived at Macy's and Casziel headed for the men's department. I hurried to keep up and joined him at a table where he stood examining ties.

"What did you mean, there is no love left in you?"

"I meant exactly what I said." He held up a black silk tie. "This."

"*That* is eighty dollars," I said. "Casziel—"

I stopped short and gasped. On our walk, he'd taken off the jacket, revealing arms of drool-worthy perfection, scars and all. But now I noticed a thin gash on the inside of his wrist, like a tally mark.

I grabbed his arm, examining the cut. It had been cauterized, the edges of it blackened and burned. "This is new. From last night?"

Casziel withdrew from my grasp. "It's nothing."

"Cas—"

"Have you not seen my scars?" he asked with a slight edge to his tone. "What's one more?"

"Did you do this to yourself?" I asked in a small voice.

"In a manner of speaking," he muttered, perusing men's dress shirts. "Don't you have business in this store?"

"Well, yes. My boss is getting married this weekend. We all have to go."

"And that's a chore?" Casziel said, not looking at me. His words dripped with bitterness. "If memory serves, weddings are joyous occasions."

"Social gatherings with a lot of people aren't my thing."

"As we've established. Go, Lucy Dennings. Find your dress."

I bit my lip. "Cas…"

"*Go.*"

He turned his back on me, and I had no choice but to head to the women's department and put his wound out of my mind. For now.

I found a pretty sundress in lavender with little green and pink flowers. It was perfect for an outdoor wedding in Central Park. Simple, with an empire waist that made me feel like Daphne Bridgerton.

Or maybe Penelope. And Guy is my Colin.

The thought made me feel a tad bit better about having to go to this wedding. I'd been dreading it for weeks, even though I loved my boss. Kimberly Paul was fun and kind, and her face lit up every time she mentioned her fiancée, Nylah. Their wedding was going to be perfect and romantic, set at the Central Park Boathouse with views of The Lake. But for me, it would be like any work function: hours of smiling and walking around as if I had somewhere to go instead of sitting in one place, alone. Jana Gill, from the accounting department, would try to include me in her group, but after a little small talk, I'd fall into awkward silence and drift away before anyone asked about my plus-one. Or lack thereof.

Casziel could be my plus-one.

I giggled at the thought. If Guy were Colin, then Casziel was the Duke of Hastings. God, I could just see the looks on everyone's faces that the handsome man with the gorgeous amber eyes had come with *me*.

A clerk rang me up and bagged the dress. I returned to the men's department to find Casziel waiting impatiently with a saleswoman who couldn't stop making eyes at him. He had changed into a new pair of black jeans, a tight black T-shirt, and a lightweight black leather jacket.

My breath literally fled my chest at how handsome he was, but I recovered fast, thanks to the huge pile of clothing at the woman's register.

I pulled Cas aside. "I can't afford all that. I mean, I have savings but—"

"Then you can afford it."

"But it's my *savings*."

"What are you saving it for?"

My jaw worked. I had no answer.

"Money is to be spent, Lucy Dennings," Casziel said, frowning. "Weddings are to be attended. Life is to be lived."

Before I could say another word, he nodded at the saleswoman— her nametag read Marcy. She eagerly got to scanning pants, shirts, jeans, and a suit jacket, all in black. I started to protest, then Marcy folded a Henley shirt that promised to highlight every line of Casziel's chest and arms.

Okay, I sort of need to see him in that.

While Marcy ran my credit card for an amount that made me light-headed, my eyes drifted again to Cas's arm.

He felt my attention and sighed. "I appreciate your concern. In fact, I'm relying on it. But not now."

I squared my shoulders. "Yes, now. Where did that come from? Tell me the truth."

"You don't need to hear the truth, nor do you want to."

"I do…"

His eyes hardened. "How can I make this more plain?" he bit out. "It's none of your fucking business."

I recoiled and let my hair fall over my face, shielding myself from Marcy who was madly scanning clothing, eyes averted.

"Fine," I murmured. "Forget it. Sorry I asked."

I moved a few steps away, pretending to be interested in a rack of wallets. I felt Cas move close, smelled the exotic, spiced scent of him that was like nothing I could identify. There was a soft touch under my chin and then he tilted my head up, his eyes heavy with regret.

"Forgive me, Lucy born of light. I'm more beast than human after living so long in the dark."

To my utter shock, his hand, heavy and strong, cupped my cheek. His touch raced through me like wildfire, down my neck, between my shoulder blades, over my breasts, tightening my nipples. The shivery heat made me gasp.

"My being here has a price," he said. "That is all you need to know. Understand?"

I nodded faintly, feeling as if time was standing still, and there was nothing left in the world but Casziel's rough voice and his soft touch on my skin.

"Never apologize for who you are." He brushed the hair from my face. "In your kindness lies my salvation."

I could've drowned in the longing in his eyes. I felt drawn into their timeless depths, falling through centuries, sunrises rising and nights falling...

Marcy cleared her throat and Casziel seemed to realize what he was doing. He snatched his hand back and looked away, regret hardening his features. The moment snapped so fast, if not for the fading tingle over my skin, I'd almost wonder if I'd imagined it. Like the raven, and the black-on-black eyes, and the feathered wings, and everything else. Every minute with Casziel was a battle with my own sense of reality. Like living in a lucid dream; I was sure I was going to wake up at any moment and he'd be gone.

And I'll lose him all over again.

The thought nearly stopped me in my tracks. It didn't make any sense, but then again, I reasoned, *none* of this did.

We left the store in silence and headed to a nearby Mexican restaurant. The bright colors and warm scents from the kitchen helped dispel some of the otherworldliness of the moment in the department store. Everything seemed so...normal.

Except for Casziel's appetite.

I watched him over my taco salad as he scarfed down a burrito, two chicken tamales, and an entire sizzling fajita platter.

"But you don't *need* to eat," I said, grimacing as he followed a swig of beer with a gulp of Horchata.

"All demons crave food, time, and sex."

Another flush of heat burned through me. "You crave *time?*"

"There is no time on the Other Side. Not as you know it. No neat, linear march of weeks, months, and years. It's a nebulous cloud in which every yesterday can be tomorrow, and a thousand tomorrows are happening all at once. On This Side, the monotony of immortality is broken with every new sunrise."

I leaned my cheek into my hand. "Despite your questionable table manners, you're something of a poet, Cas."

He glanced at me, then focused on his food. "Cas?"

"Is that okay?" I toyed with my napkin. "It just started to feel more...right."

And familiar. Because everything about Cas was growing more familiar to me with every passing minute. I lifted my head to catch him watching me. He looked away.

"There's nothing *poetic* about wasted time," he said irritably. "The ticking clock is supposed to make life more exciting and precious, yet the great majority of humans squander it. If you lived forever, you'd be an even lazier lot than you are now." He pushed his plate away, muttering almost under his breath, "And Cas is fine."

I grinned. The demon was sort of adorable when he was contrite. *And sexy.*

It was unescapable. Casziel had an otherworldly magnetism, true, but he was also just flat-out hot. I cleared my throat. "Okay, we've covered time and food, but demons also crave...um...?"

"Sex?"

Heads turned. Someone's fork clattered to their plate.

I hunched lower in my seat. "Say that a little louder; I don't think the chef heard you."

Cas shrugged, unperturbed. "Yes, we crave sex. Some more than others. One of my subordinates, Ambri, for instance, missed his calling as an incubus. But then, he's not interested in being saved."

"What do you mean?"

"There is a risk of forfeiting my redemption if I—pardon my Gallic—fuck a human."

Holy crap, the way those last three words zipped down my spine and burned like a flare between my legs stole my breath.

Get a grip, girl.

I took a long pull of cold water. "Why? Because sex is considered a sin?"

"It's not sex but the creation of Nephilim that's forbidden. The offspring of demons and humans."

"There are Nephilim here?"

"Of course."

"Would I know them if I saw them?"

"Very likely. They tend to gravitate toward politics."

I laughed, and his lips tilted in a small grin as the waiter dropped the check.

"Maybe your redemption is getting a job to help me pay for all this," I said after paying the bill and tucking my credit card back in my wallet. We stepped out onto the street. "I didn't have 'bankrolling a demon's Earth vacation' on my bingo card this week."

"This is no vacation."

"So you keep saying," I said, smiling to myself as Cas wordlessly took my dress bag out of my hands and added it to those he carried. "But I'm not feeling a real sense of urgency from you about your ten days."

He shrugged. "It serves no one if I'm desperate and panicked every waking minute."

"True, but…"

My words trailed as we came to a street corner. Our light was red, and we stood with a small group of people waiting to cross. A homeless man was leaning against the pole. Shirtless, skinny, he had shaggy hair that fell over his eyes. He mumbled a request for spare change, but no one waiting at the corner answered. No one even looked at him.

I dove into Cas's bag that held the "donated" Metallica shirt. I gave it to the homeless man, then rummaged in my wallet that had nothing left but a ten-dollar bill.

"Thank you, miss," the man said with a grateful smile that was missing a few teeth. "Have a blessed day."

"You too," I mumbled back, my throat thick, and crossed the street. Casziel fell in step beside me.

"The shirt off your back," he said quietly.

"He needed eye-contact almost more," I said, wiping my eyes. "Being seen…someone acknowledging that you *exist* matters. It matters a lot." I inhaled shakily. "Never mind. What now? We still need to figure out a plan for you."

Cas was quiet for a moment, thinking. "I wish to go exploring," he said finally.

"You just said this wasn't a vacation."

"I changed my mind."

"See, this is the lack of urgency I was talking about."

"The answer will come. I haven't seen the city in many years, Lucy Dennings." He peered down at me. "I'd like to, one last time."

The depth of his gaze and the longing that lurked beneath it made my heart pound.

Because this is his last chance for redemption. It's a big deal and has nothing to do with you.

I vowed to stop going all soft and fluttery every time Cas pinned me with those amber eyes of his and remembered he was a *demon*. A demon who had, in his own words, committed a multitude of sins. But he'd chosen the right human to help him. He deserved a chance and not just because he was gorgeous. Or because I caught him looking at me sometimes the way a condemned man looks at the world on his last day of freedom.

Ah, Silly Lucy is back, sneered Deb or K. *Silly Lucy with her silly romantic notions from her silly books—*

Casziel whirled on me, snarling. His eyes flashed pure black, and for a split second, I saw the demonic form lurking within the beautiful human man beside me. The cold dread I'd felt when I'd first found him reached for me with icy fingers. Like what I imagined Harry Potter felt when a Dementor tried to suck out his soul.

The voice went silent, and Cas's eyes reverted back to amber. He blinked innocently at me.

"Shall we?"

8

FOR THE REST of the afternoon and into the evening, I took Casziel all over Manhattan. We stored our purchases in Grand Central Station, then strolled the paths at Central Park, took in the garish lights of Times Square, and watched the sun set from the top of the Empire State Building. I'd lived in NYC for years, yet this excursion felt like the first time I really appreciated the city. As if Cas were reacquainting me with an old friend.

After a dinner of Korean Barbeque, a dessert of ice cream sundaes, and—because he was a bottomless pit—a second dinner of pizza for the demon—we grabbed our bags and headed back to my neighborhood in Hell's Kitchen.

The night was warm and soft, and I felt content in a way I hadn't in a long time. I'd been out in the world, talking easily with Cas about my studies at NYU and an idea I had to repurpose plastic scrubbed from the oceans to make athletic shoes. Somehow, being with Cas tore down the barrier between me and my feelings and my shyness about sharing them. Maybe it was because he'd scared my demons away for the time being, but I didn't feel foolish or silly. Hearing my idea out loud, it didn't sound stupid either. It sounded workable. Necessary, even.

"Perhaps it's time you shared your ideas with the people at your job," he mused as we strolled through my neighborhood. "They're all like-minded humans, desperate to save the oceans, are they not?"

"Yes." I glanced up at him. "And I know what you're going to say next—my big ideas can't go anywhere if no one hears them."

"Actually, I was going to say ocean preservation is a waste of time. In five years, a meteor is going to hit the earth and humans will share the fate of the dinosaurs."

I gaped. "What…?"

"I'm kidding." His lips twitched. "Maybe."

I laughed and nudged his arm with my elbow. Cas *almost* smiled when something across the street caught his eye. I looked in time to see two shadows fleeing from the yellow cone of a streetlight.

"Let's go there," Cas said, nodding at Mulligan's, an Irish pub just up the block.

"Something wrong?"

"I feel like having a drink. It's a well-populated establishment, therefore, it must be good."

I looked away. "I wouldn't know."

"It's ten steps from your home. You've never been?"

"Never."

I braced myself for his cutting remarks. Instead, he cast a final glance across the empty street and steered me toward the pub. I wasn't a big drinker, to say the least, but after the events of the last two days, getting a little tipsy seemed like a very good idea.

Mulligan's interior was dark with a few neon signs for Guinness and Murphy's glowing over the faces of the many patrons on a Saturday night. A TV blared from a corner, showing World Cup highlights, and competed with music from the jukebox. Even the toughest men gave the demon a wide berth, while women eyed him up and down. One caught my eye and mouthed *well done.*

Every barstool was taken. Two guys at the end were in deep conversation but froze at our arrival. Cas's eyes flashed to black-on-black again, and I felt the dread pour out. Without a word, the guys grabbed their pints and scurried away.

"Oh my God." I elbowed Cas and glanced around to see if anyone else had noticed. "You did *not* just do that."

He shrugged and pulled one stool out for me. "I don't like waiting."

I started to scold him when "Devil Inside" by INXS began to play. "You?"

His lips twitched. "Maybe."

"Now I *really* need a drink," I said, laughing. "And stop doing stuff like that."

The bartender came around and I ordered an Irish Old Fashioned. Casziel asked for a glass of red wine.

"Only wine?" I teased. "I figured you'd have one of everything and I'd have to take out a loan to cover the tab."

"Wine has been one of my few constants over the changing centuries on This Side."

"Centuries." The bartender set our drinks down, and I took a deep pull. My eyes watered as the whiskey hit the back of my throat, but it settled warmly in my stomach, making me pleasantly loose. "I can't imagine all you've seen over the years. You're a time-traveler, Cas. Which is easy to forget until you speak."

"How do I speak?"

"Like you're in the wrong era. You're a walking anachronism. No guy I know has the kind of polish and refinement you do."

Because he's not a guy. He's a man.

"You're an outlander," I continued, grateful that the dimness of the pub hid my blush. "Like the book, except if Jamie did the time-traveling and Claire stayed put."

"*The book* being a romance novel, I presume."

"Well…yes."

I toyed with my cocktail napkin, expecting his ridicule, but Cas looked thoughtful.

"Outlander," he mused. "A fitting title. I am out of my land—my home—and no longer belong anywhere."

"Were you always…what you are?"

"A demon, Lucy Dennings?"

The bartender gave us a funny look and moved to the other side of the bar.

"I was born a human."

"Oh, right," I said. "I keep forgetting, since you act like humans are beneath you."

"The internet makes a strong case."

I laughed. "You also didn't look very human when I found you."

"You discovered me in my true form." Cas gestured at himself, handsome in all black. "This was my human body. I must wear this ugly, tight-fitting suit to blend in on This Side."

"Ugly?" I snorted, already a little buzzed. "Have you seen *you*?"

He frowned, a perplexed little smile touching his lips.

I cleared my throat. "I mean, this is who you were in life."

"*In life.*" He spat the words as if they tasted foul. "In life, this body is fragile and easily broken. The form I was born into after death is powerful. Invincible."

"And demonic," I said carefully. "I thought you were trying to change. Doesn't that mean becoming human again?"

"No."

"An angel?"

"I am not, nor will I ever be, an angel."

Maybe it was the whiskey already going to my head, but his words sent a little shiver of heat dancing over my skin. But he clearly didn't want to discuss his post-redemption fate, so I changed the subject with all the grace of a tipsy person.

"Where were you born?" I blurted.

"Sumer. What you once called Mesopotamia."

My eyes widened. "The land between two rivers. The Cradle of Civilization."

Casziel's eyes flared almost imperceptibly. "How do you know of it?"

"I took an anthropology class at NYU. I don't know why; it wasn't part of my curriculum, but something about that time period fascinates me."

"Is that so?" he said into his wine glass.

"Absolutely, but no textbook can compete with someone who lived it. What was it like? Where did you grow up?"

"Larsa. A city-state in the southern region, near the gulf. I was born there in the year 1721, before the Common Era."

My eyes widened. "Holy crap. So that makes you—"

"Sumerian."

"I was going to say old."

Cas laughed a little, low and gruff, but his smile was beautiful. And short-lived.

"I am considered old by human standards, but I died in 1699 BCE at the age of twenty-two."

"How did you die?" I waved my hand. "Sorry, that's a personal question. At least, I think it's a personal question. I've never been able to ask someone how they died before."

"King Hammurabi of Babylon waged war on Southern Mesopotamia," he said. "He sought to absorb Larsa into his empire. I fought for my king, Rim-Sin the First, leading his army in many battles, but eventually we were overwhelmed. Rim-Sin fled." Casziel's eyes hardened. "I stayed."

"You were a warrior," I said, remembering one of our first conversations.

Cas nodded. "I defended my homeland to the bitter end, but it was useless. Hammurabi cut off the city, burning crops, starving the people. Women and children were dying. I had no choice but to surrender. I was captured and put to death."

"I'm sorry, Cas," I said, my fingers toying with a fresh cocktail I didn't remember ordering. "But you died defending your homeland from invasion. That doesn't sound like a bad thing. Certainly not bad enough to…"

"Condemn my soul to eternal damnation?"

"Yes…um. That. How did that happen? If you want to tell me."

He twisted the stem of his wine glass and became lost in the deep red depths.

"Hammurabi's hatred for me ran deep," he said. "We'd been at war for four years. I fended off his attacks and had led successful raids into Babylon. He blamed me for Larsa's defiance more than he did Rim-Sin."

I stared, wide-eyed, that Casziel lived through events I only studied in history books.

"Upon my capture, Hammurabi dragged me into the bowels of the ziggurat—our temple to Utu, the sun god. There, I was tortured and brought to the brink of death again and again. To punish me for my rebellion." His voice stiffened, his eyes full of memories. "He defiled our temple and Utu himself, soiling the walls of the god's house with my blood. But Hammurabi wasn't satisfied. He ordered his generals to round up my parents, my sister…" He took a long pull from his wine. "And my wife."

I remembered the strange vision I'd had when I first found Cas. His memories, I guessed, from the last night in the temple. A stab of jealousy knifed me in the chest. "You had a wife?"

He nodded. "It was an arranged marriage, as was custom. Hardly two months after our wedding, Hammurabi mounted his final, victorious attack, and Larsa was defeated. My wife was slaughtered with the rest of my family and her father, the high priest. One after the other, they were murdered right before my eyes." He inhaled through his nose, steeling himself. "Only when their blood ceased to flow was I allowed to die."

His pain slammed into me like a hammer. There was nothing I could say that wouldn't sound stupid and weak.

"The helpless rage and grief came with me as I Crossed Over," Casziel continued. "And Ashtaroth, drawn by that pain, was waiting for me on the Other Side."

"Ashtar—?"

Casziel's finger flew to my lips. "Don't say his name. You don't want him in your world, Lucy." He released me. "He must remain in mine."

"Who is he?"

"My commanding officer, so to speak. I am his servitor. His soldier." His mouth drew down in a grim line. "Stoked by Ashtaroth, my wrath worked fast to corrupt me. Under his guidance, I grew very powerful. There are few demons mightier—or more infernal—than he." He raised his gaze to meet mine. "Or me."

I sat back. "Oh."

"Ashtaroth welcomed me into a realm in which the rage and horror of my fate could be channeled. I stoked it in humans until it became something outside of me. I didn't have to suffer it; I reveled in it. My grief was no longer weakness but power."

"Grief isn't weakness," I said quietly. "It's a sign of love. It's love that endures—"

"And what of the love that is murdered before your eyes?" he demanded with sudden fire. "What is love when it screams your name on bloodstained lips, calling for help that you cannot give? Tell me that isn't weakness, Lucy Dennings. The ultimate weakness. To be unable to save them. I couldn't save them…" He shook his head with finality, his voice hard again. "Grief is not love. Grief is penance for living after love has died."

I swallowed hard. "What happened to you and your family is unimaginable, Cas. But the fact that you're here—"

"Is nothing heroic. I merely grow tired of feeding the fire of rage and pain. I'm tired of the endless hunger. The death."

My gaze dropped to the gash on his arm, hidden by a sleeve. "If we succeed, will Ash…will your commander let you go?"

"We have an agreement. Eleven days. No more."

It wasn't an answer to the question, but my head was already murky, and Cas was hailing the bartender again. A third round of drinks was set before us.

I took a deep pull of mine, letting the whiskey fortify me.

"I'm sorry about your family, Cas," I said. "My mother died when I was too little to remember her but losing my father... It's been the hardest thing. I can't imagine what you've been through."

"It was a long time ago," he said into his wine.

"Your wife..." I cleared my throat. The unwarranted little pang of jealousy seemed to be attached to that word. "Do you remember loving her?"

He whipped his head to me. "Why do you ask me this?"

"You said there was no love left in you. But if you loved her once, maybe it's still there. Maybe—"

"There is none left," he gritted out, as if each word cut him like knives. "Because I refuse to allow it to infest me like a sickness ever again."

"Love's not sickness. It's—"

"*Lucy*," he snapped. "Leave it. I have no patience for greeting card sentiment."

"I know you're angry," I said after a moment. "God knows when I'm really missing my dad or thinking about how he suffered in the last weeks of his illness, I don't want any grace or trite sentiment either. I'd burn it all to the ground to have him back."

Cas wasn't looking at me but seemed to be listening with his entire being.

"But sometimes, not very often, the grief kind of mellows," I said. "The sharp edges soften for a little bit, and I feel real beauty in it. I know that might sound crazy, but it's true. Beauty in his life, who he was, and who we were to each other. How much I loved him. In those times, the grief still hurts, but instead of getting angry or mad or scared, I feel grateful."

"*Grateful?*" he asked, disbelieving.

"Yes. Grateful that I had the privilege of knowing him. That this pain I'm feeling is strong because I loved him. I wouldn't trade it if it meant not having him. The bad stuff...it hurts. Sometimes, it hurts so much, it's almost impossible to see the beauty in life. But if we just take a deep breath and get really quiet, we can feel how alive we are.

We're here, experiencing it all, and the good stuff is all the more precious if we understand it might not stay as long as we want it to. My loss is not the same as yours, but that's how I think about it, and it makes me feel better. Maybe it would make you feel better too."

Holy moly, I didn't know what it was, but something about Cas got me talking more than my shyness usually allowed. He was watching me with a strange expression on his face. Maybe later I'd blame it on the booze, but I reached to take his hand. A scar sliced across the back that I hadn't noticed before. He stiffened at my touch, then softened into it. His fingers—a warrior's fingers, rough and calloused—curled around mine. Light at first, then tighter. He was pure power—masculine and hard and dangerous but not to me.

My hand belongs in his.

My thoughts, greased by whiskey, skidded off into slippery territory. How it would feel to have more of his skin touching mine. How other parts of us might fit together as perfectly. How there might be a kind of bliss waiting when the size and shape of every scar on his body was no longer a mystery to me.

For long moments, we sat together in that crowded, noisy pub, an oasis of silence. Then he gave my hand a final squeeze and let go.

"Your capacity for love is bottomless, Lucy Dennings," he said in a low voice. "I know what might help me."

"You do?"

He nodded. "Earlier today, I wasn't moved to offer that homeless man money or clothing, and it wouldn't have occurred to me that he needed human contact. But it occurred to you. You saw that man's plight and felt...what do you call it?"

My lips quirked. "Empathy?"

"Yes, that. And empathy cannot be taught. Neither can charity or compassion. Not to someone who has lived in darkness for centuries—and certainly not in the few days I have left.

"This puts us in a bit of a tough spot, Cas," I said, taking another pull of my whiskey.

"Indeed. Helping me is a waste of time. The key to my redemption lies in helping you."

"*Me?*"

"Yes."

"Okay," I said. "But love has to factor in somehow."

The alcohol was hitting me hard; my head felt like it was floating off my neck.

I giggled as a stray thought skittered across my boozy mind. "A fake relationship."

"Come again?"

"The 'fake relationship' is a trope in romance books where two people pretend to be together in order to achieve separate goals, like earn an inheritance or make someone jealous."

I didn't add that in the books, the fake relationship always turned out to be real in the end. Because that was impossible. Aside from the fact he was a demon, Cas was only on This Side for a handful of days. The fake relationship idea was too silly anyway, but he was rubbing his chin, wearing a thoughtful expression.

"Go on."

"Well...there's this guy at my work. I started to tell you about him earlier. I've had a major crush on him since forever, but he doesn't know I exist."

"Why not?"

"Well, look at me, for starters."

"I am looking at you."

He was. Cas's guarded, hard expression softened in the dim light of the pub, and his gaze roamed my face, drinking me in like wine, devouring me like the food he ate with bottomless hunger...

Silly Lucy, you're just drunk.

"I'm not exactly a super model."

"No, your body is fuller than the images in your magazines."

I hunched over my drink. "Gee, thanks. As if I'm not bombarded with that fact every day of my life."

"I have offended?" He frowned. "You are healthy and strong. Is that not valued now as it was in Sumer?"

"Yes and no," I said blushing up to the roots of my hair. "I don't know what they thought in Larsa, circa 17th century BCE, but in this era, the standard of beauty is not me."

"Then it has no standards," he spat.

I blinked, warmth flooding my chest. No one had ever said something like that to me before.

"Does this guy at your work subscribe to the same shallow perceptions?"

"Um, no, he's not shallow or superficial," I said. "To him, I'm just the quiet girl in the corner. But if you showed me attention, it might make him curious."

"He'll want what he can't have, you mean," Cas said sourly. "I may not have read your romance novels, but I'm familiar enough with male pride."

"Guy isn't like that," I said. "He's not a possessive jerk, but I think if he got to know me, he might see we have a lot in common."

"He is a good man?"

"Very. He works tirelessly on ocean preservation and always has good ideas. He's very popular around the office. He loves dogs…"

I dove back into my drink to stop rambling.

"And you believe if he sees you as the object of another man's interest, he'll grow interested himself."

"Maybe." I let my hair fall over my face. "Maybe not. No, definitely not. It's too risky and not monumental enough. We need something else—"

"How does this work, then? I pretend to woo you in front of this man…what's his name?"

"Guy."

"His *name* is Guy?"

"Yes…"

"Rather redundant." The demon smirked. "Is his last name Human?"

I giggled. "Guy is a real name. It's cute and it suits him. He's fun, easy-going…has a great laugh."

"Thank the gods for that." Cas rolled his eyes. "Very well, what do I do? Show up at your place of work and shower you with affection? Drop to my knees and beg you to stop toying with my heart and choose me to be your one true love?"

That didn't sound bad, honestly. I imagined the looks on everyone's faces, especially Abby Taylor, who always seemed as if she'd just finished talking about me behind my back.

"Nothing so dramatic but in that ballpark." I glanced down at my drink. "I haven't told anyone about my crush on Guy except for Cole and he's too far away to make me do something about it."

"But now we are doing something about it." Cas's voice turned low. "Will it make you happy, Lucy Dennings? To have the love of this man?"

I plucked my napkin. "Well…yes. Being in love and being loved by another in return is what we're here for, isn't it?"

"I'm here for you. This plan will benefit us both," he added quickly.

"But demons can't *make* anyone do anything," I said. "You told me that and I wouldn't want anything that wasn't real, anyway."

"I can't make Guy fall in love with you," Cas agreed, gritting out each word. Then his voice softened, turned gruff. "But if we guide him to you, I don't see how he could help it."

The words hit me hard and then sank in softly. The most romantic thing anyone had ever said to me. I basked in the feeling. A moment that could've been pulled from one of my romance novels.

Get real. This is real life, not a story with a guaranteed happy ending.

Still, it felt nice. For a little while.

I turned to the demon with a soft smile. "Thank you, Cas."

"For what?"

"It's been fun fantasizing about this, even if it's all make-believe."

He frowned. "Make-believe?"

"Well, yeah." I tucked a lock of hair behind my ear. "Nothing is going to come of Guy and me, but what you said felt good. Like having someone on my side. To have someone pretend that I'm…"

"Worthy of this man's love?" Casziel's expression was serious and grim—like what I imagine he must've looked like before going into battle. "I am on your side. And there is no pretending."

I shook my head, wishing I hadn't drunk so much. "No, no. This is not a Big Idea. It's not enough to save you."

"Probably not, given the depth of my sins. But it's the best hope we have."

I stared. "No, Cas. It won't work. It's…"

"Silly?" Casziel shook his head, his eyes like molten gold in the dimness of the pub. "Drawing a man to your light is a worthy cause, Lucy Dennings. *Your happiness* is a worthy cause. I can think of nothing worthier."

At those words, my heart beat hard, as if for the first time.

As if it'd been still and gathering dust in my chest until that night. With Cas.

I WAS DRUNK.

Like, whoa.

I couldn't remember the last time I'd been smashed.

"No, I rem'mber," I slurred, leaning heavily on Casziel as he maneuvered me and our packages from our shopping excursion out of the pub and into the night. "High school graduation. My frenn Sarah n' I got into her mom's stash of Southern Comfort. Bad idea. Do not recommend. Zero stars."

"I'll keep that in mind."

I peered up at Cas, shutting one eye to keep from seeing two of him.

"Not that two Cazzezz'z is a bad thing." I gasped and clutched at his arm. "I keep saying stuff out loud, don't I?"

His smirk deepened. "You do."

I scowled. The beautiful bastard was completely sober, despite matching me glass for glass. I vaguely remembered it was Cas who kept ordering the cocktails—which I then paid for.

Gotta get this boy a job…

I snickered and then slugged his arm, my fist bouncing harmlessly off the hard muscle of his bicep. "Why'd you lemme get so drunk?"

"You needed it," he said. "Not the illness tomorrow perhaps but to be out in the world. Your own neighborhood, at the very least."

"Pfft," I scoffed. "Just another step in your gran' plan to...what? Make me *not* be an introvert? Good luck, pal."

"I'm not trying to change you, Lucy Dennings."

"Then what's the dealio?"

He glanced down at me. My vision was blurred with whiskey, but I could've sworn there was longing in his eyes, as if he were waiting for...something. For me to say or do something he couldn't. But I couldn't guess what, and I was too busy drinking in his handsome face anyway.

God, he is really, really beautiful. For a demon.

But it was nearly impossible to think of Casziel as an infernal creature of the underworld. Or that I had two demons of my own, plaguing me. Now that I was three sheets to the wind, the whole situation was ludicrous again.

I giggled.

"Something amusing?"

"I have two demons and one of them is named...Deb. Short for Deborah? Debbie? What is K short for? Karen?"

"Their true names are Deber and Keeb."

I burst out laughing. "Stop it. Do they make cookies and live in a tree?"

He stared at me blankly. "They're quite infamous. Not many demons have been referenced in the Bible by name." He tilted his chin. "Although there are whole chapters dedicated to me in various grimoires. I'm mentioned several times in the *Theurgia Goetia* alone..."

I couldn't stop giggling. "It's just that Kee—"

Cas put a finger to my lips. "No true names. Not unless you want to summon them or bind them tighter to you."

"All it takes is speaking a demon's true name to summon'em?"

"Rituals are sometimes required. The more powerful demons, such as myself, take a great deal of wooing."

"I never wooo'd you," I said and my face got hot. "I mean...I din' summon you."

"Of course, you didn't," he said disdainfully. "I don't come at a human's beck and call like an obedient cur. I chose you."

"You chose me," I said with a smile. "You know, Cas, sometimes it feels like you and I..."

His arm under my hand stiffened. "Yes?"

"Like we—"

"Ssssh," Cas hissed and froze.

We were almost at my building. The shadows seemed thicker that night. In the alleys between buildings, the darkness felt alive. Breathing.

You're just drunk. Waaay drunk.

But Casziel's sharp eyes were narrowed, and he muttered a curse in his own language.

Sumerian, I thought. *His language is Sumerian because he's almost four thousand years old...*

The surrealism of my situation washed over me again, and I was glad for the booze that let me take a vacation from having to make it all make sense. I was too drunk, in fact, to pay attention as Cas hustled me off the street, around the corner to my back lot where I'd found him, and up the stairs. I managed to retrieve my keys from my purse but getting the right one in the lock was beyond me.

Cas juggled me, the packages from our shopping spree, and the keys, and got us all inside. He dropped the bags, then kicked the door shut. I clung to one arm as he raised the other, palm facing the door.

"*Zisurrû,*" he murmured.

I could hardly keep my head level or my eyes open, but there was no mistaking the thin light that outlined my door, glowing green in the darkness.

"Okay, so that happ'ned."

The light faded and Cas helped me to my bed. I crashed headfirst into my pillow but managed to snag the cuff of his jacket. I tugged him until he sat stiffly on the edge beside me. The exotic scent of him was as intoxicating as whiskey, conjuring images of flat land under a bright sun, cradled by two rivers...

"Wait." My brows furrowed as I tried to think through the drunkenness. "What is happening, Cas? Tell me the truth. Is this...?" I flapped a hand. "Is this all real? Or am I imagining you?"

"Would you prefer if it weren't real?" His voice was low. Gentle. "Do you want to wake up tomorrow with no memory of these last two days? Of me?"

My grip on him tightened. "*No.* I...I don't know. I can't think. Something happened tonight. You were afraid but I can't..."

"I fear nothing," Casziel said. "Not for me. But if you're frightened, Lucy. If this is too much..."

"You'll go away?"

I felt more than saw him nod.

"And I won't remember you?"

"If that's what you want."

"What about your redemption?"

"My only peace is knowing that you are safe and happy." He stroked my hair; his soothing touch was driving me down, down...

"Don't be afraid, Lucy Dennings. Nothing will hurt you. I won't let it."

The safety promised in his deep voice fell over me like a heavy blanket. Like an incantation lining me in his protective light.

I smiled and sighed as I sunk into sleep. "I believe you, Casziel."

But I don't know who you are. Or do I...?

Another voice answered, sinister and crawling with shadows.

I'll show you who he is...

A battlefield.

Bodies lie in pools of blood, soaking the dirt. The smell is unbearable. Nothing moves but ashy clouds that broil across the rust-colored sky.

And the flies.

Flies buzz over the dead like a living fog, their hum loud in my ears and growing louder. I look for an escape, but there's nothing in any direction but the dead. I brush the flies away from my face, out of my hair. But still more come and I have to run.

Blindly, I trip over motionless limbs and still the flies come at me, covering my eyes, their legs and wings tickling my skin.

And when I open my mouth to scream, they pour in...

I woke up with a scream on my lips. The dream faded and reality—searing to my aching head—rushed in. I was in my bed, in my apartment, and Casziel was nowhere to be seen.

"Just a nightmare. That's all."

I winced as morning light pierced my eyes, as if the sun were extracting vengeance on me for some unknown crime. I lay back down and waited until the nausea faded. The dream tried to creep back into my thoughts, but I pushed it out or else I was going to be sick for sure.

When I trusted my stomach again, I got up and went to the kitchen for a glass of water. Moving like an old lady, I passed the window—open a crack—and grimaced at the sight of a fly skittering along the outside of the pane.

"Stay out of my dreams, you."

I managed to get a glass out of the cupboard and filled it with water from the tap. My mouth tasted like the floor of a movie theater—I vaguely remembered the bartender at Mulligan's had put a bowl of stale popcorn in front of us at some point during last night's revelries.

My revelries. Despite drinking a gallon of wine, Cas had remained sober as hell.

I snickered and drank more water, facing my small, empty place. There were now several flies congregating outside my window. As I watched, one flew inside and landed on the bowl of fruit on my counter. The lone banana was about to go bad.

Another fly joined it. Then another.

"What...?"

I went cold all over to see a cloud of flies buzzing at the window, covering the pane, a writhing mass of little gray bodies. More and more...then they poured inside like smoke, swamping me. First in handfuls, then so thickly, I couldn't see.

The water glass fell from my hands to shatter on the linoleum at my feet. I frantically—and uselessly—batted at the swarm.

This isn't real this isn't real this isn't...

I stumbled and crashed into the tiny island counter. Trapped. I didn't dare open my eyes or even breathe as flies covered my skin, relentless. The terror enveloped me, driving out rational thought. Impossible to imagine this was actually happening.

I started to sink to the floor when the air shifted. Like a current running through the apartment.

"*Ma ki-ta!*"

Through my fingers, I saw Casziel. The demon, Casziel. He stood in the center of my apartment dressed in his black clothing. But a huge sword was strapped between the rippling muscles of his back and shoulders, between massive wings covered in glossy black feathers that draped down on either side of him, long enough that their tips brushed the backs of his boots. Even in that horror-filled moment, the dark majesty of him stole my breath.

He thrust both pale, bloodless hands toward the window and beat his immense feathered wings, once. The gust of wind they created caught every fly and drove it through the open window. Within seconds, they were gone, again leaving my senses overwhelmed and grasping desperately for what was real.

A sob escaped me as I clutched the counter. Casziel turned his head at the sound, his black-upon-black eyes like onyx pits in the alabaster perfection of his face. I cowered at the cold dread emanating from them and sank to the floor where I curled up amid the shattered glass.

In the next instant, Cas was kneeling before me in his human form, his expression stricken.

"Forgive me, Lucy. Forgive me…"

He took my face in both hands and leaned in. For one crazed moment, I thought he was going to kiss me. But he pressed his thumb to my forehead and closed his eyes.

"*Ñeštug u-lu…*"

I blinked awake and a little cry flew out of my mouth. I was sitting on the kitchen floor, pressed up against the island instead of in my bed. Broken glass lay all around me in a small pool of water. I was so drunk last night. I must've tried to get water and dropped the glass, then…passed out?

My stomach roiled at the idea that I'd been so reckless.

Cas didn't help.

Despite drinking a gallon of wine, he'd remained sober as hell…

"Whoa. Déjà vu."

Gingerly, I stepped around the broken glass with my bare feet. My apartment was empty. I looked to the open window, wondering if Cas were going to fly in as a raven and decided if he was, I didn't need to watch it happen. My poor brain didn't need another jolt.

And there was something about the window…

I cleaned up the glass, sopped up the water, and tried again. This time, I made it back to my bed with a full glass and two Advil from my bathroom. I lay against my pillows, feeling my headache pound behind closed lids.

I'd just begun to doze when my phone rang. Groaning, I fumbled around until I found it on the floor next to my bed.

"If you care about me at all, you'll whisper," I said to my best friend.

Cole's eyes widened in alarm from behind his black-framed glasses. "Are you okay? Are you sick?"

"I'm fine, just hungover."

"*You?*" Cole cried and I winced. "Sorry, sorry," he chuckled, then his concerned expression morphed into a delighted smile. "But did you get drunk on fruit wine from a local vintner who brings the musk melon goodness to his oak Chardonnay?"

"It was a lovely banana rosé." I laughed, then winced again. *Schitt's Creek* was one of our favorite shows and we never missed an opportunity to quote from it as often as we could.

"So?" he asked, reaching for his sketch pad. "Spill it. I want to hear all the dirty details." He froze, a thought striking him. "Oh shit, are you alone? Am I interrupting the Morning After? Are you with that guy I heard yesterday?"

Yesterday? Yesterday was a hundred years ago.

"Yes. No," I amended quickly. "He's not here. But yeah, we went out last night."

Cole's eyes were practically popping out of his head, his hand working over his sketch pad. "Tell me. All of it. Who is he?"

"He's a friend. I think."

Cole sagged, lips pursed. "Don't even."

"I'm serious. He's only in town for a few days."

"And then what? Then he's gone forever?"

Yes. He's gone forever.

My heart suddenly ached as much as my head.

Cole's hand stilled. "Luce?"

"Pretty much."

"What's his name?"

"Casz... His name is Cas. And you'll be happy to know he's going to help me with Guy."

God, it sounded ridiculous saying it out loud.

"Okay, and how is this Cas going to help the Guy situation?"

"It's a long story and I can't talk right now. I love you, but if I don't close my eyes in ten seconds, it's going to look like *The Exorcist* in here."

Oh my God, my life is all demons right now...

"Okay, okay, you can fill me in later," Cole said. "I called to show you something." He flipped his sketch pad back a page to show me another realistic drawing of me. "This is the one I did yesterday, remember? When your face lit up?"

"I remember," I said softly.

Cole laid his pencil to the portrait that was lightyears from those he'd been doing lately. "Note the light in the eyes and the mouth, lips parted in a little bit of a surprise. As if a pleasant thought caught you off guard. Almost a smile but not yet."

I swallowed hard. "I see it."

"You weren't thinking about Guy, were you?"

I shook my head, no.

"It was Cas. Right?"

I nodded a yes.

Cole's smile was gentle. "So, my question is, Luce, if Cas makes you look like this, why would you need to think about Guy ever again?"

10

I KNEEL IN front of Ashtaroth in the back room of Idle Hands. The lone black candle's flame is pale white and doesn't move. Under the settee, the huge serpent—also pale white—watches me warily.

Lesser servitors creep underfoot, hoping for a drop of blood or lick of fear. But even in my weak human form, they scuttle back into the shadows at my snarl.

"Are Deber and Keeb on This Side?"

"Am I the twins' keeper?" Ashtaroth muses, drawing his sword. "They are the girl's demons." He slices his sword across my arm, carving a new line into my skin, parallel to the first. "Perhaps they have come to play with her too."

I search for a sign that Ashtaroth knows more than he is saying, but he turns his blade flat, and I shut my eyes with a grunt. The scent of my seared flesh almost overpowers the stench of his breath.

Almost.

"Go, Casziel," he says when it's done. "Hopeless infatuation and concern for that girl is writ all over you. It's making me ill. If the twins plague her, they have my blessing. Begone."

My hand itches for my own sword to slice the callous words out of his throat, but the game I'm playing is a long one and I can't give up too early. I bow and head for the door.

"Oh, and Casziel," Ashtaroth calls, idly stroking the head of his serpent.

"My lord?"

"Hmm, I've forgotten what I was going to say." He wears a smile I don't like, his black eyes glittering in the black candlelight. "No matter. I'm sure it will come to me."

I go out and draw on the armor that is my demonic form. The tavern is full; every demon minding their own business. Behind the bar, Eistibus's gaze is averted. Good. He should fear me. They all should.

Especially any who dare hurt Lucy.

I close my eyes at the memory of her terror, the flies swarming her—a nightmare come to life. The helpless anguish of watching her suffer brought back our last night in the ziggurat—her eyes full of tears and love, mutely begging me for help I could not give. The flash of a blade and then the hot wash of her blood... I succumbed to Ashtaroth's servitude all those years ago because I never wanted to feel like this again—chest torn open, heart laid bare and at the mercy of that relentless agony called love.

Eistibus senses my mood and approaches slowly. "Wine, my lord?"

I nod and he sets a glass in front of me. I drain it, then hurl it at the shelf of bottles behind the djinn where it shatters.

"Ambri, to me!"

My call reverberates through Idle Hands, into the ether of This Side, across the Veil, and to the Other Side. Within moments, the tavern door opens, and my second-in-command saunters in wearing a lazy smile, black eyes set in a devilishly handsome face. His blood red jacket is as immaculate as always, his gold hair perfectly coiffed. He shows no weariness from Crossing Over; his wings—black feathered like mine—are high and arched as he stands at attention and gives me a sharp bow.

"Lord Casziel. How may I serve?"

"You're on This Side," I observe.

"Well...yes." Ambri tugs at the cuff of his velvet jacket. "I was tending to my affairs here in the city, making sure my flat and finances are all in order—"

"You were fucking humans."

He grins. "Maybe just one. Or two. Or...five."

"It's not an auction." I gesture at the stool beside mine. "Sit."

Ambri moves aside the sword strapped to his narrow waist and takes a seat with the grace of a hunting cat. Eistibus places two more glasses of wine on the bar and leaves us.

"I have a task for you," I say to my second.

"You have only to name it and it is done." Ambri's voice still carries his human accent—he'd been a wealthy British lord some three hundred years ago and spent his brief life traipsing around Europe, spending money, bedding anything with a pulse, and generally being a living embodiment of lust, sloth, and gluttony.

Not much has changed.

I sip my wine; it tastes sour. Or perhaps it's the words in my mouth. "I want information on a human. Guy Baker."

Ambri arches a perfect brow. "*Guy*? Are the humans running out of names?"

I smirk despite myself. Ambri is my favorite of my servitors and the closest thing to a friend. If one can call a demon who'll stab you in the back if it furthered his own ends a friend. But I can't judge—I was once just like him. My path to the top of the hierarchy is littered with the bodies of those who stood in my way.

"I want a full report," I say. "Who his demons are, his history, his natural weaknesses and vices, everything."

"Consider it done. Anything else?"

"If there were anything else, I'd have named it."

"Aye, my lord." He watches me over his wine glass with onyx eyes.

"Speak your mind, Ambri," I snap irritably.

"Are you not curious as to how your legions are faring on the Other Side? Maras is commanding them well in your absence, but they're still your servitors, my lord."

My servitors can go to Oblivion for all I care.

How much better would the world be without them? Without me?

But it's futile—and pathetic—to think my departure will atone for my sins. Maras, or any number of other demons from the Brethren, will rise to take my place. War and strife will continue as it always has. So long as humans harbor a spark of malice for each other, there will always be demons to stoke it into an inferno.

Ambri's shrewd, black gaze narrows on me.

"Very well," I grit out. "Tell me."

He relays news about conflicts in Myanmar, in Eritrea, in Sudan. I'm hardly listening, and he notices.

"You seem a tad distracted, Lord Casziel. Is everything well?"

They plagued her with flies...

I bite back an order for Ambri to send a battalion after Deber and Keeb, to rend the twins limb from rotted limb, then transport them back to the Other Side in pieces.

"Everything is well," I mutter into my wine.

"I only inquire because you haven't shared with me, your loyal second, why you're on This Side, taking a leave from your command." He nods at the door of the back room. "Lord Ashtaroth is here too, or so I smell. Did you get in a bad way with the old man—?"

My hand snakes out and closes around Ambri's throat. I haul him close, my hard glare boring into his wide black eyes.

"Watch yourself, Ambri," I hiss. "Control your wagging tongue or I'll cut it out of your human mouth and leave your bedmates sorely disappointed."

"F-forgive me, m-my lord," he chokes out but knows better than to struggle.

I release him with a snarl and drain my wine. "Guy Baker. Tomorrow night. Go."

Ambri straightens his collar. "Yes, my lord."

He makes his way through the tavern and out into the night.

Eistibus is at one end of the bar, giving me a wide berth. Ba-Maguje is here again tonight, lying slumped at the other, working his influence. His wet lips move as if he's talking in his sleep, cajoling his humans to have another drink. It won't hurt anyone. Just one more...

Disgusted, I turn my gaze to the demons in the rest of the tavern. A motley collection of vile devils with misshapen bodies—talons, matted hair, scales—wallowing in their revolting fluids while having a drink or two. Taking a break from stoking their humans' misery, apathy, or perversions.

I down the rest of my wine and give Eistibus a parting nod before storming out.

Just a little longer, I think as I take to the air in my raven form. A few more days and it will all be over.

And Lucy?

Hatred for my fellow demons is a joke. I'm no better than they. Worse, even. The world will not mourn me, and neither will Lucy. How could she? The man she knew is dead. He died in the bowels of the ziggurat nearly four thousand years ago, and everything she loved about him died too. Corrupted and ruined beyond redemption.

There is no love left in me.

Only a stubborn, lingering hope that she be cared for after I'm gone. That she finally finds the love and happiness that was stolen from her. From us.

Because she still has a chance, even if it's too late for me.

PART II

W HEN CASZIEL RETURNED from wherever he went at night, he brought back a foul mood that permeated the entire apartment like a fog and lasted for the rest of Sunday. He refused to tell me what was wrong and snapped at me when I tried to make conversation. All the warm words and longing looks from the pub must've been my imagination. It was hard to believe he'd stroked my hair or told me my happiness was worth everything. Worth risking his soul…

When I felt recovered enough from my hangover, I went grocery shopping for the week, buying a mountain of food for the remaining nine days of Cas's "visit." I tried not to think about the days ticking down, but the thought wouldn't leave me alone. I wondered how you could miss someone—someone you'd just met—before they were even gone.

My earlier conversation with Cole didn't help. But even if Cole were right—and he wasn't—what could I do? Casziel was leaving. Permanently.

I returned from the store to find my demon sprawled on the couch, a slant of late afternoon light falling over him. He was watching TV while stuffing his face with frozen peas straight from the bag. An empty jar of mayonnaise and a spoon littered the coffee table.

Breakfast of champions.

"So…I guess we need to talk about tomorrow when I go to work." I set the two grocery bags on the kitchen counter. "Is 'fake relationship' really what we're going with, or did I conjure that in my drunken stupor?"

"It is the best plan," Cas said, not looking up from his show. *Dr. Phil*, by the sound of it.

"Are you sure?"

"Yes."

"Because—"

"That's the plan, Lucy Dennings. There is no other."

I frowned and put a new head of lettuce into the fridge. "It's just that…I'm worried about you. It's super nice that you want to help me out with Guy, but this is your eternal soul we're talking about."

"*Super nice,*" Cas said icily. "Yes, that's exactly what I am."

I grit my teeth and wished my father were there to ask for advice. Then I remembered he was, in a matter of speaking.

"What does Dad think of our plan?"

For long moments, there was only the crunch of Cas's frozen peas, then his toneless reply, "He's in accord."

I pinned the demon with a hard look. "You're lying."

He arched a brow. "Is that so? You know me so well, do you?"

It was a rhetorical question, but something about it bugged me. Being with Casziel was like constantly living with that feeling you've forgotten something but can't remember what. I *did* know him. Or at least it felt like I did. The tone of his voice, his facial expressions, the tilt of his head…they all had a familiarity about them that made no sense. It was why I hadn't thrown him out of my house a hundred times.

I don't know him at all. We're bonded, I rationalized. *I said his true name and now he's mine.*

"He's mine."

A flush of heat swept over my face, and I almost dropped a jar of peanut butter. If Casziel heard me, he didn't show any sign; he was too absorbed with his TV show.

A demon trying to improve himself with Dr. Phil.

I smiled behind my hair.

When the groceries were put away, I pulled my desk chair next to the couch. "Dad really likes our idea?"

Casziel sighed. "I don't enjoy repeating myself."

"Does he think it'll *work?*" I persisted. "Not that Guy and I will live happily ever after... I mean, does he think it'll help you?"

Cas seemed to listen but kept his expression neutral. "Yes," he said finally. When I started to protest, he shot off the couch. "I'm going out."

"Cas, wait," I said, standing too. "About tomorrow...what do we do for our plan? Do you, I don't know...send me a bouquet of flowers to get the office's attention? I saw that in a movie once."

God, pathetic.

"I'll take care of it."

He reached for his black leather jacket on the back of the couch, and that's when I saw another gash on his wrist, a twin to the first. Two lines of sliced, burned skin in two perfect rows. The next morning, I realized with a sinking feeling, there would be three.

"Cas..."

"Goodnight, Lucy."

Then there was a raven in my apartment and then there was nothing.

I ate dinner alone and then curled up with a romance novel. But the words couldn't hold me, and I started to drift. My thoughts scattered but I saw the woman in the field with the black braids and she

enters the city walls—bricks made of mud—and into the chaos. A parade for the soldiers returning from war. It's been four years; she's been counting each day, yearning for her warrior's return. Her blue eyes scan the crowds, hopeful to find him and terrified she won't. Black-haired men and women wave cuts of colorful cloth, cheering and singing hymns to Utu and Innana. The acolytes burn tall staffs of sage as they walk among the warriors marching toward the ziggurat in the center of the city.

The woman pushes her way through the throng, following the marching soldiers, scanning their faces. But her beloved is no foot soldier. He's their commander, and the woman's soul sings louder than any hymn when she sees him at the head of the regiment. His back is to her—new scars mar his bronzed flesh—but she would know him anywhere. He is half her heart, and he is alive.

Fierce pride and fiercer desire burn through her as she follows the march to the steps of the ziggurat. Priests—her father among them— perform the Šu-il-lá i, raising cupped hands in supplication to the gods, chanting incantations while an acolyte makes an offering. The gelded bull lows in panic, and then his blood flows rich and red on the stone altar.

The king steps forward, the sun glinting off his headdress of gold and lapis. He raises his arms wide and declares the day a holiday to celebrate the glory of Innana who has graced them with victory. The speech drones on; the woman grows impatient. Men in the crowd mutter that the enemy isn't defeated, only delayed. She scoffs. There should be no talk of Babylonians on this victorious day—it's her beloved's valor that the king should celebrate.

She will atone for her pride later. Now, she wants only him. Soon, they will be joined; they've paid the price in long years of separation and war. But that ends now.

Ki-áñg ngu...My beloved.

He must hear her silent call; his head turns, and somehow, he finds her in the cheering crowds. His helmet shadows his face, but a sweet ache blooms between her legs for she can feel how he's watching her. He's been waiting too. To have her. To wed her. To take her as his and claim her under the laws of gods and men for all time.

The king calls for her beloved to stand before him. Ale is poured over his muscled shoulders, and it flows like liquid gold. The chanting voices rise as he is celebrated for bringing home victory. Prosperity. Safety.

And as the priests and the king heap their praises on him, she knows his gaze strays to her, heated and full of longing. Of love, for though he may have taken others to his wartime bed, she is the one he comes home to...

I came awake with the woman's anticipation and desire burning under my skin and between my legs.

"God, what was that?"

It was just as clear and real as the Japan and Russia dreams—I could feel the thrum of the city, the people, smell the green scent of the river, apricot and peach trees, almonds and figs... What Casziel had told me in the pub about his past came rushing back to me.

"Was that...Larsa?" I asked my empty room.

And the woman?

Cas had said his existence might infiltrate my subconscious through our bond. Something about that hadn't sat right with me then and it didn't sit right that morning either. But he wasn't around to ask, and a glance at the clock said I needed to get ready for work.

I showered and dressed in my usual work "uniform"—a skirt, shapeless sweater, and a little mascara. I made coffee and drank it slowly with a slice of cantaloupe and a bagel with cream cheese—and still no Casziel.

"The Weekend of Weird might be officially over," I muttered, ignoring the pang in my heart.

Silly Lucy is now safely tucked back into her silly little life, sneered a voice. Deber or Keeb. Or more likely just my own rampant insecurities.

I waited as long as I could, but I was going to be late and Casziel obviously wasn't going to show. I grabbed my bag and headed out.

The E train was on time and I got off at Lexington and 53rd, Midtown, and rode up the elevator to the ninth floor of The Conway building. Ocean Alliance, under Executive Director Kimberly Paul's leadership, had flourished in its three years and now we had the entire floor to ourselves.

"Hi, Dale," I said, mustering a smile for our receptionist.

"Morning, Luce." He smiled back. "How was your weekend?"

I coughed. "Oh, same ole, same ole."

I hurried away and dove behind the partition in my cubicle. The office was open-concept, with lots of plants and sweeping views of the city. Each of the forty or so employees' desks were partially walled off and all departments intermingled. Jana Gill—the head of accounting— was next to me, as was Abby Taylor, Chief Marketer, who created all of our commercials and outreach videos.

I was head of logistics, having been promoted three months in. It wasn't very challenging after my bioengineering degree, but it didn't require me to talk to anyone. And after my conversations with Casziel, it occurred to me that I took *other* people's Big Ideas and researched them to see how they could be made into reality.

That hadn't bothered me before, but that morning it did. It bothered me a lot.

Both Abby and Jana were already at their desks, their chairs pulled close to chat about their weekends. Jana gave me a warm, friendly smile. She had her blond hair pulled back in a ponytail and dark circles under her eyes—she'd recently had a baby boy.

Abby gave me a scrutinizing once-over. Her dark brown hair was fresh from a blowout, makeup immaculate, and her clothing up-to-the-minute stylish. She reminded me of the models from the opening montage of *The Devil Wears Prada* while I was Anne Hathaway in her shapeless cerulean sweater with bagel crumbs spilled down the front.

"Heya, Luce," Jana said. "You look pretty today."

"Oh, um…thanks," I mumbled, taking my seat and stowing my bag under the desk. "How's Wyatt?"

"He's lucky he's so cute," Jana said, smiling tiredly. "I don't remember what sleep is."

"What about you, Luce?" Abby asked. Somehow her "Luce" sounded condescending while Jana's was endearing. "You look a little tired yourself. Long night? Anyone we know?"

I blushed and busied myself organizing my already organized, immaculate desk. "No, no. I had trouble sleeping last night."

"*Of course*, you did, honey. I'm just teasing, *obviously*."

Because it's impossible that I might've spent the night with someone.

A current of sandalwood cologne wafted over us. "Morning, ladies," said a deep voice.

My cheeks immediately went up in flames, like an autonomic reaction. Guy Baker had his arm slung over the top of Abby's partition, a confident, easy smile on his tanned face. The executive VP wore jeans, a plaid button-down shirt rolled up at the sleeves, and Timberland hiking boots. His sandy-blond hair was a little rumpled, as if *he'd* spent a long night with a woman's hands running through it.

"Hello, Guy," Abby said, her knowing gaze sliding between him and me in a way I didn't like. "You're looking *dashing* this morning. What can we do for you?"

"Kim wants every department head in the conference room in ten." He grinned. "Our fearless leader is all work, no play. As usual."

"That woman will work through her honeymoon if we let her," Jana said fondly.

"Truth," Abby groused. "I still can't get over no bachelorette party. It's practically *criminal*, considering there are *two* bachelorettes."

"We have four days to change her mind." Guy turned his mega-watt smile my way. "See you in there, ladies."

His cologne lingered in the air, and my gaze lingered on *him*. Normally, I'd be kicking myself for not mustering even one word of greeting or small talk. But aside from my involuntary blush, Guy's presence hadn't cast its usual spell over me. And I couldn't help but compare Guy's rugged, blond, outdoorsy-ness to Casziel's sleek, dark polish. The two men couldn't be more different.

Casziel's not a Guy. He's a man.

"There she goes." Abby shook her head at me. "God girl, if pining were an Olympic sport..."

My cheeks burned. "No, I wasn't...I mean, never mind."

"Knock it off, Abby," Jana said. "Guy's a straight-up hottie. If I weren't happily married with offspring, I'd be all over that too." She got up from her chair. "On that note, I need more coffee. Anyone?"

We both declined and Jana headed to the coffee/pastry/fruit station Kimberly provided for us every Monday to ease us into the start of the week.

"I think it's impressive," Abby said, rolling her chair back to her desk with a little kick of her heels. "How long have you worked here? Two years? You're like that sad girl in *Love Actually*. The whole office—including Guy—knows about your crush."

"Mind your own business, Abby," I muttered. But I'd said it so softly, she hadn't heard.

"You should tell him," she said. "Just walk up to him and say, 'Guy, it's been two years. My body is *ready*.'"

I jumped out of my chair. "We don't want to be late for the meeting."

The conference room was a glass-walled space with one long table and ten chairs around it. The screen was for projecting stats and slides from the work Ocean Alliance did all over the world: cleaning plastic garbage out of the water, monitoring oil drilling, and doing coastal preservation.

Kimberly Paul was already there. She dressed less like an executive director of a successful nonprofit and more like a stylish factory worker in short-sleeved, army-green coveralls with heavy boots. Her blond hair was tied up by a Rosie-the-Riveter bandanna. A cluster of colorful precious stones glinted on her left ring finger.

"Good morning, good morning," she said in her rough Demi Moore voice. "Come in and get settled everyone. As you're all aware, I'll be out of the office for one week starting next Monday—"

The room broke into whistles and cheers, which she waved off with a laugh.

"Are you sure you're ready to let us kids have the house all to ourselves?" Guy asked with a grin.

"I trust you not to burn the place down, but if you want to give me a happy honeymoon, you'll keep the Big Idea train rolling at full steam."

The first of every month, Kimberly wanted presentations from the staff about innovative ideas: connections formed with other companies, celebrities we could turn into allies, et cetera. Next Monday was the first of the month.

I turned my shoe idea over and over. I'd worked out most of the logistics already, including cost, design, and environmental impact. The only thing left to do was to take the plunge and present it. While the others tossed around a few pitches, I inhaled slowly. There was too much at stake to *not* speak up, but...

They're going to laugh at you.

You're not prepared.

It's been done before.

I swallowed a lump of nerves and tried to do what Casziel had told me to do—stop feeding my demons. I knew they wouldn't magically disappear, but maybe if I talked louder than they did, I'd drown them out.

"I have an idea," I blurted from my seat at the end of the table and regretted it immediately. The entire room went silent, nine pairs of eyes fell on me.

Abby snorted. "*You're* going to present on Monday? Really?"

"Yes, really," I said, firming my voice.

"Wow, Lucy, that's wonderful," Kimberly said. "Can we get a preview?"

"I...I don't have my materials with me," I said, cheeks burning under Abby's dubious smirk and Guy's curious gaze. "But I can put it all together and present on Monday."

"Well, I'm thrilled," Kimberly said. "And a bit disappointed that I won't be there to hear it."

"I'll record it for you," Abby said, suddenly all sweetness. "You won't miss a thing."

Oh God...

It was bad enough I'd be speaking in front of the group. Having Abby's camera pinned on me was going to be a hundred times worse.

But I tilted my chin, refusing to show her any reaction. My demons had gone silent.

"Perfect!" Kimberly clapped. "Next up on the agenda—"

"Your bachelorette party," piped up Hannah from fundraising. "As in, there isn't one."

Kimberly laughed as the group booed. "I know, I know. But neither Nylah nor I am into that kind of thing."

"What about Buzz Night?" Guy said. "We could bump it up this week. You invite Nylah and we'll make it a pre-wedding celebration."

Buzz Nights were the last Friday of every month. The entire company went out to a bar or club or restaurant and hung out together, so we weren't just "coworkers." Aside from one awkward excursion right after I was hired, I never went.

"I don't hate the idea," Kimberly said, tapping her chin. "But aside from tomorrow night, I'm booked up with wedding plans, and Nylah's parents are flying in..."

"Tomorrow night it is," Guy said. "And we promise we'll all stumble in Wednesday morning on time, no matter how much fun we drank...I mean, had."

Kimberly laughed. "How could I say no to that? Thank you, all. You're a special bunch. Like family." She looked uncharacteristically emotional. Then she cleared her throat. "Now, down to *actual* business and it's not good. There's been another disaster."

She detailed how a cargo ship caught fire and rained down millions of plastic pellets along the pristine beaches of Sri Lanka. "Like plastic snow," the local officials called it. A disaster of epic proportions.

"I can be ready to go with a team by next week," Guy said.

Aside from being our VP, Guy led squads of volunteers for cleanup efforts all over the world, doing the hardest work. These trips were the fodder for my fantasies, and I waited for that tight, anxious feeling in my stomach that *this* was the time he'd ask me to join him. It wasn't there.

"Thank you, Guy," Kimberly said. "Honeymooning feels frivolous in light of this news, but if I postponed my plans for every disaster, I'd never go anywhere. Okay, next up..."

The meeting proceeded for the next forty-five minutes, and when it was over, Dale from reception was waiting outside the conference room.

"Hey, Luce, you have a visitor."

"I do?"

Never in two years had I had a visitor and the entire room knew it. Everyone looked across the open floor to reception, and there was Casziel. He wore a black T-shirt, black jeans, black boots, and a stylish black hoodie. An aura radiated off of him, an intangible magnetism that permeates a space, the same way a famous person strides into a restaurant and sends a jolt of energy into the room. Conversations hush. Eyes widen. Hearts skip a beat.

Or at least mine did. Several beats, in fact.

Most of the department heads filed back to their desks, but Abby and Jana stuck to my side like glue.

Abby gaped. "Who. Is. That?"

Cas caught us staring and was apparently too impatient to wait. He strode up, his glare trained on Guy who was standing behind me, wrapping some things up with Kimberly. The rest of the room blurred out at the edges until there was just Cas. Like a mirage or dream come to life. He'd been in and out of my imagination for the last three days, but now he was *here*. In front of my entire company. They could see him. It was all real.

"Hi," I said softly.

"Hi," he replied, tearing his demonic stink-eye off Guy. His gaze went to me and held on, no trace of his earlier coldness. "My apologies for intruding—"

"You're not intruding at all!" Abby said, sidling up beside him. "Well, well, well, Luce. Who *is* your friend?"

"This is Cas, um…"

"Abisare," Casziel said.

"Right. Cas Abisare."

His Sumerian name, I thought, and whispers of last night's dream came over me.

Jana gave him a friendly smile. "Where are you from, Cas?"

"Yes, where on this *earth* did you get those eyes?" Abby asked with less subtlety.

"Sumer," Cas answered.

I coughed. "Iraq. Sumer was in southern Mesopotamia, which is now present-day Iraq."

"Thanks for the geography lesson, Luce," Abby muttered, then turned her full attention to Cas. "How interesting! I've never met anyone from Iraq before. You'll have to tell me all about it. I have, like, a *million* questions."

I hid a smirk behind my hair. *Take a number.*

Guy and Kimberly had migrated toward us, both staring. Guy thrust his hand out. "Guy Baker. Cas, was it? Good to meet you."

Cas smiled thinly, leaving Guy's hand suspended in midair. "Ah, the infamous Guy Baker. Lucy has told me so much about you."

"Has she?" Guy withdrew his hand. "Only good things—"

"About *all* of you," Cas added dismissively. "Nothing but praise for her coworkers, striving to make a difference in the world. A commendable endeavor."

I shot him a look not to overdo it, but the team seemed enraptured. None could peel their eyes from him, as if they weren't quite sure he was real.

Take a thousand numbers.

"It's very nice to meet you, Cas," Kimberly said, starting for her office. "Lucy, perhaps you'd like to show him around?" She shot a look at everyone else: *Stop staring and get back to work.*

Abby swatted my arm. "Lucy, you're such a tease, to keep your friend all to yourself. Cas, you *must* stay for lunch and tell us all about yourself."

"I cannot stay," he said. "I was merely in the neighborhood."

"Dinner, then," Abby said. "Let's all go to dinner tonight!"

Jana waved her hands. "Not I. I have to pace myself with social endeavors these days."

"Then the four of us," Abby said. "Guy, you're down, right?"

He shrugged with a grin. "I could eat."

I looked to Casziel. I'd never been out with Guy socially. For the purposes of our plan, this was a good thing. Monumental. "Do you want to?"

"How could I say no?" he muttered with all the enthusiasm of someone about to undergo dental surgery.

Abby beamed. "Then it's settled. The four of us will go out. Get to know each other better. And of course, Cas, you're coming to Buzz Night tomorrow too."

She was gazing at him with the kind of brazenness I'd never have, but Abby may as well have been a potted plant for all the attention the demon gave her.

"Of course," he said. From behind his back, he presented me with the single red rose. "I saw this and thought of you."

"Oh." I'd read about fluttery stomach butterflies a hundred times in my romance novels, but I'd never felt them until that moment. I took the rose. "Thank you, Cas. It's beautiful."

"It almost does your beauty justice," he said. "Almost."

I could feel glances being exchanged all around me, but I was falling into the honeyed depths of Casziel's eyes and not doing a thing to stop myself. If he were putting on an act, it was a flawless performance.

He pressed the back of my hand to his lips. "Goodbye, Lucy."

"Bye," I said faintly.

"What a strange guy," Guy said, watching him go. "Old school manners."

"He's a gentleman," Jana said. "There's a shortage."

"Hmm." Guy gave his head a shake. "Anyway, I'm behind on some phone calls. Ladies... See you tonight, Lucy."

"Yep. See you."

A seed of curiosity had been planted; Guy had never singled me out like that when saying goodbye. I couldn't even remember the last time he'd said my name. And we were going to have *dinner*? The "fake relationship" plan was off to a good start and yet...

I could still feel where Cas's lips had been on the back of my hand.

"*Old school* is right," Abby was saying as we went back to our desks. "Cas smells like the inside of a pyramid. Like frankincense and myrrh or something." She pulled her chair in front of me like a detective grilling a suspect. "Okay, spill it. What's the story?"

"There isn't much of one," I said. "We met on Friday, and we had drinks on Saturday. That's all."

"That is *not* all. I refuse to let it be all."

"Did you know he was going to show up here?" Jana asked and nodded at the rose still clutched in my hand.

I set it in the half-drunk bottle of water on my desk. "No idea."

"But you like him?" Abby persisted.

"I...I don't know," I said. "I mean, yes, I like him. But it's not like—"

"How you like Guy," Abby finished. "Good on you, babe."

"Good on me—?"

"I've never seen Mr. Baker look anything but cool and collected. He had no idea what to make of Cas."

"He was very intrigued," Jana agreed as she and Abby pushed their chairs back to their desks.

Abby shook her head. "That is *not* how I expected this morning to go."

I glanced at the single red rose. "Me neither."

O N MY WAY home from work that afternoon, I found Casziel waiting for me at my subway station. He looked darkly handsome, leaning against a cement pillar. My stupid heart fluttered—the eyes of many women were on him; his eyes were only on me.

"You went rogue on me," I said as I joined him, and we took the stairs up to the street. "I had no idea you were going to show up at work."

"The element of surprise was necessary or else we'd have appeared rehearsed. And time is of the essence. I have eight days left."

"And if we forget, we can just look at your arm to count the days you've been here," I said quietly.

He looked away, as if my concern wounded and touched him at the same time.

We stepped out of the station onto the sidewalk. The sun was setting, and the sidewalks were bustling with people on their way home after the workday. Again, Cas parted the crowds like Moses parted the Red Sea. Without realizing they were doing it, the New Yorkers stayed out of his way, a few shivering as if they'd walked through a cold front.

"How was our performance?" he asked as we headed to my place. "Was Guy sufficiently *curious*?"

"Definitely. Even Jana and Abby noticed." I glanced up at him. "No one's given me a single rose before. It's almost more romantic than a whole bouquet. More…intimate."

That conflicted expression came over his face again, then he shrugged. "It's just a flower, Lucy Dennings. A prop in our plan."

"Right," I said. We'd arrived at my studio, and I unlocked my front door. "Of course."

It was all a performance. The rose was a prop and the kiss on my hand didn't mean anything. Seemed like my heart was having a hard time remembering that.

We stepped inside. Cas stretched out on the couch and flipped on the TV, as if to avoid conversation. A strange tension permeated the air, like how two strangers in a small space run out of things to say to each other. Except that wasn't right. More like when two people who are most definitely *not* strangers have *a lot* to say to each other but don't.

Or can't.

I sat in the chair beside the couch. "I did something kind of big today. I volunteered to share my shoe idea with the team on Monday."

His eyes widened and he looked to be on the verge of smiling. "You did?"

I nodded. "Deb tried to talk me out of it, but I did what you told me. Instead of listening to her, I spoke up louder. It felt good. Scary but good."

"I'm not surprised. You're one of the strongest women I've ever known."

I stared. "I am?"

He looked away. "I just meant, all humans are far more powerful than they believe."

"I don't feel powerful. I feel scared shitless, like I made a terrible mistake."

"That's K. Between now and Monday, she and Deb are going to try to stop you by any means necessary."

"God, demons make it so hard for humans to accomplish anything. It's amazing that your side hasn't won and turned this world into hell."

He arched a brow. "You think it's not? With the murders and rapes and torture and war and sex trafficking and child pornography and mass shootings and—"

"Yes, there is all that, and it's all horrible. But there is more that is beautiful than there is ugly. Sometimes it's just harder to see." I frowned at him. "I guess that's your job. To make it hard to see."

"I couldn't have explained it better myself."

"Even so. I still believe in the goodness of people."

"That, Lucy Dennings, is why I picked you."

Is that the only reason?

I decided to see how *powerful*—and brave—I really was. "How, exactly, did you find me, Cas?"

"I told you. Seen through the Veil; your light shines bright."

"But lots of humans shine just as brightly, if not brighter. Jana, for instance. She's one of the best people I know—"

"I needed someone solitary. I can't very well go about revealing my true self to just anyone."

"Okay, but...sometimes I get the feeling that you and I..." I swallowed. "I get the feeling we're not strangers."

I held my breath, waiting for him to reply.

"It's our bond—the one that formed when you spoke my name—creating a false sense of familiarity. That's all."

"But—"

He rose from the couch. "Are we not going to dinner with your coworkers shortly?"

"Well, yes. But Cas…"

His gaze swept over me, the longing in his eyes silencing my words and bringing back the dream of the woman and the warrior.

"We have a plan, Lucy Dennings." His hand came up as if to touch my cheek, then he let it fall and turned away. "Guy is waiting for you."

We met Abby and Guy at the White Horse Tavern in the West Village. Abby looked stunning in a tight black dress that was almost too fancy for the occasion. Guy hadn't changed but looked as ruggedly handsome as ever. He pulled my chair out for me and shook Cas's hand. I legit feared the demon was going to tear out Guy's throat, the way he was glaring at him.

"I don't think you and I have ever hung out," Guy said to me with a warm smile. "Aside from work functions."

"First time for everything," Abby said, shooting me a knowing look.

A man at the next table rose to his feet. He'd paid the bill and stuffed his wallet into the back pocket of his slacks. He missed, and the wallet hit the ground without him noticing.

I bent and picked it up. "Sir? You dropped this."

He took it with a friendly smile. "Thank you so much, young lady."

Abby rolled her eyes with a laugh. "That's our Lucy for you. Always the saint."

I hunched my shoulders. "Most people would do the same."

"Yeah...*after* taking a peek at how much cash was inside," Abby said with a snicker.

"That reminds me of an article I read last week," Guy said. "A psychologist did an experiment to see if people were inherently good or...not. They placed wallets filled with various amounts of money in fifteen different countries. Seventy-two percent returned the wallets with all the money intact. Isn't that something?"

"Doesn't surprise me in the least," I said, shooting Casziel a look. "I absolutely believe people are naturally good. Some just give in to their inner demons more than others."

"Guilty," Abby said and nudged Cas. "That's what makes life fun, am I right?"

He ignored her, his gaze fixed on Guy. "You believe a few returned wallets proves the inherent goodness in mankind?"

Guy smiled amicably. "I'm Buddhist. We try not to get too stuck on opposing concepts. Things aren't quite so black and white."

I could practically feel Cas's eye roll, despite the fact he'd told me the same thing the night we met.

"You disagree?" Guy asked the demon.

"I believe there are mysteries on top of mysteries that most humans cannot begin to perceive," Cas said imperiously.

"Probably true." Guy gestured around the saloon's warm interior. "For instance, they say this place is haunted."

"By what entity?"

"The poet, Dylan Thomas."

Cas snorted. "Dylan Thomas? I just saw him—"

I kicked him under the table and blurted, "I love Dylan Thomas. I love poetry in general, actually."

"Do you?" Guy turned to me. "Me too. Keats, Dickinson…but Thomas is a favorite. Everyone's always quoting his *Do Not Go Gentle Into That Good Night* but I find *And Death Shall Have No Dominion* to be more arresting."

Cas's derision was like a cold wind. "I'm partial to *Our Eunuch Dreams*."

"I love *No Dominion* too," I said, glaring at the demon. "That poem is beautiful. And hopeful. I love the line about how lovers might be lost but love never will be."

I stopped, those words suddenly taking on a new meaning. The dream of the woman and her warrior swam up again, and I glanced at Cas over the candlelight on our table. He met my eyes, a strange, soft look on his face.

"Ugh, boring," Abby groused, breaking the spell. She put her hand over Cas's. "Is all this poetry talk putting you to sleep too?"

He didn't reply but I noticed he didn't move his hand from her touch, either.

"Speaking of ghosts," Guy said, "I'm pretty sure my place is haunted too."

"Why do you think so?" Cas asked, eyes narrowed.

"Little things," Guy said. "Lights flicker off and on at weird times. Or I'll hear footsteps down the hall. Once, when I was in the kitchen, the TV turned itself on to a baseball game." He chuckled. "I hate baseball."

"Spooky," Abby said.

"The building is old," Guy continued, "but I feel a different energy in there."

"I'd love to investigate," Cas said, and I choked on my water. "I have a talent for feeling out different energies myself."

"Oh yeah?" Guy's smile was tight, like he couldn't tell if Cas were messing with him or not. Which the demon most definitely was.

"*Yeah*," Cas drawled. "I have something of an ability to communicate with those who are no longer with us."

"Shut up!" Abby swatted his arm. "Like, you're psychic?" She looked to Guy. "We *have* to go to your place."

"No, we really don't," I put in, shooting Cas another helpless glance.

"I have a bottle of '94 Terreno I've been waiting to try," Guy said with a grin. "After dinner, we'll go to my place and talk to some ghosts."

"Yay!" Abby clapped her hands together.

"Yay," Cas agreed.

An hour later, I pulled him aside while Guy stood with Abby on the sidewalk, calling an Uber. "What are you doing?"

"'I find *And Death Shall Have No Dominion* to be more arresting,'" Cas mimicked and rolled his eyes. "Is he always that pretentious?"

I glanced down. "You sound jealous. But I guess that's part of the plan, right?"

Cas hadn't heard, still ranting. "And if that man's house is haunted, I'm a swamp imp."

"So you have to prove him wrong?"

"I'd rather prove him extremely *right* and deprive him of sleep for a week."

"Cas," I warned.

He blinked, the picture of innocence. "Are we not rivals for your hand?"

"If you make a fool of Guy, he's not going to be super keen to hang out with me in the future. I'll be guilty by association."

Guy waved us over to the Uber.

"Just don't do anything scary," I muttered as we headed over.

The demon's grin was unnervingly cheery. "Who, me?"

Guy had a cozy apartment in the meat-packing district with exposed brick walls and a view of the Hudson.

"Make yourselves at home," he said, giving me a warm smile as we stepped inside. "I'll see to the vino."

Abby nudged me. "Why don't you see if he could use some help?"

Before I could answer, she plopped herself on the couch next to Cas, leaving no room for anyone in between. I headed to the kitchen, listening to his low voice and her answering peal of laughter.

Guy's kitchen was all wood and glass with a half-dozen houseplants for added warmth. For a bachelor pad, it was homey and welcoming, like Guy himself.

"Hey," I said, fighting to not let my hair fall over my face. "Need help?"

"Hey, Luce." Guy popped the cork on a bottle of chianti. "You can grab some glasses, thanks. First cabinet, over the dishwasher."

I went as directed and took down four red wine glasses.

"Your friend Cas is an interesting guy. Not sure what to make of him, honestly."

He said it with no trace of malice, just honest curiosity. I managed a smile.

"He's...eccentric."

"That's the word." Guy leaned against the counter and crossed his arms. He had nice forearms, tanned and with a silver watch on his left wrist. "Where did you say you two met?"

"Oh, umm...we sort of bumped into each other outside my apartment." I heard how random that sounded and coughed. "But he's a friend of a friend. From art school. I mean, my friend is in art school and Cas is his friend, and we sort of met...that way."

Real smooth, Luce. Gold medal in rambling at the Awkward Olympics.

"Cool. He in town long?"

For a split second, I entertained the notion that Guy hoped the answer would be no.

"Not long," I said. "A few days."

Guy's mega-watt beam returned, showing perfect white teeth. "Great. Well, the wine has breathed long enough, I think. After you, my lady."

I smiled and went out, proud that I'd survived without making a total ass of myself.

Are you sure about that?

"Shut up, Deb."

Guy took a chair at the head of the coffee table. Since Abby had claimed Cas on the couch, my only seating option was a chair opposite them.

Guy poured the wine and then sat back. "Well, Cas? What's the verdict? Your Spidey senses tingling?"

The demon made a face. "*Spidey* senses?"

Abby burst out laughing. "Oh my God, how precious. *Of course*, they don't have Spider-Man in Iraq. Guy just means, can you feel any ghosts?"

104 | EMMA SCOTT

I just about died of second-hand embarrassment but was more fixated on Abby's arm that was linked in Casziel's.

Cas, who apparently had an arsenal of smirks, put on a smug one. "As a matter of fact, I do. A little twinge, perhaps. A little thickness in the air."

Guy was nodding. "Right? That's it exactly."

"Of course, there's only one way to be sure," the demon said. "Do you have a Ouija board?"

Abby pursed her lips. "Ugh, no. Those things give me the creeps."

"Me too," I said glaring at Casziel. He ignored me, his hard gaze fixed on our host.

"Nope, don't have one," Guy said. "Too bad—"

"All is not lost," Cas said. "We need only a piece of paper of sufficient size and something to serve as a planchette. After all, the board is merely a tool for communicating between this world and the next."

"When you put it that way..." Abby turned to me and fanned herself, mouthing, *So hot.*

Guy, amicable as usual, set down his wine glass. "I think that can be arranged." He came back with a piece of drafting paper and a black Sharpie. "Not sure about a planchette."

"The shot glass on the mantle will do," Cas said. He drew a YES and NO on two corners of the paper, the alphabet, and the numbers zero through nine. Below that, he wrote GOODBYE. Then he knelt on the floor at the end of the coffee table so that each of us had a side of the "board."

Guy placed the shot glass on the paper. "This is wild. What do we do next?"

Now Cas's smirk was of the don't-be-an-idiot variety. "We each lay our fingertips to the glass and ask the spirits to make themselves known."

"Oh my God, have you done this before?" Abby asked. "You're totally giving me the shivers. Not that I'm complaining..."

I had to admit, Abby was right. The low timbre of Casziel's voice and his dark, otherworldly charisma made it obvious to me that we were already in the presence of the supernatural. I worried the others were going to get suspicious.

"Touch the glass, please," he commanded.

We reached to touch the shot glass and the lights in the apartment flickered again, three times. But for Cas, we all jerked our hands back.

"Holy shit." Guy laughed nervously.

"Holy *shit* is right," Abby said, glancing around.

Cas smiled. "An auspicious start."

I cringed and silently begged him not to get carried away. We all gingerly touched our fingers on the glass, like startled birds resettling.

"Let us begin," Cas intoned. "Spirits in this domain, are you with us?"

Nothing happened and then the glass slid to YES.

"*Eeep*," Abby screeched. "This is *so* creepy."

"What is your name?" Guy asked.

The glass slid to Z then U.

Abby wrinkled her nose. "Your name is Zu?"

The glass rushed to YES.

"Have you lived here long?" Guy asked.

The glass went to three.

"Weird. I moved here three years ago."

"Did you follow Guy to this house?" Cas asked, and the glass raced to YES.

Guy chuckled. "Okay, so that's not totally disturbing. Go ahead, Luce. Ask a question."

I decided to take this conversation to lighter ground. "Okay, um...what is your favorite color?"

"Oh my God, Luce, so boring," Abby drawled.

But the planchette was racing across the board to spell RED LIKE BLOOD

That wiped the smirk off Abby's face. "Ummm...I don't think I want to play this anymore."

"Me either," I said, mutely begging Cas to behave himself.

He gave me a brief nod of understanding. "Are you a benevolent entity?"

The planchette raced to YES.

"They're often playful and mischievous but mean no harm," he explained, shooting me an *Are you happy?* glance.

Guy relaxed. "Hey Zu, was it you who turned on my TV that one time?"

The glass moved off the YES then back on, then spelled out I LIKE BASEBALL.

The mood changed then as the questions and answers became silly and banal, more like a party game than an actual conversation with "an entity." Abby and Guy were relaxed now, having fun.

"Zu, settle a debate for us," Guy said after a while. He shot Cas a wink. "Is the basic nature of man good or evil?"

I silently scolded him to not humiliate Guy and remember our plan.

Casziel received the message because the glass spelled out IT IS NEITHER. NOT BLACK OR WHITE.

"Thank you." Guy laughed. "There you have it. Can't argue with an expert, eh, Cas?"

The demon's smile was acid. "Indeed."

We all took our hands off the glass, game over. Guy turned to me and touched my shoulder, his smile warm. "Hey, fellow poetry lover, would you like some more wine?"

"That'd be nice, thank—"

My sentence was drowned in Abby's shriek as the shot glass suddenly flew across the room and shattered against the wall.

"Oh, *shit*," Guy burst out and grabbed hold of my hand, moving himself in front of me.

A silence fell where we stared, wide-eyed.

"It would seem your home is indeed haunted," Cas said to Guy, his smile showing all his teeth. "But then again, I'm no *expert*."

Outside on the street, Cas and I waited for an Uber. The demon looked exceedingly pleased with himself. I crossed my arms.

"Was that really necessary?"

"He could stand a little humbling."

"Says the pot to the kettle. And besides, he's not arrogant. He's kind and sweet. Did you see how he grabbed hold of my hand? Like he was going to protect me."

"I did," he said icily.

"Our plan is working. He's never touched me before."

"And this pleases you?"

"Well...don't we need this to happen? For your sake?"

"Yes. This needs to happen." Cas said, his tone unreadable. "For my sake,"

A tension thickened between us and lasted the entire Uber ride home, then followed us into my place. It permeated every corner, and I was acutely aware of Casziel, his body filling my space, and how *alone* we were together. How his animosity toward Guy felt like more than an act. And how that thrilled me more than Guy's touch...

No, no, no. This is all wrong. Our plan...

"I'm tired," I said. "Think I'm going to get ready for bed. Sleep," I amended quickly. "What about you? It's early yet."

"And?"

"You and Abby seemed to hit it off. She's very into you." I cleared my throat. "I thought, maybe you would want to..."

He cocked his head. "Would want to what?"

I let my hair fall over my face. "I don't know. You said demons crave sex..."

He looked away, grimacing. "Oh, I see. Yes, that's true." His voice was low. "Goodnight, Lucy."

And suddenly, I hated every single word that had come out of my mouth since we'd gotten home. I wanted to exchange them for thousands of others. To ask him about my dream, to tell him not to go. To stay with me...

But he was going to go. He had a handful of days left on This Side and nothing was going to change that. Our plan was his only chance of redemption.

So he left—maybe to be with another woman—and I was alone.

13

"**Y**OU SHOULD HAVE seen our girl," Abby said at work the next day, grinning knowingly as she regaled Jana about last night's dinner. "The glass went flying and we all freaked. Except Lucy. She didn't bat an eye."

Jana was shaking her head. "That sounds scary and dangerous. You guys shouldn't be messing with stuff like that. Bad juju."

Abby waved a hand. "I'm sure there's a perfectly reasonable explanation. Like, too much wine. But I've never seen Guy so rattled. And did you notice how he threw himself in front of you, Luce? To protect you? Well played."

I froze, feeling as if our grand plan were written all over my face.

"Well played? No, I—"

"He was so sweet to our gal," Abby said and then stifled a yawn with the back of her hand.

I cleared my throat. "Did you stay out later? After we left?"

"Wouldn't *you* like to know?" she said with a wink, and it felt as if she'd slapped me.

Oh my God, calm down. It's not your business what she does with...anyone.

Abby gasped and grabbed my arm, jolting me out of my thoughts. "You *have* to let us take you out. Today after work. Before Buzz Night."

"What for?"

"Total makeover. I've been *dying* to get my hands on you ever since you started here, and now you have all this manly attention. We need to capitalize."

"Abby," Jana said in a low tone. "Lucy doesn't need a makeover."

"Oh, nothing major. But we have *got* to get this hair out of your face and show off this cute figure of yours. Please? We *never* go out, just us girls."

I tucked a lock of hair behind my ear. "Well…if you think it's a good idea."

"It's a *brilliant* idea. We'll have loads of fun and get you glowed up for Buzz Night."

Jana smiled gently. "You can say no."

That's what I always did. I said no, and my little life never got any bigger. But I'd had dinner with Guy, and I'd volunteered to present my idea. I was on a roll. No stopping now.

"Sure. Why not?"

After work, Abby took me back to Macy's at Herald's Square. Jana came along for moral support. "And to make sure Abby doesn't get carried away."

Abby scoffed. "Oh, please. This is going to be fun."

"Fun" wasn't my first choice of words as Abby picked out one tight dress after another for me to try on, along with shapewear to smooth me out underneath.

"Oh my God, *gorgeous*," Abby crowed as I stepped out of the dressing room in a fire-engine red dress that hugged every curve and was lower in the front than anything I owned. "See? You have the most *luscious* figure."

I had to admit, with the shapewear's help, the dress was flattering and gave me an hourglass shape.

Even Jana nodded approvingly. "Cas is going to flip."

"Noooo, it's *Guy* we're gunning for, right Luce?" Abby said. "And enough hiding behind your hair. Let's get you to the makeup counter. Guy won't know what hit him."

In minutes, Jana had wandered to the perfume section, and I was in a chair at the makeup counter, a beautician brushing and lining and dabbing my face.

"It's really clever of you, actually," Abby said, swiping a test lipstick on the back of her hand. "You've had a crush on Guy since the dawn of time, right? Then suddenly, this Cas shows up."

"I don't know what you mean."

"I mean, this is the perfect week, right? All these social engagements that put you and Guy in the same non-work space. The wedding alone—" Her eyes widened with a sudden thought. "Please tell me you didn't buy something frumpy to wear to Kim's wedding."

"Well, no..."

"You did, didn't you? If it's not in the same ballpark as the little red number we picked out today, return it. Now is not the time to back down."

I was glad to have ten pounds of blush on my cheeks already. My face burned hot; our "grand plan" was so obvious. That it was inconceivable that Cas might be with me to *be* with me and not as some decoy.

Because it is, Deb piped up. *You're a cliché. The shy little frump who could never get a man like Guy on her own...*

"I like the dress I bought," I said, my voice sounding small in my own ears.

"Pfft. I'm sure you do. But trust me, it's—"

Abby broke off as Jana returned, a small bag in her hand.

"So I don't smell like Eau de Bébé tonight." She caught sight of my face and frowned. "Well, that's...different."

I took the mirror from the beautician. She'd given me a smoky eye, blush along the edges of my cheekbones, and bright red lipstick the same shade as the dress in a bag at my feet. My hair was pulled back from my face in a messy bun with a few tendrils hanging down. I hardly looked like myself.

"Stunning, right?" Abby crowed.

Jana nodded. "But a little heavy, don't you think?"

"Nonsense. It's going to be dark at the bar."

"What do you think, Luce?"

"Umm..."

"She loves it because she knows it'll be *perfect* with that dress," Abby said. "Right, Luce?"

I must've agreed because I ended up spending seventy-five dollars on eye shadow, blush, and the lipstick that was actually called *Underage Red*.

"Now, don't change a thing," Abby said at the subway station. "I want to see you at the bar in a few hours just like this."

"Abby…" Jana shook her head.

"What? She looks amazing." Abby gave me an air kiss, whispering. "I got your back, girl."

Jana gave me a small parting wave, and we headed our separate ways. I took the subway home, garnering a few looks from men on the train…which had never happened before. At my apartment, I unlocked the door, steeling myself for Cas's reaction. It'd been ages since I'd been on a date.

This is not a date. This is part of your super obvious pathetic plan to get Guy to notice you.

"Shut up, Deb," I muttered, though she was right. Even Abby saw it.

Casziel wasn't there, and as the time ticked by, I began to wonder if he were going to show up at all. I ate my portion of the casserole I'd made for dinner and went into the bathroom to put on the red dress that suddenly looked extremely, inappropriately *red*. I reapplied the lipstick, smoothed my hair, and went out.

Cas was in my living room, looking devastating in all black. My stomach fluttered at the sight of him, masculine and potent and so very beautiful.

"Oh, you're here," I stammered. "It's about time we go…"

My words trailed at the expression on the demon's face as he took me in. His eyes widened, his lips parted. The room went still in the few seconds of his stunned silence, then his brows furrowed angrily.

"What happened to you?" he demanded. "Why are you dressed like this?"

The reaction hurt me more than I expected, especially since—for a moment—he seemed overwhelmed by me in the best way.

"The girls took me shopping after work." I smoothed down the front of my dress that felt even tighter than it had in the store. "You don't approve?"

He started to speak, and I shocked myself by cutting him off.

"You know what? Never mind," I said. "I can wear whatever I want, and I don't need—or deserve—your judgment about it. And FYI, no woman does."

"I wasn't—"

"I didn't do this for your approval. I did it for Guy. For our grand plan to save your soul, remember?" I tilted my chin up, lip trembling. "Isn't that what this is all for?"

Casziel's jaw tightened. "It is."

"Then let's go."

I grabbed my purse and headed for the door, keeping my face turned away. If I cried, it'd ruin my makeup.

14

WE ARRIVED AT the 5 Bar on West 32ⁿᵈ. The karaoke lounge was busy for a Tuesday night, but most of the patrons were Ocean Alliance staff. Abby, looking stunning in green, waved frantically as she nudged Jana by the arm, nearly spilling her drink.

"You're here and you look *wow*!" Abby crowed. "Doesn't she?"

"You do," Jana said. "But you always did."

"Now she's *extra*," Abby said. She pushed between Casziel and me. "I think I can guess your favorite color," she said to him. "Not that I'm complaining. Black is *so* you."

I'd had the same thought but never said it out loud. Hearing it from Abby felt like she was claiming a little piece of him.

"Come on. Let's all get a drink." Abby linked arms with both of us, then leaned in to me. "Guy is already here, and he didn't bring a date for a change. *Coincidence*? I think not."

At the bar, Kimberly and her fiancée, Nylah, were talking close and laughing. They both stopped when they saw us approach, and my boss's eyes widened. "Lucy? Is that you?"

I tilted my neck to let my hair fall in my face, but it was piled up on my head. I felt exposed, nowhere to hide. "Abby did it. For fun."

"Well, you look great," Kimberly said. "Cas, was it? This is my fiancée, Nylah."

"A pleasure," Casziel said, taking the woman's hand. "And congratulations to you both."

"Thank you," Nylah said. Like everyone else, she stared at him a little longer than necessary, like she couldn't believe he was real.

"I just can't get over your accent," Abby crowed at Casziel. "You really have to tell us all about yourself. Start with Iraq and finish with meeting our little Lucy."

"I'm sure Cas doesn't want to give us his life story in a karaoke bar," Kimberly said, shooting me a soft smile. "We're here to sing. Badly. Are you up for some karaoke, Cas?"

"Sure," he muttered, his eyes hardening at something over my shoulder. "I do a mean 'Sympathy for the Devil.'"

I followed his dark gaze. Guy Baker was approaching, looking wholesome and handsome in jeans and a button down rolled up at the sleeves, beer in hand.

"Good evening, ladies," he said with his usual grin. He nodded at the demon. "Cas."

Casziel's smile was barbed enough to break skin. "*Guy*."

I nudged him with my elbow, but Guy wasn't paying him any attention. He was staring at me as if he'd never seen a woman up close before.

"Lucy..." He gave a low whistle. "Wow, you look..."

"I know, *right*?" Abby cried, ruining the moment.

Not that there was a moment to ruin. I'd been yearning for Guy to see me as more than an office fixture for two years. Now that he was, all I could feel was the heat of Casziel's wrath radiating like a furnace...and the answering heat in my body. A burning desire that was exciting and new and yet had been smoldering for ages, ready to catch fire. One touch, one heated glance...

You're nuts. The dress is so tight, it's cutting off oxygen to your brain.

"I take some credit for the dress, but this is allll Lucy," Abby said. "Isn't she *gorgeous*?"

"She is," Guy said. "You are, Luce."

"Oh, uh...thank you," I managed, not daring to look at Cas. But I didn't have to. He was telegraphing his emotions with breathtaking clarity. Protectiveness. Possessiveness. Jealousy...

He's just playing the part. Like we planned.

Finally, Guy blinked as if coming out of a trance—one that *I'd* cast on him—and turned to the group, beaming.

"Shots! We need to celebrate the impending nuptials of our fearless leader."

"None for me, thanks," Jana said. "My kid doesn't need Cuervo-flavored breast milk."

Kimberly laughed, then fixed Guy with a mock stern look. "Just one for me. And I'm holding you to your promise that everyone will show up at the office tomorrow."

"Oh, we will." Guy grinned as the bartender lined up six little glasses and filled them with tequila. "I just can't promise we'll get any work done."

"Are you bringing Cas to the wedding, Lucy?" Kimberly asked. She turned to him. "You're more than welcome."

"Yes, are you?" Abby asked. "You have to. I *insist*."

I coughed and caught Cas's glance. "Um, sure. If he wants to go…"

Smooth as black silk, Cas put a hand to his heart. "I would be honored if you would have me. My thanks for the gracious invitation."

"Holy chivalry Batman." Nylah shook her head, her dark curls brushing her shoulders.

Kim nodded. "Someone's mother raised him well."

Everyone laughed and reached for their glasses.

"To Nylah and Kimberly," Guy said, holding up his shot. He turned his gaze to me. "And to new beginnings."

No one missed the smile he gave me. Especially Cas. His eyes shot molten daggers at Guy, and then the demon tossed back his tequila as if it were water. I held up my glass for the toast but didn't dare taste it. There was no chance I was going to get drunk again, not after waking up on my kitchen floor in a puddle of broken glass.

I ordered a bottle of water from the bartender. When I turned back around, Abby had her arm linked in Cas's again, and they were deep in conversation. His back was to me; I couldn't read his face, but Abby looked rapt and naturally sexy in a way that I'd never look, no matter how many red dresses I wore or how many pounds of makeup I put on my face. I studied her, as if I could tell if they'd slept together just by reading her face.

Which would be perfectly okay and none of my business.

An hour slipped by, then another. Ocean Alliance staff took turns warbling songs on a small stage set at the back of the bar. I wound up at a table with Jana, Abby, and Cas. Guy sat at the next table over, but he'd moved his chair so that it was lined up next to mine. He seemed to have started the celebrations before we arrived and got progressively drunker as the night wore on. We chatted now and then about our coworkers' singing abilities (or lack thereof). Every time I risked a glance at him, he was watching me.

And Casziel was watching us.

Even with Abby practically sitting in his lap, peppering him with questions, his gaze slid between Guy and me, and he didn't like what he was seeing.

The night was dragging, and I was more than ready to leave when Dale stopped by to chat with Jana, and Abby excused herself to the restroom. Cas and I were left alone.

"You don't have to go to the wedding," I told him. "Abby has a way of putting people on the spot. But if you don't want to go—"

"I'm only here for a few more days. The wedding will be the last opportunity to enact our plan. Which seems to be working."

"Yeah, I guess it is. But you don't seem happy about it."

He sipped his wine. "I'm ecstatic."

"What's wrong? You agreed to this—"

"I know what I agreed to," Cas seethed, his eyes hard. "I just..." He shook his head and looked away, his gaze finally landing on my empty water glass. "Would you like another?" he asked, gentler now.

"Just one more. I'm driving," I said with a small smile.

The hard angles in his face softened, almost pained. He leaned in, his eyes full of that longing that touched something so deep in me... I couldn't see it but felt it was there. Waiting.

"Lucy..."

I held my breath and then Abby bounced back to the table. Cas abruptly stood and she grabbed his hand. "Are you getting another round? Be a love and grab me another appletini? Thanks, baby."

Baby...

Cas headed for the bar. Abby watched him go, her gaze sweeping over him. She leaned toward me and shouted to be heard above someone's off-key rendition of "Love Shack."

"That man is something else."

"You can say that again," I muttered.

"There's something I can't put my finger on. So sexy but like..." She waved her hand. "What's the word I'm looking for?"

Beautiful.

Frustrating.

Familiar.

I coughed. "Polite."

"Right," Abby rolled her eyes. "He's *polite*. Was that part of the contract?"

I made a fist under the table. "If you have something to say, Abby, just say it."

She laughed. "No need to get snippy, babe! I just think it's great, how you're taking the initiative. First agreeing to present on Monday and now going for it with Guy. It's like a whole new Lucy."

I wanted to tell her it wasn't a new me. It was the same me I've always been, but Casziel was drawing me out of myself. Being with him was like uncovering something that had been buried for a long time. Years, even.

"What I'm asking," Abby said, her dark eyes sharp, "which *escort* service did you use?"

I sat back, feeling punched in the gut.

Her face broke into an innocent, disbelieving smile. "Oh, honey, we talked about this! I think it's a fab idea. Guy hasn't been able to take his eyes off you all night. He likes a challenge."

My stomach churned, and I wanted nothing more but to vanish and reappear in my apartment.

Turn into a raven and fly away...

The MC took the stage, consulting the karaoke sign-up sheet. "Up next, we have Guy Baker. Come on up, Guy!"

Our group cheered and hollered as Guy, swaying slightly, took the stage. Abby turned to watch, leaving me to stew in her insinuations.

She's not wrong, is she? Deber sneered.

I tried to ignore her and watched as Guy took the mic in one hand, holding a beer in the other. The first strains of a soft song began to play. It took a second until I recognized it, "Lady in Red." Heads turned my way as it became apparent to everyone in the room to whom Guy was singing.

Oh my God...

Jana swiveled to look at me, eyes wide. "Girl..."

"*I have never seen that dress you're wearing,*" Guy crooned. "*I have been blind...*"

Abby burst out laughing and grabbed her phone to record the scene. "Oh my God, Guy is secretly a huge sap. Who knew?" She swiveled her camera to me. "Soak it up, Luce. The moment you've been waiting for."

I shut my slack-jawed mouth and shied away from Abby's phone, my face burning as red as my dress. I felt Casziel at the bar but couldn't look at him. Every lyric of Guy's warbling serenade felt like a betrayal. A broken promise to Cas, though I couldn't fathom why.

Mercifully, the song ended, and Guy came off the stage, stumbling straight to me. He collapsed into his chair in a cloud of potent alcohol and breath mints.

"I'll give you some privacy," Abby said, giggling, and put her phone away. She hurried to join Cas at the bar.

"That was for you," Guy said.

"Yeah, I guessed that," I said, smiling weakly. "Thank you. It was very...nice."

His smile was sheepish, his blue eyes glassy. "I don't normally do stuff like that, but something compelled me. Or maybe it was just that you looked so beautiful."

No one was paying attention to Jana and Dale's rendition of "Islands in the Stream"—the entire company had their eyes on us, murmuring and nudging. Guy didn't seem to notice or care. His gaze was glued to me, looking at me like I'd imagined him doing a hundred times in my pathetic fantasies.

"You came here with Cas, right?" He inclined his chin toward the bar. "I don't think I got the whole story the other night. What's up with you two?"

The four-thousand-year-old question...

I cleared my throat, remembering we had a plan to stick to. "We just met. I don't know where it's going, if anywhere."

Guy chuckled. "You sure about that? He's glaring at me like he wants to rip my throat out."

"No, he would never..." I caught Casziel's hard stare, boring into us. "Okay, he might."

"He's your date this Saturday, eh? Darn." Guy snapped his fingers. "Missed my shot."

I stared. Guy Baker had wanted to ask me to the wedding?

"I guess so, yes. But like I said, we're not serious."

"I'm happy to hear that, Lucy," Guy said. "Will you save a dance for me? Maybe more than one?"

I risked another glance at the bar. Casziel's eyes were almost black in the dimness, watching me with Guy while Abby leaned in and whispered something in his ear.

This isn't fair.

I wasn't supposed to be jealous at how close her lips were to his skin. I was supposed to be elated that Guy Baker was talking to me, flirting with me. That he'd just serenaded me in front of the entire company should've had me floating on air.

Get with the plan, I scolded myself. *Casziel's eternal soul is on the line.*

I tilted my chin up to Guy, smiling in what I hoped was an alluring manner. "I'll do that."

"Great," Guy said and shook his head, the booze strong on his breath. "I just can't get over you tonight. The song was right. I've never seen you look like this." He brushed his knuckles over my cheek. "Or maybe you always have, and I'm an idiot for not noticing before."

My heart pounded. Was he going to kiss me in front of everyone? In front of Cas? Guy looked willing, and all I had to do was let it happen...

Suddenly, my stomach roiled and I felt sick.

"Excuse me." I pulled away. "Sorry, I...I'll be right back."

I hurried to the bar's tiny bathroom. The walls were covered in stickers and graffiti, but the two stalls were empty. I braced myself over the sink, taking deep breaths. I didn't recognize the girl in the reflection, and it had nothing to do with all that makeup.

"What the hell is wrong with me?"

A tittering laugh sounded from the stall behind me. "Poor, sweet, silly little Lucy."

I froze, the words crawling up my spine like insects. The stall had been empty but now two women—or what my brain registered as two creatures wearing woman skin suits—shuffled out. One looked like a relic from CBGB in torn fishnets and a tight black leather jacket over a cropped top that showed a pale midriff. Her hair was a dyed black rat's nest with lifeless gray roots. Yellow eyes under heavy, messy black eyeliner met mine in the mirror.

A second woman-thing shuffled out, keeping her face pressed in the arm of the first. She wore a shapeless dress, and her disheveled, snarled gray hair fell over her cheek. One yellow eye peeked out at me.

Deber and Keeb.

My blood turned to ice in my veins, and I stood frozen, watching them approach through their reflection in the mirror.

"You seem confused." Deber cocked a head and I watched, horrified, as a fly crawled across her yellowed eye. "Lost. Silly Lucy has lost her way."

"Lost, lost, lost," Keeb tittered.

More flies were now crawling across the mirror. Something nipped at my memory. Flies at my window...

"You should ask Casziel. Our dark prince will tell you everything, won't he, sister?"

Keeb giggled into Deber's shoulder. "Ask, ask, ask who you are..."

"W-who I am?"

"Silly Lucy," Deber sneered, a walking manifestation of the voice I'd been hearing in my head for years. "She doesn't know. All this time. So many years, alone."

"Alone, alone, alone..."

She trailed a finger up my arm, and flies crawled over my flesh. "Ask Casziel, silly Lucy. Ask him to tell you the truth."

"*Truth*," Keeb hissed, and flies writhed over her rotted teeth.

"Stop," I breathed, backing away. "Leave me alone."

I hurried out, tripping over my heels, obscene cackles chasing after me.

Cas and Abby had returned to the table with Jana. Abby had her manicured fingers wrapped around Cas's left arm. Even with my pulse still jack-rabbiting, I wanted to snap at her to be careful, that he had cuts there. Four of them now.

And tonight, he'll have five. Put there by another demon. God...

"I'd like to go home now," I managed.

"Already?" Abby frowned and gripped Cas's arm tighter as if I'd come to steal him from her. "It's *so* early. But if you must go, I'm sure Guy will get a cab with you."

She nodded to where Guy was talking with Kimberly and Nylah. He looked over and raised his beer bottle to me with a wobbly smile.

Jana frowned. "You okay, Luce?"

"No. I…I'm not feeling well. I want to go." I could hardly look at Cas. "Stay…if you want."

"I will take you home," he said, rising to his feet.

Abby looked distraught. "Are you sure? She's fine…"

I didn't wait to hear anything else. I hurried out of the bar and onto the street, gulping fresh, cool air. I was halfway down the block when I heard footsteps behind me.

"Lucy, wait…"

Cas caught up to me, taking my arm in his strong grip and turning me to face him. "What's wrong?"

"What's *wrong*?" I cried incredulously. "Aside from being accosted by demons in the women's room?"

He stepped back. "What?"

"Deb and K."

"You saw them? In the flesh?"

I nodded. "They said that I should ask you who I am."

Cas spat a curse in his native tongue. "They shouldn't be here. Not on This Side."

"But what did they mean? Who am I?"

He shook his head and took my arm, walking me away from the bar. "Nothing. They're sowing discord, that's all. Trying to upset you."

"Well, it worked," I cried. "Am I in danger?"

Cas whirled on me. "*No.* I'll let nothing happen to you. I swear it." He scanned the deserted streets. "But they shouldn't be here."

"Well, they are, and you're acting like you want to sabotage our plan."

"What are you talking about? Sabotage—?"

"You were hanging all over Abby tonight," I said, hearing the jealousy in my words. "I mean, that's…fine. Whatever. You can do whatever you want, but then you act like you want to murder Guy. Like you hate him."

Casziel ran a hand through his dark hair, a distinctly human gesture. "I don't…hate him. I'm playing the part. The jealous rival vying for your hand."

"It doesn't feel that way. In fact, nothing feels the way it's supposed to. It's all messed up."

"Nothing is *messed up*," he shot back. "It's all going according to plan. Did you not hear Guy's serenade?" His voice was dripping with contempt. "Did you not see how he gazed into your eyes, Lucy Dennings?"

"He's drunk…"

"He's noticing you. He's going to fall for you," he said, his voice faltering. "Isn't that what you want? Isn't that what will make you happy?"

What would make me happy, I realized with an aching heart, had nothing to do with Guy. But if we didn't at least try to make this plan work, Casziel would be relegated to an eternity of the same pain he'd been drowning in for centuries.

"Yes," I said. "That would make me happy. Guy and me. Happily ever after. That's exactly what I want."

"Then there's no problem," Cas gritted out and started to walk past me.

"*That*," I said, tugging his arm to make him stop. "That is what I don't understand. Why you look sad now instead of glad. I feel like there's a whole other story happening that you're not telling me. One that I feel like I should remember but can't. Like a dream that slips away when you wake up."

"Your imagination, nothing more."

"Is it? Because the dream I had just the other night—"

"Was just a dream."

"But—"

A group of people noisily exited a restaurant and headed our way.

"Come on," Cas said.

We crossed the street and headed up 6th, a thousand unspoken words hanging between us. The dark felt alive, like it had the night we stumbled home from the pub. Only this time I was stone cold sober. We passed a trash-strewn alley, buzzing with flies, and a hissing voice crawled up my spine.

"Casziel…"

Deber and Keeb shuffled out, just as they had in the bathroom. Flies buzzed. Instantly, Cas put himself between me and the demons. Deber wore a malicious smirk while Keeb tittered into her shoulder with a stomach-churning giggle.

"Isn't that sweet," Deber mused, sauntering closer, bringing Keeb with her. "Lord Casziel, the Nightbringer, the Prince of Demons, playing the part of the heroic—"

"*Silence*," Casziel hissed, and the cloud of flies grew agitated, then settled over the twins again, tangling in their hair, crawling over their faces across their yellow eyes.

Deber turned to me. "Did you ask your questions? Did he answer with lies?" She clucked her tongue. "Sweet, innocent little Lucy has no idea with whom she consorts."

Keeb giggled—a sickening sound—and peered at us from between strands of stringy gray hair.

"Who summoned you?" Casziel demanded.

"You can't guess?"

"Ashtaroth," he muttered, his eyes hard.

The demons moved closer, hesitantly, wary of Casziel. Only a few feet away. I felt the tension humming in him, the muscles under my hand tightening. The flies thickened, their buzzing like the static of an old TV, showing me a fuzzy image of me on the floor of my kitchen, broken glass around me...

"You're a fool, Casziel," Deber was saying. "He will never let you go. And she..." She smiled at me, showing rotting teeth. "She will know the truth and despise you for it."

With an angry snarl, Casziel thrust me back. In the next instant, he was in his demonic form—bloodless skin and eyes like black holes, sucking in all light. Somehow, his wings unfurled *through* the black leather of his jacket without tearing it. An immense sword appeared, strapped between those wings that stretched out, long and powerful and beautifully awful.

The demons shrieked and fell back as he unsheathed the sword and leveled the tip at Deber's throat, his voice dangerous and deadly.

"Leave her alone or I will hunt you on This Side and the Other until your very existence becomes a burden and you beg for Oblivion."

Keeb let out a little shriek. The fear in Deber's eyes was alive and electric, but she smiled in triumph. She backed away, taking Keeb with her into the cloud of flies.

"Beautiful threats, Casziel. But empty." She leveled a wasted finger at me. "She's ours now. Not yours anymore. Never again."

The demons' bodies disintegrated into more flies that dispersed into the night, leaving the alley quiet and dark. Casziel turned to me, his black-on-black eyes like endless pits of darkness in his pale face. I recoiled and he reverted to his human form.

My throat was dry, my head reeling. "I don't...I can't..."

Casziel approached me slowly, hand outstretched as if he were afraid I'd run. But where would I go? Demons lurked in every shadow.

"What just happened?" I asked through trembling lips. "What did she mean that I'd despise you?"

"Nothing. All lies. A demon's word isn't worth anything, remember?" His lip curled, and then he raised his eyes to mine, heavy with regret. "Come. Let's get you home."

Feeling lost, underwater, and drowning in a hundred different emotions, I let him guide me to the subway station. The car wasn't even half full—a few friends ending their night out, a few solitary people scrolling their phones. The glaring light was like a slap to the face, and I calmed my harsh breathing, though my heart didn't stop pounding, even back in my apartment.

Casziel held his palm up. *"Zisurrû."*

Green light outlined my door, then faded, and I was overcome with a sense of déjà vu.

"What you just did to the door...I've seen it before. The night of the pub."

"A protective ward," he said. "I'll do the same to the window after I leave tonight."

"And the flies. I've seen them too. I remember, I was in the kitchen..." I shook my head, my thoughts wading through a dreamy murk. "You were there... Did you use another word? To make me forget?"

He took another step toward me. "Lucy..."

I took a step back. "No. Tell me the truth. What is going on?"

"I never meant for any of this to happen to you. Please. Sit down. I'll explain everything."

"You will?"

"I will. But the truth is not going to be easy for you to hear."

I backed up all the way to my bed and sat down hard. "Okay," I said warily. "Tell me."

The demon kneeled at my feet, and the longing in his eyes drew me in until I wanted to sink to the floor with him, wrap my arms around him, hold him and be held by him.

"Gods, Lucy..."

"What is happening?" I asked, suddenly on the verge of tears. "Why do I feel this way? Everything about this is so strange and scary, and yet..."

He reached up, both hands cupping my face, softly. Reverently. Holding me as if I were precious to him. "And yet?"

"I know you…don't I?"

His head bowed, his eyes fell shut. When he opened them again, they were filled with pain. Grief. It called out and something inside me answered. I gasped, my heart pounding so hard, I thought it would break. For what I never had.

No. For what I had and then lost…

"Tell me," I whispered. "Who am I? Who are we to each other?"

Casziel's lips parted, and he pressed a gentle kiss to my forehead. "Forgive me, Lucy. Somewhere in those dreams of yours, I hope you can forgive me."

"What? Wait—"

He touched his thumb to my skin where I could still feel the warmth of his lips.

"*Ñeštug u-lu.*"

The TV's volume was on low, its light flickering in my darkened apartment. My clock radio said it was after three in the morning. I was still wearing that ridiculous dress, but the bedcovers were tucked around me. Makeup smeared my pillow. I sat up slowly. My head felt heavy, as if I'd gotten drunk after all.

"Cas?"

No answer. I climbed out of bed. The couch was empty and the window that Casziel always kept open was shut. Something nipped at the corner of my mind, but I couldn't grasp it. I couldn't recall leaving the bar or how I got home. The last thing I remembered was Guy singing to me and telling me I was beautiful…

"The plan is working."

The words sounded hollow. Empty. But Cas needed the plan to work. To save his soul.

What about mine?

I washed all the makeup off my face, brushed my teeth, and changed into my sleep T-shirt and sweatpants. I wanted Casziel to come back. I wanted Casziel to come back more than I wanted Guy to think I was beautiful. That was the only truth I had.

I opened the window.

I SLAM OPEN the door to the back room at Idle Hands. The gust of wind from my wings makes the black candlelight flicker but does nothing to lessen Ashtaroth's stench.

"*We had a deal,*" I seethe.

"Watch yourself, boy," the demon lord snarls, his hand resting on the sword strapped to his waist. The serpent coiled around the settee narrows its black eyes at me in warning. "You are to kneel before your master."

I ignore the command. "Every night I pay you in blood and pain. Every night. And in return—"

"*You dare defy me?*"

The air shakes with Ashtaroth's wrath. He rises off the couch, his own wings beating his foulness to me, his sword at the ready. Imps snicker and cower at his feet, hungry for my fear.

"Kneel, Casziel, or I'll send a horde of my servitors to your pretty little Lucy, and you will spend your remaining days on This Side watching her descend into madness."

Though he looks wasted and rotted, Ashtaroth is more powerful than I. A fact I will rely on in a few days' time, but now I must watch myself.

I clench my teeth and it takes everything I have to force myself to one knee.

"Better." Ashtaroth lowers his sword. "Your enduring regard for that human girl is disgraceful to our dark purpose."

I raise my head. "Deber and Keeb."

Ashtaroth smirks, a mockery of innocence. "What of them?"

"You and I made a pact. Lucy is not to be touched."

"What the twins do is none of my concern."

"You brought them to This Side."

"Do they need my help Crossing Over? Besides, they're the girl's demons. Our agreement, Casziel, is between you and me. But we can modify the conditions if you so desire."

My jaw clenches. "What do you want?"

"You know me better than that, my sweet prince," Ashtaroth's words are carried on the currents of his foul breath. He taps the hilt of his sword. "There is only one thing I ever want."

I transform into my human body, then roll up the sleeve of my shirt to reveal the four cauterized cuts on my inner arm that mark my time on This Side. Ashtaroth adds a fifth.

"It's become obvious that this payment is not enough," he says, still looming over me. "You have forgotten to whom you belong. If you wish to keep your Lucy safe, you'll allow me to remind you."

My frail human form trembles against my will. "I do this, and the twins don't touch her."

"I can arrange that."

A demon's promise…worthless. But there is no choice to be made. My pulse stutters as I strip out of the jacket and shirt and bow my head. I half-expect Ashtaroth's sword to cleave it from my neck and send me into the nothingness of Oblivion.

Not yet. Not yet…

He exchanges his sword for a curved dagger. The room is dank, the air rancid and cold on my scarred flesh as Ashtaroth circles me, taking his time. Drawing out my fear. The imps slaver and mewl in the dancing shadows cast by the lone candle. The dagger begins to glow pale yellow. I feel the blade's heat before Ashtaroth chooses his mark.

Then I know nothing but searing agony.

Again and again, he touches his dagger to my back, carving, cutting, burning. Ruining the flesh between my shoulder blades that hadn't yet been scarred.

I don't have to see what Ashtaroth does to know he's branding me with his seal. A pentagram, bracketed with vertical lines that are tipped with circles and bisected with horizontal lines that curl at the ends. I keep the screams he hungers for locked behind my teeth until I can't hold them back.

Then I surrender.

I give him my pain, throwing my head back and releasing it for him to drink down, to gorge on. The minutes drag and the torturous agony returns me to the night in the ziggurat, where I was beaten and burned to the brink of death. That pain I could take, but it's married to the visions of my family dying, one by one.

And then it's her turn.

She dies and then I scream for me. For what I've lost and will never get back.

When Ashtaroth is done, the agony seeps into my skin, into my heart. The blackened husk still has tender flesh left in it, even after all these years. A part of me that clings to the life she and I once had.

The love...

Ambri is waiting for me when I emerge from the back room. I've returned to my demonic form, sending the pain of Ashtaroth's branding to sleep for now. It will wake with a fiery vengeance the moment I revert back to my human body and make the new cut on my arm feel like a kiss.

My second-in-command has intelligence enough to appear as if he hadn't heard my screams. Every demon in the tavern, in fact, averts their eyes.

But for one.

A lesser duke is playing cards with another demon. He looks away but too slowly for my like. The cards in his hands drop from trembling fingers when he feels my attention.

"Good evening, Druj," I say, leaning over the table. "Might I borrow your dagger?"

"My Lord Casziel, I-I did not mean to—"

"Your dagger, Druj."

He withdraws it from his waist sash and hands it over. His friend tilts back in his chair and raises his fan of cards like a shield. Without a word, I take the dagger by the blade, flip it nimbly in my hand, then drive it into Druj's lone eye. Brown and green ichor sprays over the table.

His companion tosses his cards down with a sigh. "Pity. T'was a good game, too."

I lean in to Druj. "Do I make my point?"

The demon nods, the dagger nodding with him, and then he slumps dead over the table, driving the blade deeper into his head. Blood pools.

"Good."

I head for the bar while behind me, a cloud of foul smoke plumes and roils. In moments, Druj's chair will be empty, him having Crossed Over to the Other Side where he may consider his actions.

I put on a smirk to remind those gathered—including Ambri, watching everything with keen eyes—who I am. But disgust churns within.

"Good evenin', my lord," Eistibus says, placing a glass of wine in front of me and replacing Ambri's with a fresh one. The djinn wisely backs away, leaving us to our business.

"You were merciful," Ambri observes. "The Nightbringer would have burned this tavern to the ground and every demon in it."

"I'm not in the mood for your commentary, Ambri. Make your report."

"As you wish. Guy Baker. Age twenty-seven. Graduated from Columbia University with a degree in environmental science. Honors student, gives to charity, recycles..." Ambri smirks into his wine. "Flosses daily, calls his mother once a week, always tips twenty-percent—"

"Ambri."

"He's nauseatingly decent, is my point. A few minor demons on him. No one special."

"Who?"

"Servitors of Belphegor and Rishk."

I nod, thinking. "So he's a little vain, has tendencies toward jealousy. But he's a good man?"

"It would seem so." Ambri heaves a sigh. "A pity."

Guy's light shines bright. And must, for her.

"Was there anything else, my lord?"

I sip my wine, debating. Confiding in a demon is never wise, but the turmoil in my mind and heart are distinctly human and Ambri spends an inordinate amount of time on This Side. Humans are his playthings, on the battlefield and in the bedroom. I'd never call him soft, but he's not nearly as bloodthirsty as the rest of my Brethren. A romantic...if insatiable sexual appetite is *romance.*

I'd have to ask Lucy.

A small, soft smile touches my lips and Ambri sighs.

"So it's the girl."

There's no point in refuting it. "Yes."

"Who is she? Who is this human you've been following through her every lifetime for the last four millennia?"

Anger at his brazen question flares and then flames out. Denial dies on my lips. I haven't the strength for either anymore.

"She is my wife."

Speaking the word aloud is like releasing a burden and invoking a curse at the same time. It's sweet on my tongue and burns like Ashtaroth's blade.

Dam-gá. Ttsuma. Zhena.

The most beautiful word in any language because it describes her. She was mine for a handful of moments in the brief candle-flicker lives of humans. My eyes shut at a memory that roars up at me. Her pleading stare, her mouth gagged, and then the blade at her throat...

My hands flinch, the glass upends, and wine spills along the bar. Like blood.

Eistibus hurries over to clean the mess and refill my glass.

Ambri has gone silent. When the djinn is gone, he leans in. "And this Guy is your gift to her?"

"I'm paying a debt, that is all." I hunch over the bar, twisting the glass stem in my fingers. "I watch her, Ambri. Lifetime after lifetime, always alone. She's never loved another. Not once since Larsa."

"Because she loves *you.*"

My chest tightens, my wings tense and fold close. "There is nothing left to love. I'm a moth, battering itself against a lamp, trying to get to her light. But it's too late for me. The best I can hope for is to leave her with a chance to love someone else."

Ambri's perfect eyebrows rise. "Leave? As in...*leave?*"

I nod.

"How? Who...?" His eyes widen. He knows who. The only demon in our sphere powerful enough. He lowers his voice to a hissing whisper. "You're going to get Ashtaroth to send you to Oblivion."

I nod again.

Ambri clears his throat and says with a false smile, "Are you certain, my lord, this is the wisest course of action?"

"I'm certain."

He shakes his head. "I've heard of our kind giving up immortality for the eternal sleep. I've just never met anyone who was willing to do it."

"I'm not *willing*," I say. "It's the only tactic that satisfies my intentions."

"Intentions that baffle me. What of your duty on the Other Side? Have you lost your taste for it?"

I'd begun to lose my taste for it years ago. The fire of my rage and pain was burning out, leaving nothing but ash and wasted years. Centuries of human misery that paid for my grief. I say none of this to Ambri. There is only so much weakness I can trust to relay in a single night or else he *will* betray me on general principle.

"I'm weary Ambri," I say, one facet of the truth, at least. "When you're as old as me, you might feel the same."

He snorts. "So long as there exists cocks and cunts, I'll exist to enjoy them. Because that's all humans are to me. Toys. Playthings. Vessels." A brow arches. "I wonder, my lord, if that's something you've forgotten."

"*You* forget, Ambri, my outrage at the murder of this particular *vessel* is why I've been laying waste to humankind for centuries."

"Aye, and what a glorious run it's been." Ambri touches his glass to mine. "But I still fail to see the allure of Oblivion. Is there nothing holding you here?"

"No."

His shoulders hunch, and then he looks almost angry. "I don't believe you. The utter lack of consequences, of conscience, is what makes it fun. Perpetual irresponsibility…what could be better than that? To give it up for a mere girl…"

I shoot him a dangerous look and he holds up a hand.

"If you're set in your course, I'll not sway you," he says, deflated. "Your secret is safe with me."

I believe him. Not that I have a choice. Time will tell how foolish I am to bare my soul to a demon.

I drain my glass in one gulp and set it down hard. "Give me some money."

Ambri frowns. "What for?"

My eyes widen.

"I meant, how much does my lord require?"

"All of it."

He rummages in his coat and pulls out a wad of American money. I take the entire roll—several thousand dollars in hundred-dollar bills by my cursory count—and stuff it in my trouser pocket.

He sighs dramatically. "I had plans with a lovely little tart this evening…"

I smirk; he's a dramatic little tart himself. Ambri has collected enough wealth on This Side over the course of his three hundred years that he'll not miss what's in my pocket.

Sure enough, his cocky grin returns. "I can always plead that I've been mugged. Sympathy is a sure ticket to a human's heart. And bed. They enjoy caring for the downtrodden…when they're not busy killing each other, of course."

I nod. Lucy cares for others. Even those scarce few lifetimes in which her despair drove her to sleep her way from one human to another or fill the emptiness with drugs or alcohol, her light has never dimmed.

But how she suffers…

I never dreamed her love for me was as bottomless as mine for her. I never imagined my corruption would condemn *her* to endless lifetimes of loneliness, searching for me without ever knowing whom she sought. I'm Forgotten, until she dies and Crosses Over. Then the memories rush back in, and she calls my name. But I'm not among the heavenly host; I'm in hell. Then she Forgets and begins a new lifetime with the same nameless hunger.

A vacancy in her heart where I once lived.

By the time I realized she hadn't let me go, it was too late. My sins guarantee there will be no redemption for me. No second chance. *Her* best chance at freedom from this terrible cycle is my Oblivion. Perhaps then her soul will finally understand what she does not—that our love died in the bowels of the ziggurat.

And it's never coming back.

CASZIEL DIDN'T COME **back**.

He wasn't there as I got ready for work Wednesday morning, which was bustling due to Kimberly's upcoming honeymoon and the disaster in Sri Lanka. Guy was busy making his own departure plans, and Abby hinted more than once that he might ask me to go along with him.

"And you'll say yes, of course. You and Guy…close quarters in a foreign land. Perfect, right?"

Just a short week ago it *would* have been perfect. My favorite romantic fantasy come to life. Instead, all I could think about was Casziel. Something had happened after we left karaoke, but I couldn't remember. Just like everything else with him, it danced at the edges of my awareness. *He* lived at the edges of my awareness like an unspoken promise. But it seemed every time I tried to grasp the truth of it, it slipped away.

I dragged myself through the workday, then rushed to get home. My place was empty. I wondered if Cas was in trouble with that terrible Ashtaroth. God, even the name sounded monstrous and evil. Or maybe he went back to the Other Side. Except he had eleven days here, which was sort of random, when I thought about it.

He's not coming back, Deber offered. *He grew bored with you— Silly Lucy and her silly, uneventful little life.*

My apartment's silence became deafening. Twilight became full dark, no stars, and still, Cas didn't return. I heated some leftover casserole, changed into my sleep shorts and T-shirt. I checked and double-checked that my window was open, then went to bed to read. But for the first time, the romance couldn't hold me or make me fall in.

I shut off the light and lay in the dark, trying to remember what happened after karaoke night. My thoughts began to scatter, turn slippery and indistinct...except for the woman at the warrior's homecoming. She appeared, and I teetered on the edge of sleep, watching as she

waits for him on the upper floor. She has already greeted him properly with the family, and now her heartbeat is a drum when his heavy footfalls enter the room. She can hardly see his face; the lone candle's light is low and the night, thick. But she can feel how his eyes burn with want. She rushes into his arms. He's real and solid, after living in her dreams for years. He smells of ale and sweat, of cloves and honey. His mouth captures hers in a brutal kiss.

"Too long," he moans, his hands roaming her back, his fingers sinking into her thick black hair. "It's been too long. You're so much a woman now. Gods, a treasure..."

His words make her heart sing as her body aches for his. Four years of war has brought him new scars, new strength. He is a stone monument, hard and strong, when he was already both. She kisses him ferociously, bites at his lips, presses herself against him.

"Li'ili," he grits out, and she feels his stiffness between them.

"Father says we'll be wed within the moon's turn," she says, her hands slipping down to the rigid length of him in his trousers. She strokes him and kisses him with increasing urgency. "But I ache for you now..."

He grunts and takes one full breast in his large hand, squeezing. "Did you wait for me, Li'ili?"

"I would wait for you until the sun goes black and the stars fall, beloved."

The sound he makes is part emotion, part dire need. She gasps as his hand slips under her dress. His fingers tease her opening that is wet and ready for him.

"Are you still mine?" he breathes hotly against her neck.

"Always... ki-áñg ngu." She presses against his touch, wishing he'd plunge his fingers inside and take her. "My beloved."

"We must wait," he says, reading her thoughts as usual. He uses her arousal so that his calloused touch glides over her nub of pleasure, rough but slick. "I'm going to make you my wife and then I'm going to take what's mine."

"Yes," she hisses, taking his lower lip in her teeth and sucking. Her grip on his cock tightens. "And this." She meets his eye with her own heated gaze. "Mine."

He chuckles, though it's quickly burned up in the fire of lust. "Fierce woman. Yes, yours." He grips her hips, hauling her against him. "I dreamed of you while at war. Every night."

"Because you love me," she says, pushing him down into the wooden chair carved with ravens and straddling him.

"Because I love you," he replies, his voice soft.

He kisses her gently. Deeply. Then harder. His fingers are between her legs again, stroking her. She cries out and rides his hand while palming the thickness in his pants.

They strive to bring each other to release—there are many clothes separating them. But the eyes of the gods are watching and will withhold their blessings until the wedding. That night, they will be together. Joined. Complete.

And whole at last...

I blinked awake Thursday morning, an old—ancient?—longing alive in my heart and a fierce orgasm throbbing between my legs.

"Oh my God." I squeezed my thighs together, as if I could capture it and hold on. Not just the physical pleasure but the love I'd witnessed. Raw and all-consuming. The dream was like the others I'd told Cas about but a hundred times more potent and even earlier than Japan.

Like, Sumerian-earlier?

I sat up, the dream and the pleasure both ebbing away. My thoughts swirled with possibilities, each more overwhelming and unimaginable than the last.

"It's what he said. His existence seeping into mine. That's all."

With a full body orgasm on the side?

I rubbed my eyes, feeling as if I'd come to the end of my suspension of disbelief. There had to be a plausible, scientific explanation for all of this, and if I didn't talk to someone and get out of my head, I was going to go insane.

"That's the most plausible explanation of all."

It was a little after seven a.m., around noon in London. Cole was likely in class or working on one of his masterpieces. I hated to bother him with my crap, but when he moved to the UK, he told me again and again to never hesitate to call.

I grabbed my phone.

"Three times in one week," Cole answered with a tired grin. "I don't have my sketch pad ready. What's up, Luce? Everything okay?"

"I was going to ask the same of you. Rough night?"

My friend was a night owl but mostly because he didn't sleep well. Sometimes not at all.

Cole ran a hand through his shaggy light brown hair. "I'll sleep when I'm dead. Isn't that how that morbid motto goes?"

You won't do much sleeping then, either.

"I wish your insomnia would give you a break."

"You and me both, but it's actually useful now. The deadline for the June issue of *Art for Life* is racing at me like a runaway train."

Cole was editor-in-chief of his university's student-produced visual arts magazine—a huge honor for a second-year post-grad.

"I'll let you go if you're busy."

"Nope, I need the break. Plus, I *always* want to talk to you, Luce."

Love for my friend flooded me. He never complained, was always kind.

If someone deserves all-consuming love, it's this boy.

"Well, you're the smartest person I know, and I have a question. It's silly, really."

Silly. God, I was getting tired of that word.

"Shoot," Cole said.

"Do you believe in reincarnation?"

"Haven't thought about it."

"You've never been curious?"

He shrugged. "I figure there's no way to know what happens when we pass on, so there's no point in serious speculation."

"But lots of people believe in it, right? There are stories of kids who can speak languages they can't possibly know. Or people having vivid, detailed memories of past lives, from different eras in history that come to them, maybe...in dreams?"

"I guess. But there're also stories of white lights and ancestors gathering to welcome them on to...wherever. Like I said, no one knows for sure. It's not like there's anyone around to ask."

Yes and no...

"Right. Okay, one more question. Is there something special about the number eleven? Like, in an occult kind of way?"

"Occult kind of way? What does that mean?"

I shrugged one shoulder. "I just meant, do you know if eleven holds some special meaning. Seven is lucky, thirteen is unlucky and eleven is...?"

"A character in *Stranger Things*? Cute kid. Bad haircut."

I snorted a laugh. "I'm being serious."

"So am I," Cole said, the silvery-blue of his laptop reflecting in his black, square-rimmed glasses. "But while we're chatting, this numerology article is telling me that the number eleven represents intuition." He read from the screen in front of him. "*It asks us to look beyond our senses and be receptive to hidden meanings.* Does that make sense?"

"Yes, a lot. Actually."

He read on. "*Eleven may also indicate transgressions, indiscretions, and sins.*"

"Sins? It says that?"

"Yes, and it talks about being drawn to something unknown. Something unresolved."

That was the perfect phrase to describe that strange, déjà vu feeling I got when I was around Casziel: something unresolved.

"What are you doing over there, Luce?" Cole asked, shutting his laptop. "Having seances? Playing with a Ouija board?"

"Not...lately."

"Don't. It's not safe."

"I didn't know you were a believer in that stuff."

"I'm not. Not really. But there are energies out there and it's not smart to poke at stuff we don't understand. Who knows what you might wake up?"

"That is very good advice," I said. *That I could've used a week ago.*

"But Luce, you're a researcher. You could have looked it up yourself."

"You mean, you don't like being my personal Google?"

"I know your face, and you've got something on your mind. How are things with you and Cas? Or is it you and Guy?"

"Not sure yet," I said. "My boss's wedding is on Saturday, and I have a feeling a lot of *unresolved somethings* will be figured out then."

"Is Cas your plus-one?"

"I think so. Maybe. But as friends."

A lie. Cas would come as a decoy. As the escort Abby thinks he is. But not as a friend. Casziel Abisare wasn't a *friend*.

He's so much more that all of those things. If only I knew what.

"I take it Operation Get the Guy is still in effect?"

I forced a laugh. "Guy asked me to save a dance for him. I think something might be happening." Cole frowned but I cut him off at the pass. "What about you? How's your love life going?"

"Me? My love life is represented by the number zero, which indicates there will be no indiscretions or sins any time soon. But that's by choice. I've sworn off men."

"Noooo, you can't. You need to share your awesomeness with *at least* one other person."

He laughed. "I see what you did there. Nah, guys are too much drama." He glanced at his watch. "Shit, break time's up. But before I go, let me ask *you* a question. You're at your boss's wedding. Cas and Guy are both standing across the room—"

"No rooms. It's at the Loeb Boathouse in Central Park."

"Okay, the Boat—wait, really? *Nice.* So Cas and Guy are standing on the other side of Bow Bridge. One of them crosses to you, sweeps you into his arms, and dances with you until the sun comes up. Which one is it?"

My cheeks warmed. "Jeez, Cole. For someone who's sworn off men, you're quite the romantic."

"You're avoiding the question."

"It's more complicated than what I want." I plucked at my ratty couch cushion. "Someday I'll explain it all to you. When it all seems less crazy."

"Fine, you're off the hook. Because this magazine no one reads isn't going to edit itself. Love you."

"Love you."

I blew him a kiss and ended the FaceTime, then got ready for work, feeling better after the injection of real life from talking to Cole. I grabbed the Macy's bag with the dress I'd bought for Kimberly's wedding. Abby said it wouldn't be alluring enough for Guy, so I was going to take it back on my lunchbreak and get something better.

Do I care if Guy likes my dress?

I had to care. For Casziel's sake. Our grand plan's success was necessary for his redemption. But...

"If a Guy falls in the forest and there's no one there to hear it...?"

I snorted a laugh; my dork game was strong, but the dream clung to me, whispering possibilities.

Impossibilities, I insisted. *He's a demon and I'm...*

I didn't know what I was. Someone who was holding a tiny flickering candle in a vast, dark cavern—I could see only bits and pieces, but the darkness hinted at something so much larger and deeper. My aching sense of loss. My endless search for love in books.

Scientists search for the truth but what if the truth was too incredible to believe?

The office was a bustling hive of activity. Before nine, I had a pile of papers on my desk, logistics to be worked out. Guy Baker came by with a manifest for his upcoming trip to Sri Lanka. His smile was as warm as ever, but he didn't linger to chat. It was as if his drunken serenade hadn't happened.

He probably wishes it hadn't.

Jana leaned over from her cubicle after he'd left. "What are you doing for lunch?"

I nudged the Macy's bag at my foot. "Returning this dress and getting a new one. As per Ms. Taylor's orders."

Jana pursed her lips. "Want some company?"

"Um...sure. If you want."

"I want."

At noon, we headed to the department store, but Jana steered me into a Greek deli on the way.

"Let's eat first," Jana said. "I'm starved, as usual. Don't believe them when they say you can eat whatever you want while breastfeeding and not gain weight. Lies, all lies."

I managed a smile and waited for the anxiety to grip my stomach. The kind that usually came at the prospect of sitting in front of someone—*eating* in front of someone—and having to barrel through a conversation without making a fool of myself.

But instead of a squeezing fist, the anxiety was a pinch. I'd survived dinner with Guy and Abby, and I supposed having a demon as an on-again off-again roommate had a way of making lunch with a coworker look like child's play.

We ordered our food at the counter, the deli smelling of freshly baked phyllo—the owner made his own right there on site—and took our number to a table near a window.

"So," Jana said, her blue gaze direct but warm. "We've worked together for two years, and this is the first time we've hung out, Abby's makeover notwithstanding."

"Yeah, I guess it is."

"I'm not trying to put you on the spot. I'm just as guilty—"

"No, you're not," I said. "You've asked me to lunch or coffee a bunch of times, but I've been too shy to say yes."

She smiled. "I'm glad you said yes. But I don't want to make you uncomfortable or self-conscious for being shy. Or is it introverted? Or both? I don't know that there's a difference."

"There is," I said. "Introverted people don't hate socializing but draw more energy from being alone. I used to be able to go to parties and talk and have fun, but they'd leave me mentally exhausted."

A waiter brought our food and departed.

"And shy?" Jana said, taking a bite of one of the dolmas we ordered to share.

"Shy is more like fear. Or self-consciousness. It comes from…" *Demons.* "Negative self-talk, I guess. I've made peace with my introversion, but the shyness has been isolating."

I poked at my salad and years of that isolation were suddenly right in front of me, so I could feel every second of it.

"Sometimes the loneliness is so much, and the silence is so loud, I read romance novels until my head aches, and I *think* until it feels like I'm drilling into myself. Like excavation. As if I'm mining for memories I don't have, certain that there is more to me than this. There has to be. But I can't find it. Whatever it is, it's always out of reach. I drop a stone into the well of my heart and I keep listening for it to hit something real. But it never does."

I blinked out of my thoughts to see Jana watching me, her jaw slack.

"Oh my God, sorry," I said, my cheeks heating. "I don't know where that came from. I just...dumped all that in your lap."

"It's okay," she said. "It's *really* okay. That's real talk, Luce, not bullshit chitchat, which I hate. I'm sort of honored that you said that to me. I get the impression maybe you needed to get it out."

I nodded. She was right; a week ago, I would've run out of the restaurant for baring myself like that.

"Thanks for not giving up on me."

"Never." Jana smiled gently. "Can I ask you a question? You said you *used* to be able to go to parties. When did that change? I know your father passed and I'm so sorry about that, Luce. I don't know that I ever told you."

"You told me." I smiled back. "But no, it was earlier than that. It was..."

I searched my memory, trying to find a moment or incident that might've made me withdraw like the proverbial turtle into its shell. It was before Dad died. A much longer stretch of years. Centuries, even...

"It was gradual," I said. "The negative voices in my head grew louder and I grew more tired, somehow."

"Tired of what?"

Not having him.

The thought had risen up from the deepest recesses of my mind, like a flare, wanting to illuminate the empty spaces in me. The dream of the woman and her warrior rushed in after it, daring me to believe it was merely a remnant of Casziel's life.

"The reason I ask..." Jana frowned. "You okay?"

"Oh, um...yes."

"You look a little pale."

"Fine. I promise." I took a sip of water "What were you saying?"

"Okay, well...this might sound completely condescending so feel free to tell me to jump off the Brooklyn Bridge—but I feel sort of maternal toward you." Jana laughed, looking a little sheepish. "It's one hundred percent new baby hormones, I'm sure, but when you said you were going to present on Monday, I was bursting with pride. And I really, really want to see what you do, because I bet it'll be amazing."

The presentation. Monday, at work. That was real life.

"Thank you," I said to Jana. "I don't know if my idea will be any good. It feels like it's missing something, but I'm going to go for it anyway."

"Well? Let's hear it," she said and took a bite of her gyro. "I'll be your dress rehearsal."

"Okay. If you want…"

"I want."

I told Jana about my shoe idea and her eyes got wider and wider as she chewed her food.

"Holy shit. Luce…"

"It's not exactly new," I said. "Other companies make sustainable apparel, but…"

Jana's head was bobbing as she took a sip of water. "Bracelets and stuff but not actual shoes. Can it be done? As in, will the shoe hold together?"

I nodded. "I've done the research. Instead of using real rubber, plastic can also be used to create synthetic rubber polymers. No sense in robbing the forest to save the ocean."

"I think it's genius. But you're right, it's missing one thing."

"What's that?"

"A celebrity endorsement." She leaned in confidentially. "My hubby plays golf at Douglaston. Since Wyatt was born, he's been forbidden to play more than once a month. But do you know who his favorite golfing buddy is?"

"Couldn't guess."

"Jason Lemieux. He's a hotshot sports agent. Has a huge roster of big-time clients under his belt. Clients like Kai Solomon."

"Um…"

"The tennis star? Won the Australian Open and a bunch more tournaments after that." She arched a brow. "You see where I'm going with this? I'll force my hubs to force Jason to force his client to sign on to your shoe."

"That's a lot of forcing," I said with a laugh.

"Think of the possibilities. The exposure. The more shoes we sell—"

"The more of that damn plastic gets repurposed. And every penny of profit goes right back into cleanup." I shocked myself by offering my hand for a high five, which Jana obliged. "You have to present with me."

She shook her head. "No, no. This is your baby. I won't have Jason on board by Monday, anyway. It's all you, girl."

The thought should've given me hives, but the twinge of anxiety in my stomach had faded altogether.

Take that Deber and Keeb.

"Now can we talk about this?" Jana nudged the Macy's bag under the table. "Is it really so frumpy?"

"Well…"

"Let me see."

I wiped olive oil off my hands and held up the dress.

Jana pursed her lips and cocked her head in a mildly reproving way. "Luce, it's gorgeous. Moreover, you love it, right?"

"I think it's sort of perfect."

Jana brushed her hands together. "Welp, seeing as we no longer have to wrestle with the returns line at Macy's, we have time for dessert."

I grinned. "Yeah, we do."

After we finished strong Greek coffees and shared a slice of baklava, Jana gave me a hug. "Let's do this again sometime. Please?"

"I'd like that." I held up my bag. "We're close to my place. I'm going to drop this off and hang it so it's not bag-wrinkled for tomorrow."

"An excellent idea. See you back at the office."

We parted ways, and I went back to my apartment. I rounded the corner and stopped short. Casziel was sitting on the lowest rickety step of my staircase, his head bowed, his arms dangling off his knees.

The first emotion that swept through me was anguish because he looked like he was in terrible pain.

The second was an overwhelming, unwarranted rush of joy that he was still here.

With me.

I CLIMBED THE stairs and sat next to Casziel, setting my dress bag aside. "What happened?"

When he didn't reply, I took his left arm in my hands and carefully rolled up the sleeve of the black Henley that made him look just as devastating as I suspected it would. Seven burned slices marched up his arm now, one fresh, the skin an angry red.

"This isn't right. It's horrible. Cas, I—" I'd laid my hand on his shoulder and he flinched away from my touch. "There's more?"

He smiled grimly. "A souvenir."

I tugged down the back collar of his Henley and bit back a cry. Something had been burned into his skin. *Branded* into him.

Anger burned in me too, swift and hot. "Come on. We're going to take care of this."

"Leave it, Lucy."

"Absolutely not. This is wrong. Just…wrong."

I offered him my hand, and he let me pull him to his feet. Inside, I dumped the bag on the floor and guided him to the couch.

"Show me."

"You don't want to see it."

Based on what little I'd seen so far, that was probably true, but I fixed him with an unwavering stare. He relented with a small smile, shaking his head at a private thought, and started to remove his shirt. He winced and hissed a curse.

"Let me help." I moved to stand in front of him. "Raise your arms."

He obeyed, and I reached around his waist and lifted, careful to keep the material away from his back. The shirt covered his face for a moment and then it was off, ruffling the dark curls on his brow. Our eyes locked, my mouth inches from his, his bare chest brushing my breasts.

Heat rushed through me, the kind I'd read about—and craved—in romance novels for years but had never experienced. Especially not with Jeff Hastings in college. Our awkward fumbling had been a candle to my body's fiery, visceral response to Casziel. To be in his space, this close to his shirtless and scarred skin, lit me up from the inside so fast, it stole my breath. Like the woman in the dream, I trembled with anticipation and ached with want, yearning for a release that was years in the making…

For a heartbeat, we shared the same air and then I took a step back. But I couldn't stop staring. My eyes gorged on him, the brick wall of muscle that was his abdomen, the rounded bulge of his shoulders that tapered to defined forearms striated with veins.

I put my hands on those shoulders to turn him around—a pathetic excuse to touch him—and a cry caught in my throat, the desire stamped out by horror. A pentagram, about the size of a dinner plate, was burned into his back and bisected with strange lines and loops. His skin was red and raw, blackened at the edges.

"My God. What is this?"

"Ashtaroth's mark. A reminder to whom I belong."

I swallowed hard and blinked back tears. "You need medication. For this and for your arm. This is a human body. It can be hurt. It *is* hurt and you have to take care of it."

"If you insist, Lucy Dennings."

He sounded defeated, but maybe it was only the pain. I hurried to the bathroom and returned with a tube of Neosporin. I sat on the couch and Casziel moved to the floor, his back to me. As gently as I could, I coated the strange lines with the clear antibiotic. He never flinched, though now and then, the muscles in his back would move and bulge— he was all elegant lines and sculpted masculinity.

And familiar.

I put the medicine on his skin and touching him rekindled the fire of need that burned deep in the center of me. My fingers itched to stray, to trace his scars. I longed to kiss them, to reacquaint myself with the lines and contours of him because the sense that I'd had him before—and far more intimately—was alive and bright in me. The dream of the woman reuniting with her warrior hovered in the thickened air between us like a secret waiting to be broken open. Or the proverbial door to Narnia, waiting for me to walk through it...

You don't have the guts, silly Lucy. Stick to your books.

I blinked out of my thoughts and Deber's insinuations and finished tending to Casziel's back.

"You should really go to the hospital, but I suppose that's out of the question." I took his arm to tend to the cuts. "Why does he do this to you?"

"To feed on the pain that comes from wounding this human body," Casziel said. "To remind me that I am vulnerable in my human form."

"Can he...kill you? I mean...worse than sending you to the Other Side?"

Cas didn't reply and the mountain of things unsaid between us grew taller, more precarious. I set the medicine on the table.

"Do you want something to eat? Or maybe watch TV, to keep your mind off the pain?"

"Are you not supposed to be at work?"

"I'm taking the rest of the day off." I fished my phone out of my bag to call the office. "I haven't called in sick or taken a personal day since Dad passed. They'll survive without me for one afternoon."

And you have only a few days left on This Side.

The pang in my heart was familiar too. The woman in Japan. The girl in Russia. Both had been left feeling as if they'd come close to something real, only to have it—him—vanish into smoke. Like a dream...

I called into work, then hung up my dress for the wedding. I returned to the couch and turned on Netflix, scrolling shows.

"See anything you might like?"

Cas cocked his head. "*Schitt's Creek?*"

"This is the best show ever. I've seen the entire series three times over."

"Why?"

"Because it's special to me. It's special to a lot of people. Hilarious but so sweet too." I moved through the episodes. "It's about a wealthy family who loses everything and learns to love and appreciate what they have in each other, that they're rich in all the ways that really count. Then in season three, David meets Patrick and oh my God... Their love story is so beautiful."

I glanced down to see Casziel looking up at me, and I laughed self-consciously. "I know, I know. Me and my romance. But I just love this show so much. You interested?"

He shrugged, and I turned on a random episode, mostly to fill the silence between us. It was the one where Johnny dreams of how the Rose family's life used to be before they lost all their money.

Of course, I had to pick the dream episode.

I thought I caught a whiff of pipe smoke and steeled myself.

"Do we live more than one lifetime?" I blurted.

Cas faltered for a split second. No one would have noticed it but me. A small tightening of his mouth. A blink, then gone again.

"No. As the poet said, you have only one wild and precious life." He smiled, though it looked forced. Pained. "And that is the question, Lucy Dennings. What will you do with the rest of your one life after I'm gone?"

"I-I don't know," I said, his last words like a chill wind running through me. "Give my presentation on Monday. Hopefully, the team will take it up and we'll rid the oceans of more plastic. Though it's sort of like trying to bail out the *Titanic* with a spoon. In thirty years, there will be more plastic in the water than fish. Ninety percent of seabirds have consumed some kind of plastic waste. *Ninety* percent. It's heart-breaking."

"A tragedy."

I knocked his shoulder. "It *is* a tragedy. And most people would agree, but the problem is so big, it's hard to grasp the enormity of it."

"And you will dedicate your life to showing them how," Cas said, his eyes on the TV. "You will marry Guy and produce children and save the world together."

"That's a little presumptuous," I said, tucking a lock of hair behind my ear. "I mean...I don't know what's going to happen at the wedding tomorrow or beyond. Honestly, I'm only going along with our plan for your sake."

His head whipped to me. "*My* sake? What of yours? What of your romantic fantasies? You've loved Guy from afar for years—"

"I haven't *loved* him. I had a crush on him, but I don't really know him. The *idea* of him is stronger than the reality."

"But we've broken the ice, so to speak. He serenaded you at the singing bar. He is eager to see you tomorrow. You'll soon get to know him and see that he's a good man."

I frowned. "How do you know that?"

"His demons are weak. His light is bright. He is a man worthy of you, Lucy Dennings."

I didn't know what to say. Except that Guy was far from my thoughts and all I could think of was the ticking clock that was going to take Casziel away from me.

"What if I don't want Guy at all? What if I want...something else?"

Cas stiffened. "What else do you want?"

I heaved a breath. "I had another lucid dream, like the Japan and Russia dreams I told you about before."

"Okay."

Be brave. Be brave.

I relayed the dream of the woman and her warrior. How I felt the love and desire between them. When I was finished, Cas's eyes watched me in the glow of the TV for a long moment, his face impassive.

"And?" he said finally, his tone like a locked door.

I recoiled as if I'd been slapped, tears of frustration pricking my eyes. "And? So? I studied Mesopotamia at NYU, remember?" I inhaled and let it out in a rush. "I think the city was Larsa, you were the warrior, and the woman was...your wife."

"Probably."

I stared. "That's all you have to say? Probably?"

"What do you want me to say?"

His callous dismissal hurt more than I expected. There were a thousand things I wanted him to say. To erase this longing and let me know I wasn't crazy. That there was something real happening that wasn't my imagination.

I crossed my arms, trying to keep my lip from trembling. "Why am I having these dreams?"

"We've discussed this before. We're bonded," he said, his voice low and heavy. "My energy is spilling into your dreams—"

"No! What about Japan and Russia? I had those long before I met you."

"I can't speak for how your subconscious works, Lucy Dennings," he said bitterly, scornfully. "But if I had to hazard a guess, I'd say those dreams are manifestations of your romance novels. Romantic interludes with heroes and heroines."

I shook my head. "You're lying. Or there's something you're not telling me. You're making me feel stupid. Like…gaslighting. Like I'm holding the truth in my hands and you keep insisting there's nothing there."

"*Because there is nothing there*," Cas seethed with sudden fire that flared and then burned out. "There's nothing there," he said, shaking his head. "Nothing left."

My voice wavers. "I don't think that's true."

His head bowed for a moment, shoulders slumped. He got off the floor and reached for the Henley.

I jumped to my feet. "Where are you going?"

"Out. Where I always go."

"No!" I tore the shirt out of his hands, shocking him. Shocking *me*. "No," I said, softer. "I don't want you to go."

A silence fell, thick and heavy. The TV show played on distantly, but my eyes were on Cas, memorizing him—his eyelashes that were long and thick. A sharp jawline but lips that were full and soft. And the scars on his body where he'd fought for his city. For his woman. I'd miss every part of him when he was gone—all those parts I could see and touch and all those that I could not. The invisible parts of him that I felt like I knew so deeply.

The shirt fell from my hands and I moved closer.

"So many scars."

He nodded, watching me. "Earned in battle. But for one."

"This one," I said, touching the silver dollar over his heart.

"The killing stroke," he said, his voice gruff. "That night. The last night."

Without letting myself think, I bent and put a kiss there. His skin was warm, his pulse thundering against my lips, an echo of mine. Up, higher, I moved my mouth to the jagged slash near his throat, my tongue flickering, tasting the salt and spice of him. Up, up to his chin, his mouth…

"Lucy…"

His voice was a growl, and he gripped my hair, hauling my lips away from his. His eyes blazed in the dimness, and for a split second, we hovered in delicious, heart-pounding need, and then something in him relented. Gave in. He kissed me ferociously. Possessively. A little cry escaped me at the pure ecstasy that flooded my senses.

At last. At long last....

My lips fell open, letting him take my mouth. My warrior, invading and plundering. The biting, sucking pull of his kiss drawing me into everything that was him.

I wrapped my arms around his neck, kissing him deeper, my tongue sliding against his with a boldness I hadn't known I was capable of. His taste...I could've cried to taste him again. The scent of his skin in my nose, the feel of him beneath my hands was like coming home.

With a growl, he kicked my rickety old coffee table away, and wrapped an arm around my waist, taking me to the floor. Our bodies were like interlocking pieces finally falling into place. He fit perfectly into the V of my legs and my fingers sank into his hair as if I'd done it a hundred times. The weight of him on me...both new and familiar. Fresh lust swept through me, lifetimes' worth, now unleashed.

My legs wrapped around his waist, my hips strained against his, and I let out a groan as he ground into me again and again, the hard length of his erection seeking entry through our clothes. He braced himself with one arm while his other hand explored, roughly hiking my dress up to get at bare skin. His hand slid up my thigh, under my dress, to my breast. He palmed me, then pinched the aching nipple. All the while, his mouth plundered and plowed mine, the power in him stealing my breath—otherworldly and barely restrained.

Mindful of the burn on his back, I skimmed his bare torso, feeling the muscles move and slide under my touch. Like a starving woman, I feasted on him with my hands, utterly unafraid of the power every touch ignited in him. I wanted it. I'd go mad if I didn't have him inside me. My own power that had been sleeping for centuries was waking, along with the pure joy that my lonely search for him was finally over.

My Casziel.

My beloved...

"*Ki-áñg ngu,*" I whispered, the word slipping easily and perfectly from my lips as if I'd spoken it a hundred times.

Cas froze, then reared back, wrenching his mouth away. His eyes widened, boring into mine in the dimness.

"What did you say?"

"I…I don't know. It just slipped out. But I think—"

He tore himself off of me, and I was bereft at the sudden loss of his heaviness. He stood in the center of my small place, staring at me, his hand carving through his dark curls—a gesture so thoroughly human it made my heart ache.

I got to my feet. "Cas, it was us, wasn't it? In Larsa…"

"No. No, you can't… Gods, I'm a bastard. A careless, selfish bastard."

"You're not. Finally, I know who I am. Why I've been feeling like I've been missing something." I swallowed hard. "It was you. I've been missing you."

"No! No, Lucy," he said, pleading. Stricken. "We're nothing because I am lost. You must forget me." His mouth drew down in grim determination. "I'll make you forget."

He took a step toward me, and I backed away.

"What are you doing?"

"The right thing. Because there's no hope for me."

I put out my hand to ward him off, keeping the couch between us. "*No*," I said, my lip trembling. "You made me forget before, didn't you? I remember…the flies. And you holding my face…"

He took another step, and I raced away, nowhere to go in this tiny apartment. I put the kitchen island between us.

"Lucy." His voice was agonized. "You don't understand."

"I understand everything," I cried. "Years of loneliness. Years—no, *lifetimes* of it. Wanting you. Waiting for you. You were taken from me and I'm not going to give you up again. No more forgetting—"

I shrieked, as suddenly Casziel disappeared and reappeared in front of me in his demonic form. He gripped both my wrists in one large hand. His huge body pushed me against the sink, feathered wings filling the tiny space while his black-on-black eyes bored into mine. The cold, dreadful sucking pull came with that onyx gaze, but I pressed back, let his hips move in tighter.

His eyes flared, and my heart pounded, fear and want warring in me. Every nerve ending sang with terror, even as I gave myself up to him, offering. Wanting the touch, wanting *him*. A demon with my beloved trapped inside.

I was helpless against his immense power, but I mustered courage from the deep well in me I didn't know I had.

"Don't," I said, meeting his black gaze, unflinching. "Don't do it. Don't leave me. Not again."

He shook his head, anguish and lust writ in every conflicted line of his face.

"There is no hope for me, Lucy." His voice was rough and hard but frayed at the edges, betraying his pain. "You *will* let me go. I'll make you…"

"*No!*"

I struggled to free myself, but he was too strong. His thumb pressed the skin between my eyes. Pained regret suffused his voice as he said the word that stole him from me all over again.

"*Ñeštug u-lu…*"

THE ANGUISH IN Lucy's dark blue eyes fades. Her gaze sharpens, then widens with fear; I'm still in my demonic form, one hand gripping her wrists, holding her tight to me.

"Cas…?"

"*Usa nganu,*" I murmur. "*Usa nganu.* Sleep, my love."

Her eyes fall closed and she slumps in my arms. I gather her to me and press my nose into her neck, inhaling her sweet scent. I stay there for long moments, feeling the beat of her heart against me and the softness of her body.

You have to let her go.

I lay her down gently on her bed and smooth the locks of dark hair from her face. A different face in this lifetime but no less beautiful in my eyes. And recognizable. I would know my Li'ili in any form; she is the other half of me. I should stop inflicting myself on her, but I can't. She is my weakness. The sweetest vice. Lifetime after lifetime, I find her and protect her.

Because I was your rōnin, Lucy. I was your Shura.

I curse myself for showing her so much of us. I hadn't lied that it was my existence spilling into hers—our souls are entwined. But Hammurabi ruined me when he killed her, and I surrendered to damnation because I couldn't save her. Her eyes were pleading, and then they opened her throat…

Now I'm a fiend. She's an angel. She won't find love again until she's free of me.

But gods, kissing her…

I can still feel her mouth on mine after so many millennia—soft and sweet, warm and wet. I taste her on my tongue, feel her body pressed to mine, eager and willing, *wanting* to take me inside her. I fight the overwhelming urge to climb into her bed, to wake her and finish what we started…

But I can't. I shouldn't.

And Ashtaroth is waiting.

I transform into a raven and take flight through the open window. I'm not a meter from the apartment when the pain wells in me, anchoring me down. The rage and anguish. Touching and kissing Lucy have awakened it like a beast.

I want my wife.

I change course, tilting my wings to circle back to the empty lot behind Lucy's apartment. I take my demon form and let my huge wings bring me to the ground, where I hunch down and curl with rancor, the vile infection of my corruption. I let loose an inhuman scream of rage that no living ears can hear. My hands make fists in the dirt, grabbing handfuls. The grains fall from my grip, slipping away.

"Her life. I let it slip through my fingers…"

"Oh, jeez, don't be so dramatic."

I stand and whirl, my sword already drawn…then bite off a curse and return it to its scabbard between my wings.

"You again," I snarl.

"Me again. Can't get rid of me, can you?"

He's leaning against the wall, glowing with an aura of blue-white light. His hands are tucked in the pockets of his Hum-free Bo-gart and a hat is pulled low over his brow. He clenches a pipe in his teeth, and his shrewd but kind eyes regard me through the curling smoke.

"What do you think?" He tugs the brim of his hat. "I always felt the fedora completed the look, but Lucy refused to be seen in public with me if I wore it." He chuckles. "Kids."

"What do you want? I'm late for a meeting."

His jovial smile tightens. "To offer your pound of flesh? Your *meeting* can wait. I have something to say, and you *will* listen."

I start to protest but like the obedient son-in-law I'd been, I nod grudgingly.

"That's better. I just have one question: *What the hell are you doing?*"

I squat on my heels and fold my wings tight to me. "I'm doing the best I can. But I shouldn't have kissed her. I should've left—"

"You should've stayed. You should love her. Let her love *you*."

"I can't stay. There is no redemption for me. I lied to her. Over and over, I lied to her."

He purses his lips. "Yes, you've made quite a habit of that, haven't you?"

"A habit?" I snort. "I've done more than spin a lie or two, old man. You know this."

"I know what you've done," he agrees. "But I also know what's in your heart. Russia. Japan. All the lifetimes she can't remember. *You've* been her guardian angel. Imagine *that*."

"Tell your god, then, I'm waiting for my absolution." I rise and throw my arms and wings open to the heavens. "Well? Here I am. I'm ready."

Of course, nothing happens. The night sky is silent and impassive.

I drop my arms. "It appears what's *in my heart* is inadequate."

"She's not the only one plagued by demons," he mutters.

"Enough talk. Go away, old man. It's too late for me."

"You sure about that?" His endless patience radiates off of him as strong and vibrant as the blue-white aura. "Tomorrow, at the wedding. Take her in your arms. Dance with her. Hold her and tell her the truth. Stop erasing her damn memory. Stop erasing *you* from her mind, because no matter how hard you try, you can't purge yourself from her heart."

I cast my gaze to the ground. "I can. There is a way."

"Oblivion?" He shakes his head gravely. "That is not an answer, son. No answer at all."

"Then tell me what to do, priest. How does it end?"

"With your death, of course."

I bite off a curse and spread my wings to take flight.

"Casziel," he says, arresting me with the gentle authority imbued in him, the same that was there four thousand years ago. "What is death but a new beginning? And every new beginning comes from some other beginning's end." He cocks his head. "I think I heard that in a song once."

I fume with impatience, unwilling to let hope take root in the blackened soil of my soul. There will be no more beginnings for me. Only an end. A final end.

He moves off the wall toward me, his aura growing brighter, hotter. Searing my eyes. If I touch him, he'll burn me. Because I'm damned and he's pure. His gaze bores into me. Dark blue eyes like Lucy's. Like Li'ili's. The deep blue of lapis lazuli, the divine gemstone of Sumer.

Even then he was holy. And she…she was a gift from the gods.

"You were always so hard on yourself, my boy," he says. "And stubborn? My word! But good too. Honorable down to your bones. Hammurabi tried to torture it out of you. Ashtaroth tried to burn it out of you. The others…they've tried to convince you it's too late. There's no such thing. Remember that." He tips his fedora at me with a grin and says in an odd voice, "Here's looking at you, kid."

Then he's gone, and I'm left alone, the night thick and black but for the stars. Pinpricks of light. Like tiny spots of hope in a canopy of darkness that stretches to forever.

My heart swells with every emotion I'd been trying to block out. A barricade that had been falling to pieces, bit by bit over the last days with Lucy. Her father's words give me hope that I hadn't earned.

But maybe he was right and all I had to do was love her…

PART III

I GASPED AWAKE, anxiety boiling in my stomach, as if I'd overslept and missed something monumental.

The wedding...

I jerked to sitting and glanced at my alarm clock. Not quite seven a.m. I slumped against my pillows. I had hours yet. But a fuzzy, hungover feeling made my head heavy. I took in my empty apartment. Sunlight streamed in through the windows, over Edgar, my wilting houseplant. I was in my bed, but last night I'd been on the couch...

Hadn't I?

I struggled to remember what happened. Cas was injured. I'd tended that terrible wound on his back and then...

"Dammit," I said, tears of frustration pricking my eyes.

Something had happened. I'd touched something beautiful, and it slipped away. Again, like Japan. Leningrad. The woman in...where? A few days ago, I'd had another dream but that was slipping away too. My only certainty was that sense of loss, like a cry echoing down a long hallway, finding nothing, just emptiness.

I started the coffee and took a shower, hoping one or both would help wash the mud from my thoughts. Nothing helped, and then it was time to dress for Kimberly's wedding. I examined myself in the mirror. The empire-waisted dress flattered my figure, highlighting what I wanted to highlight and concealing what I wanted to conceal. I piled my hair on my head like the beautician had done the other day, leaving a few tendrils to curl prettily around my cheeks.

I was pretty. It felt like arrogance to think it but only for a moment because it wasn't just physical. Despite my tumultuous thoughts, there was color in my cheeks and my eyes were brighter. Maybe this last week had brought out a spark of life in me.

Or maybe it had always been there.

I sighed. But so what? Was I finally pretty enough that Guy would sweep me off my feet? We'd live happily ever after and that would somehow save the demon I'd been harboring in my apartment for the last eight days?

"I'm an idiot," I said before Deber or Keeb could.

The wedding was at noon. By eleven, there was still no sign of Casziel. The sense of longing and frustration swelled like a broken limb that refused to heal. I needed help. Guidance. *Something.*

I glanced around my empty place. "Daddy? Are you here?"

Cas had said he was close because he had unfinished business, whatever that meant. But there was no answer.

"I miss you so much and could really use some advice right about now."

Silence. And time was running out. I called an Uber just as my phone chimed a text. No name or number, only: #######

I'm outside.

Considering I hadn't given Cas my phone number—not to mention the fact that he didn't own a phone—I thought I handled his phantom text well. I didn't even flinch.

"I've dealt with worse," I muttered.

I grabbed my purse and a lavender wrap and headed out.

Cas was at the bottom of the stairs. He wore a charcoal gray suit, black shirt, no tie. He was even more devastating, somehow, for *not* wearing all black. He looked like a human man who'd had a rough night. A scruff of beard on his angular cheeks, his hair loose and flyaway in the wind. I couldn't stop staring at his mouth. His hands. I could practically feel his soft lips on mine—deceptively soft; they concealed biting teeth and a hard, sucking pull that drew me into him…

Those hands have touched me. I've kissed that mouth…

God, I was so damn tired of *almost* remembering.

Cas was staring at me, his gaze moving up and down. "You look…beautiful."

"So do you," I snapped. "Did you rob someone for that suit?"

His eyes flared at my confrontational tone. "It's paid for, Lucy Dennings."

"I hate it when you call me by my full name. Where did you get the money? Did you rob *me?*"

"The funds are from a coworker. I intend to pay you back for all you've spent on me—"

"Keep it. I don't want your money."

He cocked his head. "Something on your mind, *Lucy Dennings?*"

"Yes, as a matter of fact," I said, crossing my arms. They pushed up my boobs, amplifying the cleavage in the square-cut bodice. His eyes flared again, and I felt an answering heat in my belly. I cleared my throat. "What happened last night? Tell me the truth."

"We watched a favorite television show of yours and then you fell asleep."

"That's it?"

"You drank some wine. Perhaps that's why things are a bit hazy."

"I don't believe you."

"What you *believe* is of little consequence to me," he said, and I caught a flash of pain dart across his face before he looked away.

Tears sprang to my eyes for a thousand different reasons, none of which I could grasp. *Because* I couldn't grasp them. Because Casziel was lying, and it hurt him to do it. I could see the anguish in his eyes and hear it in his voice, hiding behind his cold tone. He was holding me at arm's length while I wanted to wrap those arms around me…

Silence fell, as thick as the air that was heavy with the promise of rain. A storm was coming, and I wondered what would be left of me when it came.

"Come on," I said as my phone notified me that the Uber was here. "Let's get this over with."

The car took us to Central Park, where we joined a few stragglers—other late-comers hurrying into the Boathouse. The restaurant had been opened up so that guests would be able to move inside and out, between the bar and the patio that would become the reception after the ceremony. Dining tables and chairs had been cleared away from the deck that overlooked The Lake, and white foldouts had been arranged in rows facing an arch of gardenias that laced the air with their delicate scent. The water rippled gently in the breeze that was almost a wind but not quite. Wedding planners kept nervously glancing at the sky.

Ushers guided Cas and me to our seats, one row behind Jana and her husband. She was holding an adorable baby boy in a mini suit of powder blue. His chubby cheek was smooshed against his mama's shoulder while he slept, oblivious.

I leaned in and whispered, "I'm never going to make it through the ceremony if I have to stare at that cuteness the whole time."

Jana turned. "Hey, you! You look beautiful. And don't keep it down for Wyatt's sake. This guy sleeps through anything. Oh, except *the night*." She nudged the man next to her. "Brian, this is Lucy, she of the ingenious shoe idea that you're going to make Jason attach his tennis star to."

Jana's husband craned around in his seat with a friendly smile. "I sure am, though I don't think Kai will need much convincing." He extended a hand to Casziel. "Brian Gill."

The demon dragged his gaze to Brian's hand, then away.

I coughed. "This is Cas Abisare. He's...not feeling well."

"Sorry to hear that," Brian said, shooting his wife a look. He turned around quickly; the back of his neck above his suit collar had broken out in goosebumps.

Jana raised her brows at me, but the ceremony was starting. Kimberly took her place under the arch, looking radiantly happy in a white suit with a cobalt blue tie. She glanced nervously at the officiant, which made me smile. Kimberly was never nervous.

The bridesmaids and groomsmen walked down the aisle and took their places—a mix of both on either side. Then Nylah, on the arm of her father, took her turn. She was stunning in a white dress with blue flowers embroidered up the hem, the same color as Kim's tie. She and Kimberly both had tears in their eyes as they clasped hands.

I was flooded with happiness to witness their happiness—a romance novel playing out right before my eyes. Without thinking, I took Casziel's hand, squeezing hard, needing an outlet so I wouldn't make a fool of myself by bursting into tears.

To my shock, his fingers curled around mine and held on. I didn't dare look at him, afraid he'd change his mind and push me away. But he sat with my hand engulfed in his as we watched the ceremony.

The officiant began her opening, but her voice sounded distant. Nylah and Kimberly grew blurry and indistinct. A new image superimposed itself over them—a different wedding, high on a stone roof. A temple. Two rivers glistened distantly on either side...

I gasped and blinked. The image vanished and I turned to Cas. He was looking at me with the same ache I'd felt for so long. His longing a reflection of mine and now so close to the surface...

Dimly, I was aware that Kimberly and Nylah were kissing, the guests cheering and clapping, more than a few wiping their eyes. Then the newlyweds came down the aisle hand in hand and everyone got to their feet.

I wet my lips. "Cas, I—"

"There you are! Snuck in last minute, eh?"

We both flinched, and Cas let go of my hand while releasing me from the intensity of his gaze. Abby had her hands on her slender hips, her eyes only for him, as if she were starving and he was her next meal. She was supermodel stunning in a tight-fitting purple dress that hugged her curves, her hair falling in soft waves down her back. Guy was with her, handsome as usual in a beige sport coat and slacks, as if he'd stepped out of a Ralph Lauren catalog. Everyone said hi and cooed over the baby.

"That was a beautiful ceremony," Guy said and nodded his head at Cas warily. "Hey, man."

I braced myself for Casziel's acid tongue or dagger glare. But he looked at Guy with a strange expression I couldn't identify. As if they'd run a race and Cas had lost.

He shook Guy's hand graciously. "Good to see you."

"Uh, yeah, you too," Guy said, surprised and then grinning. "Here's hoping I left Zu at home, right?"

"I doubt he'll bother you again."

My heart clenched with sudden pain.

He's saying goodbye.

"Can we *please* get a drink now?" Abby griped.

The Lake was growing gray under a heavy sky. Jana and Brian hung back to talk to some people, while the four of us headed for the bar. Abby slung her arm through mine and slowed me down while the men went ahead.

"I'm not feeling the loose cut of your dress, but the cleavage makes up for it. Great rack, babe. Guy is going to flip."

"Oh yeah?" I asked without energy. "He hasn't said a word to me."

"Of course not. Why would he when you're sticking so close to Cas, staring into his eyes like that? You looked like you were about to kiss."

My fingers went to my lips. A flicker of...something came and went. Abby was shaking her head.

"I think you're safe but don't do it again. I'll run interference for you, and just watch how fast Mr. Baker comes running."

"Interference...?"

We joined the men at the bar.

"You look pretty, Luce," Guy said, and Abby mouthed *I told you so*.

But his friendly grin showed no signs of the drunken devotion he'd had at karaoke. "Something to drink?"

"Water, please."

"Borrrring," Abby drawled. "Come on, Luce. Live a little."

"Nope, I'm good," I said, my voice uncharacteristically firm. I didn't believe for a second that I'd drunk too much wine the night before, but I wasn't taking any chances.

"Good idea," Guy said. "I'll stay sober with you. Abby?"

"Vodka and soda for me," Abby said. She wedged herself next to Cas, hip to hip, and gave him a seductive grin. "Vodka makes me reckless. How about you?"

He turned a flat gaze on her. "It gives me a headache."

I almost burst out laughing and took a swift sip of water. Abby pouted but recovered quickly. She linked her arm in his. "Maybe you just haven't found your liquor," she purred. "Or the right person to drink it with."

Cas glanced at Guy. "Maybe not," he said with a faint smile, and my laughter drained away.

We took our drinks and headed back out to rejoin Jana and Brian. Baby Wyatt was awake now, blinking sleepily at the scene around him. Kim and Nylah had come outside too, wading through well-wishers as they made their way to us.

"Beautiful ceremony," Guy said. "Congrats, you two."

The rest of us echoed his sentiment and then Casziel bowed low.

"*Šùde niñ-mí-ús-sá*. My best wishes for a joyous life together."

His voice was low and deep, his native language flowing off his tongue like rich wine. Everyone stared, charmed but confused, no doubt feeling that peculiar sense that something was...*off*.

Abby broke the silence with a screech. "Oh my *God*, what was that? Iraqi?"

THE SINNER | 171

"It was beautiful, whatever it was," Kimberly said, exchanging smiles with Nylah. "Thank you, Cas."

"I believe Arabic and Kurdish are spoken in Iraq." Guy frowned a little. "I'm no expert, but that didn't sound like either."

Because it wasn't. I'd learned in that anthropology class at NYU that Sumerian was a language isolate. It had no connection to other languages. No roots and no branches.

Like Casziel, I thought, watching him— elegant, dangerously dark and beautiful and utterly alone in the world. *A true outlander. A wanderer. A rōnin...*

I froze, my chest constricting, as if I'd been doused with a bucket of ice water. Then heat rushed through me like a fuse racing through every nerve ending. Last night flooded back. Everything flooded back. Demons in dark alleys, flies, and... My hand flew to my mouth; I could barely hold the water glass in the other. We'd kissed. Just like the warrior and his woman kissed in my dream. Because it wasn't a dream.

It was a memory.

He was the warrior and she was...

A gasp slipped out of me but was drowned in conversation, music, and the *clink* of glasses. Somewhere in my deepest self, I'd known the truth, but it had lived in the shadows. Now it stood naked and raw in the bright light of day. The ramifications flooded me, too many to take in all at once. The sense of something unresolved between us, now resolved, rushed through me, taking my breath away.

I gazed at Casziel, standing in that light of truth, new and yet achingly familiar. I knew every line of him. Every expression, every curl of his lips, every glance.

Because he's mine. He's always been mine.

My hand curled tightly around his arm as if he might be ripped away from me again. "I need to talk to you."

He glanced down at me and read it all in my face. Understanding dawned in his eyes. I waited for him to tell me I was crazy or drunk or maybe speak the word that would put my memories back to sleep.

Instead, he shook his head, a faint smile on his lips.

"Maybe he was right. I just have to love you." He touched my cheek. "Li'ili."

Tears sprang to my eyes as my heart felt like it was breaking and healing at the same time. The warmth and *fullness* were unlike anything

I'd ever known. The missing love of this lifetime and a hundred others now had a name too.

Abby nudged me out of my thoughts with a sharp elbow. She cleared her throat meaningfully, head inclined to Guy. "Oh my God, I love this song! Cas, come dance with me."

She took his arm, tugging him to the small dance floor at the edge of the deck. Jana and Brian had been muttering to each other and digging in the diaper bag slung on his shoulder.

"If I had two hands, I could find it," Jana said. "Do you mind, Luce?"

She plopped Wyatt in my arms as Cas let Abby drag him away. But he shook his head, letting me know everything was going to be okay.

He's *going to be okay*, I thought. *Someone is watching. They have to be...*

"Forget it. It's too late now," Jana grumbled at her husband, and they called a bickering cease-fire. She gave me a grateful smile and reached for the baby. "Thanks, Lucy—"

Wyatt burped, and a splat of white landed on the shoulder of my dress.

"Oh no, I'm so sorry. Shit, your dress..."

"It's perfectly fine," I said, laughing. I patted the baby's back. "You okay, sweet pea? You want your mama?"

Jana took the baby and flapped her free hand at Brian. "Get a wipey, quick."

Her husband began another search. "I don't see any wipies in here..."

"You have got to be kidding me..."

The bickering began anew, and I laughed. "Don't worry about it, Jana. I'll get a wet cloth from the bar."

Inside, every stool at the long gleaming counter was occupied but for one at the end. I sat at it and asked the bartender for a wet cloth. He obliged, and I cleaned baby spit-up off my shoulder. I stood to go when a terrible stench, barely concealed behind cologne, wafted over me. Something cold and clammy clamped down on my wrist. Fingers wearing antique rings with rubies and burnished gold gripped me tightly. I raised my petrified gaze.

The man was middle-aged, but his pale blue eyes told me he was older than counted time. His suit was pure white, complete with tails

THE SINNER | 173

and a top hat. Another lie—there was nothing pure about him. His hair
flowed down his back in soft brown waves, and elegant spectacles were
perched on his nose. He brought to mind Gary Oldman in *Bram
Stoker's Dracula*—a hideous monster wearing the suit of a dignified
man.

Ashtaroth.

As I stared, a snake slithered out from under his sleeve and over
my skin, cold and smooth. I tried to jerk my hand back, but the demon
held me fast.

"Lucy Dennings," he said, his voice as old as the grave. "The girl
my beautiful prince cannot relinquish. At last, we meet."

"Let me go."

He leaned in. "You first."

I stared, the sheer malevolence in his empty blue eyes making my
insides shiver. His breath had my eyes watering—a stink that was
everything rotting and spoiled in the world. He released me from his
gaze but held my wrist tight.

"Your hold on Casziel has been a nuisance for centuries. His
weakness for you disgusts me. A liability I can no longer tolerate. Your
infatuation for him is equally baffling. Do you know who he is, your
beloved?"

"Yes," I managed through a dry throat. "I know exactly who he is.
Finally..."

Ashtaroth snorted and the stench intensified. "I'm not speaking of
the man you knew in one pathetic lifetime thousands of years ago. The
lifetime you both cling to like barnacles on a sinking ship. I mean *who
he is*. What he has become under my care."

"Care?" I barked a laugh, short and fearful. "Doesn't matter. He's
still himself. You failed—"

"Failed? *Failed?*"

Ashtaroth's voice boomed so loud that I felt it in my chest. I
glanced around for help and let out a small cry. The entire room had
frozen, every person in it an unmoving tableau. As if this were a movie
and Ashtaroth had paused it mid-scene.

"I don't fail, girl," the demon sneered. "Others fail *me* and must be
punished. And replaced."

"No." I shook my head, marveling at my own defiance. "You failed
because love is stronger than whatever you tried to do to him."

"Love." He scoffed. "Love cannot save him. He's a liar. A sinner. A fiend of the highest order. Did you believe his little tale about his redemption?" He laughed, mirthless and cold. "Foolish girl. There is only one way out for him."

"H-how?" I asked through trembling lips.

"A trade. A soul for a soul." Ashtaroth traced a line down my cheek with one long fingernail. "So sweet, Lucy Dennings. So ripe and good. How deep does that goodness go, I wonder?"

I squeezed my eyes shut, dread squeezing my heart just as hard until I couldn't breathe.

"Casziel has sacrificed his eternal soul for want of you. I can't imagine you would allow him another millennium of agony. Not if you loved him, sweet Lucy. And you do love him…" He cocked his head with mock curiosity. "Don't you?"

The demon released my wrist and stood up, snakes slithering at his feet and across the bar. He touched my chin with the side of his finger, tilting my head up, studying me. I could feel his dead-eyed gaze everywhere on my skin. A wormy tongue touched the corner of his mouth.

"So ripe…" He exhaled, and the fetid stink of rot and decay gusted over me. "I'll be listening, Lucy Dennings."

Ashtaroth disappeared into the crowd and then the scene around me began again, everyone resuming their lives, unaware. I rubbed my wrist, feeling as if a hundred showers wouldn't begin to wash his touch off me.

Casziel rushed to me, his sharp gaze scanning the room. "Something's happened. I felt it… Why are you so pale?"

"Ashtaroth," I managed. My hands were shaking.

Cas's eyes widened and he bit off a curse. "Gods, no…"

He led me away to a less-crowded section of the deck. I took deep breaths of cool air. Overhead, the clouds were thickening.

Casziel gripped my shoulders, his eyes boring into mine. "Tell me everything. What did he want?"

"Me."

He froze. "What were his exact words?"

"A soul for a soul. Me for…you."

"What did you tell him?" he asked, his tone hardening slightly.

"I didn't have a chance to tell him anything. I—what's wrong?"

Right before my eyes, his demeanor shifted. The worry left his expression, fell away like a mask, leaving him cold and stony. Empty. "Cas?"

Slowly, a smirk curled his lips, and he heaved a sigh. "I suppose the game is up. A pity. You've been a delight, Lucy Dennings. The most entertainment we—Ashtaroth and I—have had in long years."

"What...what are you talking about?"

He grabbed a glass of red wine from a waiter's passing tray. "You know," he said conversationally, "humans are fools, but most have sense enough not to fall so thoroughly for our machinations."

"Machinations..."

"But you are astonishingly naïve. Gullible." His smile became a sneer as he sipped his wine. "Silly Lucy. What a treasure of amusement you have been."

The blood drained from my face, and I took a step back. "What is happening right now? What are you doing?"

"Please allow me to introduce myself," he said in a sing-song voice and gave me a mocking bow. He straightened, and his wicked smile fell away, leaving a countenance of pure malice. "I am the Nightbringer. King of the South. Slayer of men and archduke of hell."

"No..."

"*Yes.*" The demon's eyes flashed black, and a cold wave of dread washed over me. "I am as you found me, Lucy Dennings." He held up his wine, swirling the red liquid in the glass. It thickened until it became like blood. "A creature of the night. Of the damned. Commander of legions..."

The glass was suddenly as big as an ocean, the wine swirling like a vortex, taking me down, down. Red all around me—the sky, the clouds, the ground was muddy with blood. A battlefield. And demons—hairless and slavering like rabid dogs—raced across the wasteland, thousands upon thousands of them. More filled the sky, their wings black, their screams drilling into the center of me.

At the rear of the legion, Casziel rode in a chariot drawn by horses, the flesh hanging off their bones, flapping and showing rotted tendons and yellow eyes. His black eyes were as merciless as his whip, his wings outstretched like an endless night.

I saw all this, while at the same time, an image drifted over the first. Superimposed. A battlefield under a blue sky. Human men raced along a field, swords drawn, their faces curled in rage. Humans and demons blurred and merged, the sky was blue and then bloody again.

And I understood what I was seeing. Casziel led demons on the Other Side, while the humans were on This Side, and the Veil was the mirror that reflected them both. I watched in horror as Casziel drove his legions of demons across the landscape, whipping them into a fury. And on the other side of the Veil, the fury seeped into the human men, and they fought and died...

I gasped and staggered a step back, blinking out of the vision. "Stop. Why are you doing this? This isn't you—"

"No?" Cas cocked his head in mock curiosity. "Who am I? One of the heroes of your stories, willing to do anything for his lady love?" His voice turned sinister, his eyes flashing black again. "I told you before, Lucy Dennings, I am not, nor will I ever be an angel."

I shook my head. "No..."

His gaze went to something over my shoulder. Abby stood at the railing, overlooking The Lake. She twiddled her fingers at Casziel suggestively, and he smiled back, promise in his eyes.

"Did you ever wonder where I spend my nights?" Cas asked. "Whose arms I fall into? Whose legs part for me? Whose warm cunt I sink my cock into—"

"Stop it," I cried. "You're lying."

"Am I?" he inquired, and every single thing I thought I knew about us was disintegrating in the cruelty in his eyes.

No! I know what I saw. Who I am...

"I know what you're doing," I said. "You're trying to push me away. To protect me from Ash...from him. It won't work." I sucked in a breath. "I-I'm your wife."

Casziel stared and then, to my horror, he threw back his head and laughed. "My *wife? You?*" His laughter died and he moved in close, all seething malice and barely constrained disgust. "My wife was fierce and brave. She didn't hole up in a small dark room, living her life between the pages of books. She was remarkable in every way." He moved even closer, brushing his nose against my cheek to whisper hotly in my ear, "The only remarkable thing about you, *Lucy born of light*, is how easily you are fooled."

It felt as if the floor had fallen out from beneath my feet to the center of the earth. My hand went to my heart that was breaking.

"No. Don't...please."

His face was impassive. Cold. He sipped his wine with a final shrug that dismissed me completely. "It's what we do."

"Uh, hey. Am I interrupting something?"

Guy Baker was there, raking a hand through his hair.

"Not a thing." Casziel's eyes were like stones on me. "You're here for your dance."

"Well, yeah. But if this is a bad time, I can come back..."

"There is no other time." The demon took my hand and placed it in Guy's. "Goodbye, Lucy."

For a split second, Casziel's hard façade cracked, and the pain seeped out. His eyes flickered to mine, agonized...

...or maybe it was just my imagination because he walked away and didn't look back.

I watched him go, stunned and hollow, while Guy cleared his throat. "Are you okay?"

"Fine."

"Would you like to sit down?"

"No."

"Maybe some water...?"

Stop talking.

"You're asking me to dance. Let's dance."

Guy pulled me onto the dance floor. I moved like a zombie, as if I'd felt every emotion I could possibly feel in one week and was now drained. Wrung out. There was nothing left.

"You look really beautiful, Luce," Guy said, holding me close. His breath was strong and pungent with alcohol and a mint working overtime to cover it up. His blue eyes were glassy and vacant as they drank me in. I guessed he'd decided not to stay sober after all. "Kind of funny, isn't it?"

"What is?"

"That we've worked together for two years and I'm just now really seeing you."

"What do you see?"

"Someone who's kind, and smart, and...beautiful. You're very beautiful, Lucy."

"What else?" I asked, tears stinging my eyes.

Tell me everything, Guy. Tell me everything I've been waiting two years to hear. Right now. When it's too late.

"Well, it kind of sucks that here we are, finding each other after so long just as I'm leaving for Sri Lanka."

Finding each other after so long.

I thought I'd be sick.

"I'm still putting my team together," he continued. "But it looks like I'm outta here at the end of next week."

"I know. I helped work out the logistics."

"Right, right," he said with a short laugh. "But it's not easy to find people who would drop everything and fly halfway around the world to scoop plastic off a beach." He cocked his head as a thought occurred to him. "You've never been on one of my expeditions, have you?"

"No, never."

This is it. My fantasy coming to life. Right now.

"Well, there's a first time for everything." He chuckled. "What do you say, Luce?"

"You're asking me to go with you."

"It's short notice, I know but...yeah. I want you to come with me. I don't know what happened this week, but it suddenly feels like the two years you've worked at Ocean Alliance have flown past me and I feel every second of it. All that lost time." He held me closer. "I don't want to waste one more minute."

Tears filled my eyes, and I hid them by pressing my cheek against his broad chest. Guy's scent filled my nose--nothing like Casziel. No fire and spice. He felt different from Cas too. *I* felt different in his arms. Stiff and uncomfortable instead of perfect. Across the deck, Abby was alone but had her phone out, filming everything.

"I'll go with you to Sri Lanka," I said.

"You will?"

I felt him want to pull me back, to look in my eyes, but I held tight.

"Sure. Why not?" I pressed against him, not sure if I would laugh or cry.

Cry. Definitely cry.

"Great! Let's talk about it at the office on Monday. Work out the details." He sighed, content, and held me tighter. "It's going to be perfect."

"Perfect," I nodded, my tears staining the front of his jacket. "Happily ever after."

"What was that?"

"Nothing. Nothing at all."

THE HEAVY CLOUDS that had been building on Saturday broke into a steady rain that didn't let up all day Sunday. The weather app said a huge storm was coming and would last until Tuesday night. Casziel's last day on This Side.

My thoughts tried to turn to him, but I kept steering them away and spent the dreary afternoon prepping for my presentation. Going through the motions like a robot. Rain battered the window—now closed.

Because it had all been a lie.

My phone rang with Cole Matheson's number. I ignored it. My BFF tried again and then a text popped up with a thumbnail of his latest sketch—me, looking radiantly happy and surprised about it. Shocked I could actually feel that way.

This is your heart on Cas. Any questions?

My heart clenched with actual physical pain.

Another text followed. **OK that was cheesy, even for me, but you're beautiful, Lucy. I hope the wedding was everything it was supposed to be. Call when you get a chance.**

A great sob welled up in me, but I pushed it down. If I started crying now…

I tossed my phone aside and noticed that Edgar, my houseplant, was dead. All the water he needed was pouring down the panes of glass outside the window.

"I'm sorry, Edgar," I murmured, touching his dried leaves. "I'm so sorry. I got so wrapped up in…"

My words trailed. I didn't know how to describe the last nine days. A nightmare? A fever dream? Or maybe the entire thing was a hallucination. Maybe I had a brain aneurism. Maybe I was lying in a hospital bed in a coma on the brink of death.

Dad's voice sounded gently in my head. *You're alive, kiddo. You're here. You're strong and you're not done yet.*

I wished I believed him. I wished I believed it was my dad. That he was still with me, just in the next room. But maybe that had been a lie too.

The next morning, I dressed for work and packed my presentation materials in an old briefcase Dad had given me when I went to college. "To hold all my big ideas." It'd sat empty in the closet for years.

Now, I put in my notebooks and my laptop loaded up with a very plain Google Slides presentation of my shoe idea. I didn't know why I was still going through with it. I guessed I had a shred of dignity left because the idea of lying around all day, feeling sorry for myself, was nauseating. Then again, everything in my tiny, empty, simple little apartment made me sick. The rows of romance novels were pages and pages of lies. There were no happy endings in real life. Real life was brutal and full of cruel jokes.

Like the fact Guy had finally noticed me and wanted to take me with him to Sri Lanka.

I searched my entire soul and found no feelings for him. I'd been waiting for real, true love my entire life. Probably longer. And now I had a chance, and I couldn't bring myself to care.

"Fake it 'til you make it," I muttered on the subway.

If Guy wanted to take me out of my silly little life, I'd let him. There was nothing for me here. And while I knew I'd never feel anything real for him, he was better than more loneliness. More solitude.

You don't have nothing, pumpkin, Dad insisted. *You have you.*

And what was I? I had no clue. But I could give this presentation and clean plastic off a beach and maybe do some good in the world.

At Ocean Alliance, I headed straight for Guy's office.

"Hey, Luce, what's up?" he asked. Maybe it was my imagination, but his smile felt forced, and he had a hard time looking at me.

"Um, well we have a lot of details to work out for Sri Lanka. Don't we?"

"Sri Lanka?"

"Yeah. What we talked about on Saturday. At the wedding."

He cocked his head, his face scrunched up. "What did we talk about?"

I tensed all over. "You don't remember."

"Oh shit. Did I get drunk and say something inappropriate?" He frowned. "Funny, I don't remember drinking at all. Sorry, Luce, what did I say?"

Either he was the greatest actor in the world, or his confusion was genuine. My stomach twisted and I recalled the strange smell and the breath mints, the weird emptiness in his eyes...

"Oh my God..."

"Shit, Luce, I'm really sorry. I don't know what happened but if I gave you the wrong idea—"

"You didn't," I said quickly. "We were talking about logistics. That's all."

"Really?"

I managed a smile while inwardly, I felt like puking. "Yep, really. You asked me if I'd help calculate supply arrival times and I said yes."

"Oh." Guy blew out a laugh. "Well...great! That's such a relief. I'd hate to think I might've been a dick."

No, you were just possessed.

The ramifications slid deeper. There was no Sri Lanka. No happily ever after for me, pretend or otherwise.

"But you still look a little shell-shocked." Guy's smile softened into something like pity. "Does this have something to do with Abby's video?"

"What video?"

"Listen, Luce. I think it's sweet, and I'm flattered. But I have a strict no-dating-coworkers policy. Keeps me out of trouble—"

"What video?"

"It's nothing. She's been playing matchmaker between us, I think. Silly, really."

"Silly." A heavy ball of something ugly settled in my stomach. "I don't understand. Is it your song from karaoke night?"

Guy's confused expression returned, and my stomach clenched all over again.

He has no idea what I'm talking about.

"I don't remember singing that night." He chuckled. "Good thing too. No one wants to hear *that*." He cleared his throat and shuffled through a small mountain of papers on his desk, missing my incredulous stare. "Sorry, Luce, I have a million things to do before my trip. Was there anything else you needed?"

"Not a thing."

"Good luck on your presentation," he called as I backed away. "Can't wait to hear it."

I exited his office to see clusters of my coworkers bent over phones or gathered around laptops, snickering and murmuring. They stopped when they saw me, identical guilty expressions on their faces.

I stormed up to where Dale was huddled with Hannah from fundraising, my hand out. "Give it to me."

"Oh, uh, Luce, it's nothing," Dale said, exchanging glances with Hannah.

"You don't need to see it." Jana strode up, shooting daggers at the others. "Come on, Luce. Let's talk about your presentation. I have good news—"

My outstretched hand didn't waver. "Show me."

Dale looked sheepishly at Jana, then handed over his phone. Abby had posted a video to TikTok—a montage of me over the last few months gawking at Guy in the office, staring like a puppy dog when he walked by, gazing up at him while he spoke in a meeting. A documentary of my pathetic crush, set to a song called "Notice Me."

My skin felt hot and too tight.

"Luce." Jana's voice sounded far away. "Forget it. The presentation…"

The presentation. Right. I had to stand up in front of all these people and talk about *shoes.*

No way.

I rushed to my desk to gather my things. Permanently. I'd get another job. Somewhere no one knew me. I'd sit in the corner and mind my own business and not talk to anyone. Because this last week had made it abundantly clear what happens when you put yourself out there. Humiliation and pain. My "demons" were right all along. Silly Lucy had ventured out of her silly little life and had been slapped for it. Hard.

In minutes, I'd thrown all my belongings into my bag—there wasn't much. Jana hadn't followed me. She was probably in the conference room waiting for me along with everyone else. She could run the shoe project without me.

I shouldered my bag to go when my eye caught the single red rose Casziel had given me in its water bottle. It was brown and wilted, having dropped all its petals. But for one. One petal remained, and it was as red and vibrant as it had been a week ago.

There's still time.

Time for what? I'd lost everything. I thought I'd touched on something real with Cas, some deep truth about us—about *me*—and it'd all been a lie. His redemption and our big plan to make Guy fall for me? More lies. Every deepest wish of my heart had been exposed and burned to ash.

Tears flooded my eyes, and I sank into my chair, staring at the rose.

Hey pumpkin. Dad's voice was as clear in my mind as if he were sitting right next to me. I even thought I caught a whiff of pipe smoke. *Don't give up. It's not too late.*

"Yes, it is, Daddy," I whispered, the rose blurring in my vision. "I can't…"

Yes, you can. You've never given up, not in thousands of years. You're strong. Fierce. You've just forgotten for a little while.

The truth of it seeped into the broken cracks of me. I'd done more and seen more and *felt* more in one week than I had in my entire life.

I danced with the devil in the pale moonlight.

I stood straighter, shoulders squared. My personal life might've been reduced to a barren wasteland, but I was still standing. There was no one beside me, holding my hand. No all-consuming love, but I still had me. In that moment, it wasn't much, but I still had work to do. The oceans weren't going to magically rid themselves of the nearly ten million metric tons of plastic dumped into them every year.

I tossed my bag on the chair and grabbed my briefcase. The jumble of nerves in my stomach didn't vanish—they tightened until I was nauseated at the idea of standing in front of the group, my humiliation still fresh in their minds.

But I felt Dad's proud smile as I made my way to the conference room, clutching that briefcase handle in my sweaty hands. His voice in my mind—and heart—was so much louder than the demons that clamored I was making a huge mistake.

Thatta girl, pumpkin. I knew you could do it.

The water hit my face, and I held my cupped hands to my cheeks, the bracing coldness the best thing I'd ever felt. I looked up from the bathroom sink, and the woman staring back at me in the mirror wore a smile. They'd loved it. Kimberly had insisted on being patched in from Cancún and began giving orders to put my plan in motion. Jana, who'd been blinking back proud tears, announced that Kai Solomon had agreed to sponsor the shoe when it was ready. Guy was impressed, but I could tell he was already halfway out the door without me.

But maybe that's how it was supposed to be. No Guy or Casziel. There were worse tragedies than not having a man, including the one in Sri Lanka.

That's right, Deber sneered. *Silly Lucy, back to her silly life. Alone. And that's how you'll stay. Because no one wants you. No one.*

I ignored the insinuations that were so tired and old, like faded wallpaper, then jumped as a bathroom stall opened. I half-expected the demons to shuffle out but it was Abby. She had toilet paper pressed to her eyes and stopped when she saw me.

"Oh, hey, Luce."

"Hi," I said flatly as she joined me at the sinks.

Her eyes were smudged with mascara and brimming with tears. "Lucy, I—"

"I don't want to hear it."

Don't be bitter, pumpkin, Dad said. *It's not your style.*

I snorted. "Maybe it should be."

"Huh?" Abby shook her head. "Listen, I need to tell you something. Lucy…I'm a bad person."

I crossed my arms. "Okay."

"I know, shocker, right? I don't know why I do half the things I do. Do you know why I was so eager to help you with Guy? Because I don't want him. He's wholesome and good and we don't vibe *at all.*

But me and Cas? He's got a darkness that I *totally* vibe with. Getting you with Guy was literally just so I could have Cas to myself. But he's not interested in me and—*wow*—did he make that crystal clear at the wedding. I felt so *invisible*. Humiliated. So I humiliated *you* with that stupid video. As if all my shit is your fault, and I'm sorry, Lucy. I really am."

I uncrossed my arms. "So, you and Cas…?"

She snorted. "What *me and Cas*? He never gave me the time of day, despite my best efforts."

"You never slept with him."

Abby gave me an incredulous look in the mirror. "I *wish*. He wouldn't even kiss me. I mean…how humiliating is it when even an escort won't touch you? That's his *job*."

I almost laughed. Abby's insistence that Casziel had only been with me because I paid him was still insulting, but the fact he never touched her was like a burst of hope that tried to crack the brittle shell around me.

Abby started to cry again. "I don't know what's wrong with me. I get these urges to do terrible things like make videos, and I give in. Like it's a thrill to see the number of likes and all the nasty comments, and then I just feel like crap afterward. Why do I do stuff like that?"

Because you have a Deber and Keeb too.

"We all do," I said. "We all have little voices in our heads that tell us bad stuff is a good idea. I used to think there was something wrong with me. Like my own brain had become a bully and turned against me. But those voices are not the real you and they have no actual control. You have the power to ignore them until they just become noise." I smiled. "I'm not saying it's easy but maybe if we ignore them long enough, they'll disappear altogether."

"That would be really nice," Abby said and sniffed. "God, you are being so nice to *me* when I don't deserve it. Because you're a good person." She huffed a shaky breath. "I'm quitting Ocean Alliance."

"You don't have to do that."

"Yeah, I do. I only signed on because my parents have more money than God and threatened to cut me off if I didn't *contribute to the world in some meaningful way*. Working here fit the bill but it's not my style and—clearly—I have too much time on my hands."

"What are you going to do?"

She wiped mascara from under her eyes. "I'm going to do something *I* want to do. I'll get my own place and pay my own rent. Get a roommate and struggle for a little while. But who cares? Lucy, I don't expect you to forgive me, and you *definitely* don't need to take advice from me but don't let my stupid video mess things up for you and Guy. God, I hope it didn't. Because you deserve to be happy."

I managed a tight smile. "It didn't mess anything up, I promise."

She threw her arms around me in a short hug. "Thanks, Luce. And I think your shoe idea is really good. It's going to make a real impact."

I waited a few more minutes after she was gone, then headed out. Coworkers congratulated me, and Jana—on the phone at her desk—waved at me like she wanted to talk but I couldn't stay in the office another second. Tomorrow, I'd return and get back to work, but I was going to take the rest of the afternoon off.

Outside, I hunched against the rain—the storm had arrived in full force. In all my turmoil over Casziel, I'd forgotten a raincoat, and my dress and cardigan were soaked instantly. I should've called an Uber, but my thoughts were scattered, my chest feeling hollow and carved out. They say what does not kill you makes you stronger, but I just felt numb.

Go back to your little life...

Deber was relentless, but even out there on the deserted streets, soaked to the bone, I knew there was no going back to my *little life*. I wasn't the same person I was ten days ago. I didn't know who I was. Lost in a kind of purgatory with no idea what lay ahead. The pride of giving my presentation had already drained out and all I wanted was to get to my place, take a hot shower, and dive into a romance novel. Because I enjoyed reading them.

There didn't need to be any other reason.

My head full of these thoughts, I stepped off the curb.

Too late, I saw the splash of headlights against the rain-washed street.

Too late, I heard the horn and the screech of tires that weren't going to catch in time on the slick pavement.

I exhaled my last breath. "Casziel..."

A heavy weight crashed into me, tackling me from the side, and I was flying. I felt the wind of the truck at my ankles while staring into black eyes. Strong arms—and wings—were wrapped around me. Cas twisted midair and hit the ground on his back, cradling me and taking the brunt of the hit. He rolled so my back was on the asphalt, and his immense body was shielding me from the rain. From the world.

I stared into his face—bloodless white with black pits for eyes. The cold dread emanating from them was defeated by the love in my heart that swelled until I thought it would burst.

Because he's mine and I'm his. Always.

I traced the line of his jaw, the rainwater running in rivulets down the sharp contours of his cheekbones, off his full lips.

"Li'ili," he said, his voice gruff.

I cupped his face in both hands. I was staring too long; his eyes were drawing me down, but I couldn't look away. Not yet.

"Say it," I whispered just as the dark consumed me.

"My wife…"

21

THE APARTMENT WAS dark, and the storm raged outside the windows. I sat up in my bed, shivering in damp clothes. Casziel was at the window, hard and still. A statue in the dark, standing guard. His vigilance was written in every tense line of his body. Lightning flashed, illuminating his sleek, black wings.

"Casziel," I said softly.

His shoulders hunched, wings lifting slightly. "Ashtaroth is getting bold. I won't let him hurt you, Lucy." He scoffed. "More than he has."

"He possessed Guy," I said, slipping off the bed. "To ask me to go to Sri Lanka. Why would he do that?"

Casziel's jaw tightened. "To drive you blindly into a street in a rainstorm, hopeless and alone. To lure you with all the same fiendish promises he made me." He turned his black gaze to me. "He was waiting for you on the Other Side, Lucy, ready to catch you as you fell."

"You did your part to make me feel hopeless," I said, moving closer. "What you said at the wedding..."

He flinched as if I'd whipped him, his voice ragged. "Gods, forgive me, Lucy. It broke my soul to wound you. Ashtaroth wants you any way he can have you. I was terrified you'd make an unspeakable bargain. For *me*."

A small cry choked out of me as Casziel whirled with sudden fury, his wings flaring like night and his eyes emanating cold. He gripped my shoulders, fingers digging in. "You must not listen to him, Lucy. There is nothing you can do. No bargain you can make. You can't save me. Do you understand? *You cannot save me.*"

The sucking pull of his black gaze was making me weak. My lips parted but no sound came out but a little whimper. He let me go with a curse and then turned away, crossing his arms tight as if to keep from touching me.

"So that's it?" I asked, hugging my elbows. "In a few hours it's just…over?"

Tears of frustration threatened. Worse than frustration. I was losing him. The minutes were ticking away, his departure yawning like a black chasm, and I was falling in.

"What about all that stuff with Guy?" I demanded. "More lies? If it can't save you, what was it all for?"

"For *you*, Lucy. Your happiness. That was no lie. I want your happiness more than I want my next breath. But your kindness was an obstacle. The only way to help you was to let you think you were helping me."

"So you tried to pawn me off on another man? I don't want to love someone else. I *can't.*"

"But you have to."

"Why? Because you're going back to Ashtaroth forever?"

He didn't answer, his jaw tight.

"You should have told me the truth. Let me decide for myself."

"Maybe so," he admitted. "It was a farce from the beginning. I've loved you too long and too hard to give you up. But I tried. For your sake and mine, I tried."

Tears brimmed again. How long had I waited to hear a man tell me that I was loved?

Not any man. This man. I've been waiting for him, my husband.

"I'm not giving you up," I said fiercely. "Now that I finally have you back—"

He shook his head. "There is no hope for me, Lucy. You have to let me go. I should make you forget. Erase all this horror—"

"Don't you dare!" I cried. "I'm done forgetting. You've given me no say in my own life—"

"To protect you," he retorted. "To leave you with something more than dreams. Something real."

"With *Guy*? What's real is what I feel for you, Casziel. I love—"

"Don't say it. You can't love me. Not like this. Not when even looking into my eyes is dangerous—"

"*You are not my bodyguard!*" I cried, and thunder boomed outside the window. I turned Cas to face me, muscled arms crossed tight, his hands in fists. "Do you know what happened this afternoon on that street? I wasn't calling for help. I didn't *summon* you. I had seconds to live—less than that—and I said your name because my entire being was filled only with you." I tugged at his arms, forcing my stubborn man to let me in. He kept his gaze over my head as I pressed myself against the hard wall of his chest. "What I feel for you is real, Casziel, and the only thing that scares me is losing you again."

"Lucy…"

"I don't need rescuing. I need you."

I laid my hand on his arm; it looked so small on the bulge of his bicep. He towered over me, tall and imposing. A beast of darkness, smelling of old leather, heated metal, blood and ash. I closed my eyes and rested my cheek against his arm. His pale skin was hot and cold, burning with the fires of hell and the bloodlessness of death. His feathered wing brushed my cheek.

My touch softened him; his big strong body shuddered at my words, and he heaved a sigh. When he let it out, his arms—and wings—went around me, and we held each other for the first time in so many long years. Tears seeped beneath closed lids as I settled into his embrace, a perfect fit, safe and secure because this is where I belonged.

"I'm sorry, beloved," he said, his mouth against my hair. "For bringing darkness to you. For the horrible things I said. For making you feel less than you are, when you are everything to me, Li'ili. My wife. My life…"

"I'm not sorry for one minute of it," I said. "I fell in love with you twice—four thousand years ago and again, ten days ago. But that's not true, either. I've never fallen out of love with you."

"Nor have I."

"That has to count. It has to."

His chest rose and fell against my cheek in a heavy sigh. "I've loved you for a hundred lifetimes, Lucy. If it could've saved me, it would've done so by now."

"I don't believe that. Love is stronger than anything. I feel it in you. How can there be nothing left if we're here right now?"

"I don't know," he whispered. "I'm afraid to hope..."

"I'm not." I pressed a kiss to his heart. His throat. His chin, seeking his lips. "Just love me, Casziel..."

His body tensed as my mouth found his in a trembling, feather light touch. He made a growling sound—barely restrained need that snapped all at once. Cas crashed his mouth to mine, his tongue invading, teeth biting my lips, then sucking them, leaving no part of my mouth unexplored. The taste of him was metallic and electric, lighting me up from inside.

I kept my eyes shut as the cold fire of his demonic form seeped into me. I wasn't afraid; I surrendered to it. Sensations I hadn't known existed were unspooling in me—the hottest desire tinged with a chill of fear. Every part of me on fire while shivers danced down my skin. This kiss...otherworldly and ethereal. A fever dream I didn't want to wake from.

But Casziel wrenched his mouth from mine, leaving me breathless and bereft.

"We can't," he groaned. "Ashtaroth is strongest at night. I can't face him in my human form. Not yet."

"Not yet...?"

"When the dawn comes, I'll take you to bed." Casziel's tone became thick and heated. "I've waited centuries to feel you again. I can wait a few more hours."

"No." I took his face in my hands, staring directly into the dead black of his gaze. "We only have a few hours *left*. I want them all. I don't want to wait."

"My brave woman," he said and kissed my eyes closed. "There is a hell in me, Lucy. Look into my eyes long enough and you will see your death."

"I want to see it. Our last night."

"Lucy, no—"

"You're doing it again." I pressed myself into him, tilting my chin, blindly seeking his mouth. "Trying to protect me. From that night. From your touch. I want you to touch me."

"Gods, woman. You don't know what you're asking," he said gruffly into the small, heated space between us. "It wouldn't be what it is with a human. I am distinctly *in*human."

THE SINNER | 193

"Would you hurt me?"

"Never. But gods, you're an angel, to take me in this body."

"I want to," I said, even as my heart hammered against my ribs. "You are this way because you loved me. Besides..." I smiled, my own boldness shocking and thrilling me as I slipped my hand down to the immense erection straining against his pants. "Maybe I'm not as pure as you think."

His eyes flared and he captured my mouth in a searing kiss. The sensations—hot and cold, fire and ice—rushed back in. His kiss devoured me, raw and feral. Overwhelming.

And this is just kissing.

A twinge of apprehension shuddered through me but was burned up in the need that electrified my every molecule, calling out for his skin on mine, his mouth and hands on my body, him inside me...

Just the thought made me dizzy.

He carried me to the bed, kissing me hard and working fast to strip me out of my clothes. The cardigan fell to the floor and then he pulled my dress over my head, leaving my curves on full display, my breasts spilling from my bra. I knew a moment of uncertainty, self-conscious that there was more of my body than he wanted.

But Casziel licked his lips, his hungry gaze grazing over me as if he didn't know where to feast first.

"Gods have mercy," he breathed. "I've dreamed of having you. Every night for years. Every lifetime, wanting to kiss and touch and fuck you until I was nearly mad."

And just like that, my self-consciousness burned up like a dried leaf.

I removed the last of my clothes and lay on the bed, stretched out and waiting. "Come here," I said, my voice trembling at the edges.

"Close your eyes, Lucy, and keep them closed. No matter what happens."

I nodded and did as he asked. The demonic despair lessened but I'd never felt more vulnerable in the dark, with a storm raging outside and the rustle of wings over me. The bed dipped with Casziel's weight as he moved into the circle of my arms, heavy and hard on top of me. My pulse thundered while want and nervousness twined together and danced along my skin.

I felt him place a kiss to the hollow of my throat, his hair tickling my chin.

"Lucy, your heart…"

"Is yours," I said, pulling him closer. "I want this. I want you."

"You're certain?"

"I've never been more certain of anything in my life."

The weight of his body on mine was solid and real, everything I'd been yearning for. It slowed my crashing pulse and blanketed me with the solidity of him. This was real. *He* was real and not a dream. This wasn't someone else's story but ours. His and mine.

"If you need to stop, we stop," Casziel said, his lips brushing, tongue flickering, sending icy hot licks down my throat and chest, hardening my nipples. "You tell me if it's too much."

It was already too much and not enough. A rush of adrenaline-laced lust was flooding me, every particle of my being wanting him. Needing to feel him at long last. I couldn't remember all of us, but I felt every minute of the long centuries when I didn't have him. My body deprived of him.

"Hurry," I whimpered. Begged. "I want…"

"You want me to fuck you," Casziel growled, breath hot against my skin. His tone was no longer refined but rough and raw. He put his mouth to one heavy, aching breast and sucked. "You want me to take this luscious body, don't you, Lucy? You want me to sink my cock into your tight flesh and fuck you hard. And I will because you're *mine*."

I moaned, his possessive words filling me with a heat I'd never known. Lust and love. Surrender and desire. I was in his hands completely; he could do with me what he wanted because what he wanted, I wanted too.

Him, inside me…

I arched myself wantonly against his hips. He was naked now—all hard muscle, smooth skin, and his heavy erection pressing between my thighs. He was impossibly huge, the head of his cock sliding against my slick entrance. The urge to open my eyes was both tantalizing and frightening.

"Eyes closed," he gritted out, moving back up to my mouth. "My Li'ili. My beloved…"

He kissed me with his unearthly cold fire that electrified my nerve endings until I was panting, then moved upright to kneel on the bed, taking me with him. My legs went around his waist, and he slid into me with one swift thrust.

I sucked in a breath and then choked as it caught in my throat. Every part of me was suddenly too small. Too tight. Too filled with *him*. His mouth was everywhere. He had a dozen hands, caressing, stroking, pinching. And his cock... I was filled completely in every way a man can fill a woman, all at once. My hands scrabbled at his back, powerful muscles moving underneath smooth skin and the brush of his wings...

"Oh my God," I whimpered. "Oh my God..."

"Li'ili," he said, tightly. "Gods above, you are everything. Everything..."

I had no breath to speak. I could only clutch him around the neck, dizzy with the sensation of him inside me at long last. In the dark of pure sensation, I was reduced to mindless desire, my thoughts breaking apart, every part of me filled with him.

"H-how are you doing this to me?"

But I already knew.

Possession.

Casziel possessed me in every sense of the word. Every touch went beyond physical—hands and mouths everywhere, all of him touching all of me, inside and out. He was in my body, my heart, my soul...

"Tell me if it's too much," he said against my lips.

It was too much. I could hardly contain him. I was stretched to breaking, filled with him so completely and overwhelmed with sensation...and I wouldn't give him up for anything.

Beneath the fullness, the intensity, there was pleasure. A molten pool of it, miles deep. Casziel lit my skin wherever we touched, his mouth taking mine with possessive need, our bodies moving in perfect tandem. I rode his cock with abandon, feeling wild and reckless, even locked in his embrace. His arms held me tight, leaving no space, while mine were wrapped around his perfect back. The muscles slid and moved under my touch, the skin hot and flawless.

I let my hands venture. Tentatively. Daring them to find the impossible. I gasped into his mouth when I touched the hard junction where his wings met his shoulder blades. I explored further, my hands feeling the strong shape of one wing, the arch of bone covered in soft, glossy feathers. He never stopped taking me, making me ride him, while I was lost in the delirium of all that he was. The impossibility of him.

This is real.

A sudden, fierce pride rose in me that was taking all of him, even if it felt I would burst at the seams. Ready to explode into stardust with the ecstasy that was building where we were joined and a thousand other places where I felt him.

Finally, just as my sanity felt as if it were stretched to the breaking point, as if I couldn't contain it one more second, the pleasure released, flooding me. Consuming me like a wildfire run rampant. My nails dug into his perfect flesh, raking over the bunched muscles between his wings. I clung to him as an orgasm unlike anything I thought possible ripped through me. The pleasure went beyond physical sensation. I was given everything I'd longed to feel for years. Lifetimes. I became the heroine in every romance novel I'd ever read. Passages that thrilled me, or brought tears to my eyes, or made my heart pound or my stomach flutter. Every first heated glance. Every first kiss. Every first touch. Every longing to be protected, safe...*owned*. Every need to be desired, cherished, and wanted with fierce animal lust...I felt it all, all at once.

At the same time, Casziel became every tough hero whose walls are crashed in by love. Every stoic, stubborn man brought to his knees by his woman. His rough sounds of want and lust were a chorus of male need, all coalescing in me. I was a trembling puddle of sheer sensation, surrendering to everything he was doing to me and giving to me and yet powerful too. More powerful than I'd ever been.

I bit into the slope of muscle between his neck and shoulder as I rocked on his cock, rolling and grinding, drawing the ecstasy out until I was wrung out, sopping wet and drained.

Then he released me and lay me on my back. Urgently, he withdrew from me, and the impossible fullness fled with him. I let my eyelids blink, needing to witness him in this moment, just once.

Casziel was kneeling between my splayed legs, black wings outstretched to their fullest length and breadth—a kind of awful, dark majesty. His pale, muscled body was tensed, his head thrown back with an expression of agonized ecstasy. With one hand, he gripped his immense cock, stroking himself to the finish.

The sight was so impossibly erotic. So wrong and dirty and impure. I lay beneath him like a vessel waiting to receive. My fingers went to the throbbing wetness between my legs, stoking the aching need while he made a sound deep in his chest. He came on my stomach and breasts, his release like hot candle wax. I moaned and quickly squeezed my eyes shut before he caught me.

Too late.

"You peeked," he said, a mischievous edge to his tone. "And why are you touching what's mine? That beautiful cunt...it belongs to me tonight."

His dirty, greedy words lit new fires in me. I stroked myself brazenly. "Is that so?" I managed, still catching my breath. Somehow, still wanting more. "Then take it."

His eyes flared, black and ferocious. I shut my eyes tight and gasped as he moved my hand away and bent his huge, powerful body to the V of my legs. My tentative cry became a scream as he voraciously drew another orgasm from me with his tongue. He soothed the raw, throbbing ache his cock had left and drove me to another crescendo, until I was arched off the bed, hands grasping at the sheets.

When the last wave of ecstasy had shuddered through me, I fell back, limp and utterly drained. Now I couldn't keep my eyes open if I wanted to. Casziel's weight settled beside me on the bed, and he hauled me to him. His arms went around me, my head pillowed on his warm skin.

"Sleep, Li'ili. My fierce woman."

I was sinking into him, my body wrung out and perfectly heavy. Beneath that, the pain of losing him was like a fresh, ragged wound opening wider and deeper with every passing second.

"I can't..." I murmured. "I won't..."

"Ssh," he whispered into my hair. "Sleep, my beloved. We'll have the dawn."

But I took my vow down with me. I had Casziel back and I wasn't going to let him go without a fight.

I WOKE TO watery, gray light streaming in from the window. My body felt as if I were anchored to the bed, every part of me utterly drained but satiated.

Cas lay on his back, his amber eyes staring at the ceiling. His hair was rumpled and messy. Human. I didn't move but just watched him, soaked up his presence because now that I had him back, it was all ending. The clock read a little after ten a.m.

Seven hours. Seven hours and he's gone.

He'd told me that he'd go back to Ashtaroth's servitude and there would be no returning to This Side. But there was more he wasn't telling me. Something worse. A finality that scared me to my bones.

The daylight was like an insult, throwing our limited time together in my face. I remembered *Romeo and Juliet,* where the morning's arrival means Romeo has to flee Verona for killing Tybalt. Juliet holds him tight, unwilling to let him go, and pretends the day hasn't come. It was a playful moment, but Romeo's response sent a chill over my skin.

Let me be taken. Let me be put to death.

Cas turned his head on the pillow, misreading my expression. "Last night…it was too much. I suspected it would be. Forgive me. I was desperate to have you and—"

"No, last night was perfect," I said, moving into the crook of his arm, his bare skin warm under my cheek. "I don't want you to go."

He pulled me close and pressed his lips to my hair.

"Can you really not come back? Or maybe die and have a new lifetime as a human? Maybe we can find each other next time…"

"I wish that were so."

"I can't believe there is no forgiveness for you," I said angrily, tears pricking my eyes. "I refuse to believe it."

Cas said nothing but held me tighter. I ran my fingers over his skin, tracing the lines of his scars to the killing stroke over his heart.

"Tell me more about us," I said. "At the Irish pub—which feels like a million years ago—you told me that our marriage was arranged."

"It was," he said. "Marriage in Sumer was more of a business transaction between fathers than anything else. But you and I were different. Our fathers were friends, and our families were close. From the moment we met, there was love."

"I wish I could remember."

"I was eighteen. You were fourteen and—"

"*Fourteen?*"

Like Juliet…

Cas's chuckle rumbled under my cheek. "It was a different era. I'd already risen in the ranks of King Rim-Sin's army when our fathers arranged our engagement. Before we could be married, Hammurabi attacked, and I was called away to war for four years."

"And then you came back," I said, snuggling tighter to him. "I remember that. But I want the rest of our story."

"I can give it to you, Lucy."

I craned to look at him. "Even that last night?"

"That nightmare is best left in the dark."

"I want it, Casziel. I'm not afraid."

"Of course, you aren't," he said. "You're my fierce woman. My Li'ili…"

He kissed me, and while there was no icy heat or otherworldly aura behind it, it held its own power. The simple power of a man kissing the woman he loved. My tears spilled from under my closed lids as his mouth gently captured mine, tasting and touching. So familiar. The memory of us was a thousand years old and yet alive in that moment. But unfinished. I wanted the rest of us—our brief love that burned so bright and hot but was stamped out just as quickly.

Like Romeo and Juliet.

Now that my thoughts had latched on to the comparison, I couldn't stop, and the dread in my heart grew heavier with every passing second. Cas kissed me, beautifully deep and slow, with love and goodbye.

Thus with a kiss I die...

I pulled away, the sobs wracking me. He gathered me to him.

"I'm sorry, Lucy," he breathed into my hair. "If there was something else to do, I would do it. But I've made my fate. I ruined myself when you died and gave myself to darkness. The sins I've committed are not washed away by your sweet tears."

"I'm not giving up," I said, wiping my eyes. "And we have time yet. Tell me more about us. Our wedding. Was it beautiful?"

His gaze was steady and soft. Sad. "It was perfect."

"Show me the rest of our story."

"I will. But not yet."

He gave me a final kiss and then rose from the bed. My gaze trailed him, taking in his naked body that was perfect, scars and all. Except for that terrible brand burned into his back. It looked better, but the lines were stark and black on his olive skin. He pulled on a pair of boxer shorts from his pile of clothing at the foot of my bed and padded into the bathroom.

I heard the bathwater running, and the scent of lavender bubbles wafted on the air. He reemerged and wordlessly scooped me naked out of the bed, holding me under my knees and around my back.

"Are you going to join me?" I asked as he deposited me into the water that was just how I liked it—a few degrees below scalding.

"No," he said. "This is for you. For last night."

"If you insist," I said with a groan. I lay back, luxuriating in the perfect water. My body was pleasantly sore and aching, feeling as if it had been turned inside out with the intensity of...

Fucking a demon?

I pressed the back of my hand to my mouth, a crazed laugh trying to burst out. I'd really done that. Like performing a cliff dive when you're afraid of heights. Thrilling, death-defying, pushing oneself to the very limits... And you know you'll never do it again.

Cas took a washcloth and ran it over my face, my neck, under my hair and down my back. Then over my breasts and then lower. Even as wrung out as I was, I couldn't keep from arching into his touch. But he moved on, running the cloth down the length of my arm, ending with my fingers that he pressed to his mouth. He tossed aside the washcloth and folded his arms on the edge of the tub. I did the same so that our elbows were stacked one on top of the other.

"What happens next?" I asked as steam curled around us.

"I have until five tonight."

I nodded and realized the only way to survive this was to pretend Cas was going away on a long trip and I wouldn't see him for a while. Not never again.

Because it's not never again. It can't be.

"Is there anything else you want to do?"

He shook his head, his chin pivoting on his wrist. "I want to do whatever you want to do. Or nothing. Just be with you. That's all I've ever wanted."

"You were with me in Japan and Russia, weren't you? In the other lifetimes?"

He nodded. "Always from afar, wanting to make sure you were safe."

"My guardian angel, a demon."

He arched a brow. "I believe the term you hated was bodyguard."

I laughed. "You probably could've been a bodyguard-with-benefits in any of those lifetimes. But you weren't."

"No. It would've been wrong, to be with you like that." He held up a hand when I gave him a smart look. "Yes, I have perpetrated deception after deception upon you, but that would've been unforgiveable. To use you when I had our history and you didn't."

"Or maybe it would've given me dreams. The same sense of us knowing each other that I've had this entire time."

"Perhaps. I couldn't risk it. Back then my appetite for blood and death was sharp. It's since dulled and now I'm just weary."

I opened my mouth to ask him what it meant to return to that existence under Ashtaroth, but Cas shook his head and put a finger to my lips, then leaned over and kissed me. The kiss turned deeper, more dire. I had thought my body would never again be ready, but I ached for him in every way.

I stood up, the bathwater running over my body in rivulets. Cas's gaze drank me in, and I never felt more beautiful or at home in my own skin. I didn't need Casziel to complete me; his love showed me that I was already whole.

The water drained out. He wrapped a soft towel around me and lifted me onto the bathmat. He took his time, running the cloth over my body leaving my skin warm and dry.

Then he took me to bed.

The hours melted away—too rapidly—as the storm grew fierce outside, the rain battering the windows. Inside raged our own personal storm of anguish and love, ecstasy and despair, as each touch, each kiss, each thrust of his perfect body inside me took us closer to goodbye.

Finally, we lay in the quiet of my place, letting the storm howl for us. My head pillowed on his shoulder, my arm draped across his chest, and him holding me tightly. It was after one in the afternoon, and I was drifting toward sleep.

"Cas? I need to ask you a question."

"Anything."

"Where is my mother?"

I braced myself for a hard answer, but he said softly, "She's with you. She's always with you."

"But not like my dad."

I felt him nod. "How to best describe it... Each human has his or her own family of loved ones, though they're not always related by blood."

"Like a team?"

"Yes, a team. And they're with you through every lifetime, though the positions change, each member taking lesser or greater roles."

"They sit on the bench or they're your starting player."

He nodded. "In many lifetimes, you and your mother were very close. In others, one of you stepped back. But never away. Never away."

"They're just in the next room," I murmured and pressed a kiss to his shoulder. "Thank you, Cas."

I couldn't afford to lose a minute of our dwindling time together, but I was growing sleepier. When his time was up, I intended to do...something. I didn't know what, but I wasn't just going to let him walk out the door and into Ashtaroth's waiting arms.

Casziel kissed my forehead, each cheek, one eyelid then the other. I felt myself drift down. I fought it, but the current was too strong.

"I want to sleep for just a little bit. Just a little. But I want the rest of us. Will you show me?"

"I will."

"All of it. Our last night, too. Don't protect me from it, Cas. I'm not afraid."

"As you wish," he said softly, and I felt his lips on mine in a last gentle kiss. "I will give you us. Li'ili, my beloved."

I floated down to sleep and journeyed backward at the same time. Thousands of years to the mud-brick house that is filled with guests come to celebrate. It's dusk. The lamps are lit and she

wears her thick black hair piled on her head, and a dress decorated in gold and blue. Her eyes are lined in kohl and more gold and lapis lazuli glint from a circlet on her brow. The groom steps forward. He is wearing a kilt of leather, his jerkin decorated with gold coins. He lays a heavy necklace around his bride's neck. When he reaches around to fasten it, their eyes lock; they see no one but each other.

He places a veil on his bride's head and pours a few drops of scented oils over it. Behind the veil, her eyes glitter with tears.

"This is my wife," he announces to those assembled.

A great cheer goes up in the front room of the house. Her father— the high priest of Utu—smiles and nods knowingly. Men make lewd jokes. Women nudge the bride and whisper the hope that her new husband's axe has sufficient weight and heft to it, now that she's allowed to handle it.

Carried on this tide of lascivious merrymaking, the bride and groom lock hands and hurry upstairs to the bedchamber. A wedding bed of fresh rushes under soft sheepskin awaits. Laughing but with urgency fueling them, they strip each other naked and kneel on the bed, facing each other.

His fierce expression of want softens as he takes her face in both hands. His eyes roam, taking in every detail of her body. Under his armor, he's as magnificent as she suspected, proudly bearing the scars of battle. She cranes for his kiss, lips parted, breath hot. But he waits, draws out the moment. One by one, he removes the delicate hair clips of lapis and carnelian. Long ribbons of thick black hair pour down her bare back.

Her lips reach for his, restrained by his strong hand.

"Take me, my love. My husband. I'm yours," she whimpers. Begs. "Spill your seed inside me and I will give you sons. Fine, healthy sons. Strong, like their father."

He grips her neck, moved by emotion and barely constrained desire. "How have I earned the gods' favor, to be blessed with a woman like you?"

She shakes her head. "We cannot know the gods' will. Just love me, Casziel. Love me as I love you..."

"I will never stop."

She moves onto his lap, and he kisses her and thrusts deep, breaking her boundary with rough need. A cry rises to her lips, but he drinks it down and thrusts again. Taking her completely. Conquering her. She surrenders and is victorious at the same time. Her hands clutch his shoulders, nails digging into his skin, and she rides him fearlessly. The fire between them burns hot in every heated gaze, in every scorching kiss. Bodies move, bronzed skin sweat slicked in the torchlight. Her hair clings to her back; his hands are tangled in it as she comes down onto him. As he drives up into her.

Their love is raw and rough but deep, sinking into the marrow of their bones now that they can finally share their bodies. His devotion to her is complete. Her desire is for him and no one else. They are perfect in their love—Casziel and his wife. They move and breathe and touch as one. One soul in two bodies.

Their movements become more frenetic, more urgent as they drive each other toward bliss. He is darkly beautiful in his lust and tenderness. His animal need and his reverence. He fucks her as he loves her. And she

She is me.

The thought—the truth—nearly jars me from the dream or vision, but I fight to stay so that it can flood me completely. Centuries of dammed up love finally breaking free. Somewhere I hear my gasp, as my love for Casziel is all I know or feel. It ceases to hover at the edges of my awareness or reverberate down the long corridors of time like a mournful echo. It's real and restored to me in all its potent ferocity.

Tears blur the scene before me, but I blink them back. I don't want to miss anything. I want everything. Every touch, every sigh...

No more watching. Somehow, I will it to happen and I become her. I am

me and he's inside me—huge and stretching. He holds me tightly, protectively, his mouth taking mine, breathing his love into me. Sweat, sex, and the perfume in my hair hang heavy in the air. The scent of his skin, salty and spiced, fills my nose and I want to lick him and bite him, consume him completely.

The pain of our joining is still raw, but I want that too. I want to feel where he marked me. Where he took me for the first time. I'm filled with her fearlessness, her courage. But then, those were always mine, I'd just lost them for a while. Lost myself. Now I'm restored too.

I reach down between us, my fingertips running over his slick cock that is moving in and out of me.

"My warrior." I draw my finger down one cheek, then the other, my blood his war paint.

His breath catches then releases, like a gust of wind that stokes the fire higher. His hands are exquisitely painful, digging into my hips as his thrusting cock drives deeper and harder. I ride him just as ferociously, taking him to a peak as he takes me to the edge and over. I feel the pleasure in every part of me, erasing all pain. It consumes me until I'm delirious and crying out his name. Because there is nothing but him. My world, in memory and reality, is only Casziel.

And there is nothing for him but me. I see it in the fire burning in his eyes. I feel it in his hands that grip me and hold me tight to him. I feel it in the thunderous beat of his heart against mine, one answering the other.

He comes in me, grunting, his release hot and thick. I'm wrapped around him so tightly, sealing us together so there is no separation. For long moments, there is only the slowing of our rocking hips and our gusting breaths. At last, we're still. I remain impaled on him, not wanting to feel his absence.

Never again...

"Beloved." His voice is ripe with concern as he brushes strands of my hair that are stuck to my cheeks by sweat and tears. "I hurt you..."

I shake my head and bury my face against his neck. "No, I'm overcome. I love you so much."

He chuckles. "My Li'ili is overcome? Now I have lived to see everything."

I pull back to see him, hold his face in my hands. I'm changing the memory but maybe he'll understand.

"You are my light. My life. I will never love another as I love you."

His eyes darken with his own boundless love and lust that ignites at the fierce conviction in my eyes.

"Ki-áng ngu," he says. "My beloved. I will love you until the end of time."

He kisses me. Gently. Deeply. Then his hands slide down to cup my heavy breasts, to knead and caress, then move lower. To where we're still joined.

"I want this again."

I nod, and my eyes fall shut as he strokes my aching core of pleasure. My own need to have him is rekindled too, even though I'm raw and sore. I want him again. All night. Every night...

But we're out of nights.

The truth kept coming even after I gasped awake. I saw our last horrifying night in all its bloody clarity.

Babylonians stormed the house, taking us all to the ziggurat. Casziel was already there, on his knees. Torchlight flickered, casting slices of light over his blood-spattered skin. They'd tortured him to the brink of death, but his fire still burned. They brutalized him but he was still fighting. For me. For his family. His sister, his parents, and my father, the high priest—we were all bound and gagged and forced to kneel on the stony floor. One by one, they fell with necks sliced open and blood pouring.

And then it was my turn.

The horrified anguish on Casziel's face tore my heart to shreds. They hadn't gagged him, and his screams were ragged as the dagger was laid against my neck. With my eyes, I begged him to give himself mercy. Saving me was impossible. My death was inevitable, but I'd wait for him to join me in the afterlife.

My hand slipped to my belly, not yet rounded—we both would.

But he didn't understand and blamed himself. Then the blade opened my throat, and my last image was of my beloved screaming, head thrown back, neck corded, eyes bulging, every muscle taut and pulling against his bonds. His scream followed me into darkness...

And then there was nothing.

I shot to sitting in my bedroom, tears brimming in my eyes. The horror of what Casziel had endured wracked me while the love I had for him washed over every bloody memory. I clutched my abdomen.

A baby...

Joy flooded me and just as quickly curdled to anguish. My bed was empty.

"No. No, no, no. Not yet. Please…" I drew a breath. "Casziel."

Nothing.

"*Casziel.*"

Only the rain striking the windowpane—closed tight—answered.

Tears of frustration and fear pricked my eyes, but I wiped them away angrily. "No. Not when I just got you back…"

My gaze fell on a piece of paper sitting on my bedside table. I grabbed it, devoured it, even as it tore me to shreds, word by word.

My beloved,

Now the truth is wholly yours. But somewhere in your deepest self, you've always been Li'ili. Brave and fierce and so beautiful, my heart weeps with joy that you were once mine. Forgive me for concealing us, but there is no hope for me. I cannot cross the Veil and into the light. It's too bright and pure for a sinner like me.

You'll be safe. When I'm truly gone, Ashtaroth will be powerless, and you'll have others more powerful than me watching over you—loving you. That's the lesson it's taken me four millennia to learn: love is stronger than hate. You taught me that. You called my love forth—summoned it—and it rose up through the murky, bloody depths of me and broke the surface. I regret that it took so long; I'd have loved to spend an eternity of lifetimes searching and then finding you, loving you again and again. But I can't, and you must not let your light go out for me. You're too bright for one man. There is nothing small or silly about you and never has been. As the poet said, you contain multitudes.

And I'd like to think that even in Oblivion, there will be a part of me that remembers loving you, and I'll know peace at last.

I release you, Lucy Dennings. May my eternal sleep sever the chains that bind you to my damnation. You are free.

All my love is yours,
Casziel

23

I SOAR OVER the city in my anicorpus, riding the currents of air. The rain beats at my wings—little weighted drops that want to drive me to the ground. The wind gusts against my face, pushing me back toward Lucy.

But there's nowhere else for me to go. Part of me wondered if I'd wake up to a new life that morning, having been granted a second chance. But everything is the same. All doors closed to me except for one. So I left Lucy with what she asked for—the rest of our too-brief story.

And then I kissed her goodbye.

The old anger and rage flares in me as I land and transform into my demonic form in front of Idle Hands.

What did you expect? Redemption? You haven't repented. You awakened Lucy's memory, fucked her, and then left her.

I snarl at the unwanted thoughts and shove past the bouncer at the door.

The tavern is nearly empty, only a half-dozen tables occupied. Eistibus is in his usual spot behind the bar. Ba-Maguje, too, is at his post—head resting in a pool of his own fluids, inciting his humans to drink.

But I stop short to see Ambri sitting at the bar looking unlike himself—unsettled and anxious, like a peacock with its feathers ruffled. Indeed, his wings look less than immaculate. A faint smile—an echo of his usual cockiness—touches his lips.

"Casziel, my lord and friend, please join me."

"I have business here," I warn in a low voice. "You know this."

"Yes, yes, of course," he says, flapping a hand. "But the old man isn't going anywhere. We have time for a drink."

"Ambri…"

"Oh, come now. Let's have a round of shots and pretend like we can get drunk." Ambri signals to Eistibus. "Tequila, my good man. Ha! Has the absurdity occurred to anyone else that our meeting place on This Side is a pub? How peculiar. All of us sitting around, drinking like twits, nary a buzz to be had."

Ambri's stalling, but I give in and sit with him. He can't deter me, but his efforts touch me more than I want to admit.

I'm going to miss him too.

The djinn lines up two shot glasses and pours the liquor.

"Tip one for yourself, Eistibus," Ambri says, and we all lift our glasses. "To Lord Casziel. A bloody fine fellow."

"Hear, hear," Eistibus says, and the finality of it all weighs heavier.

We start to drink, but Ambri's jovial demeanor slips off like a mask, his voice taking a sharp edge. He holds his glass higher, his black eyes hard on mine.

"To my friend Casziel, the fool. A right bloody wanker." Ambri crosses himself with is free hand. "Forgive the daft arsehole, for he knows not what he does."

Eistibus holds his glass uncertainly. "Cheers?"

"That's enough, Ambri," I say and down my shot. The tequila burns a path down my gullet, and then it's gone.

Ambri tosses back his drink then slams the glass on the bar hard enough to shatter it. "Apologies, Eistibus," he mutters. "Hand slipped."

"Not at all, mate," the djinn says, still glancing between us. But he knows better than to meddle in the affairs of archdukes. When he goes to retrieve something to clean up the mess, I shoot Ambri a glance.

"Something on your mind?"

"Bloody hell, man, it's *Oblivion*," he hisses, leaning into me. "There's no coming back. Perhaps you haven't considered that as deeply as you ought. Because I have."

"I've considered everything."

"And your wife? I can't imagine she's happy with your choice."

"Her safety is all that matters. If it were just my soul on the line, I might seek a different way out. But now she's in real danger." I lower my voice. "Ashtaroth wants her, Ambri. If I'm gone, there is no reason for her to be tempted by his promises. And she'll be free to love again."

Ambri snorts as Eistibus returns with fresh glasses of tequila.

"You don't approve?" I ask and nod gratefully at the djinn.

"I prefer making decisions about the course of my own existence," Ambri says with a smirk. "But that's just me."

I scoff. "And risk condemning her to Ashtaroth's depravities? Because she would, for my sake."

"A horrid fate to be sure, and I'm no expert on such matters, but..." Ambri turns his black eyes on me. "It's her life."

He's right. The Li'ili I know would despise being a pawn in this game, even if every action I take is to protect her. Always to protect her.

I shake my head. "She cannot fathom what lies on the Other Side, and apparently, you've spent too much time on *This* Side and have forgotten. No, I won't risk it. I won't condemn her to endless suffering. Not when I can save her."

"While you simply cease to be."

"Is there an alternative?"

"Maybe there is," Ambri says with scorn. "I'm just spit balling— as the American humans like to say—but did you ever consider that the forgiveness you need is your own?"

For a long moment, I stare, then toss back the second shot of tequila. "Ah, Ambri. You've always been able to make me laugh." I lay my hand on his shoulder. "Thank you, my friend. I will miss you."

His lip curls, and he turns his gaze away, muttering to himself.

I wave Eistibus over and clasp his wrist. The djinn's expression is confused and fearful at the same time.

"My lord?"

"Farewell, Eistibus. And my apologies. It's about to get messy in here."

"Farewell?" Eistibus shoots a glance at Ambri who hunches deeper over his drink, still pouting.

I turn away from them both before I let Ambri talk me out of it. I stride for the door to the back room, unsheathing the greatsword from between my wings as I go. Other demons watch me with wide eyes, apprehension thickening the room like smoke. I struggle for a moment to get my blood up, to let the anger and rage for Ashtaroth flow through me. For the demon whose lies had coaxed me into this existence. But the truth is ruthless—he had no power except that which I gave him.

And I gave him everything.

The rage comes then, not at Ashtaroth but at myself. That I've been so foolish and weak. I failed to protect my wife and then had taken the worst possible way out of the agony, ruining us forever.

With a snarl I kick the door in, shattering it to kindling. I step inside. The darkness is lifted by the light spilling in from the common room, adding to the flame of the single black candle on its little table. The stench is ungodly.

Ashtaroth lounges on the settee, waiting for me, petting the head of the giant serpent coiled on the floor. The white python emanates its own ghostly light, its black eyes watching me.

"Such a dramatic entrance," Ashtaroth drawls lazily and then makes a face. "You stink of her." He cocks his head, smirking. "Been saying your goodbyes?"

My fist tightens on my sword handle.

"It doesn't have to be goodbye," he continues. "It will be easy to draw sweet Lucy into our realm. I'm quite willing to share her—"

I let out an inhuman bellow and swing the sword into the small antique table. The table's legs are reduced to splinters and the black candle hits the ground and rolls toward me, its flame never wavering.

"You will never touch her," I snarl between gritted teeth. "You'll have nothing to do with her."

Ashtaroth looks amused, my threats utterly inconsequential to him. "It's not entirely up to you now, is it? That irks you the most—that you've completely lost control. Your lies and selfishness have brought her to the brink. It'll be nothing for me to tip her over—"

Another roar and I bring my sword up with both hands and bring it back down in an executioner's blow; I cleave the serpent's head off. The body writhes and then goes still before evaporating into a pungent stink, back to the Other Side.

Ashtaroth's wings bring him to his feet, wrath snarling his features. "You go too far, boy," he seethes, drawing his own sword.

I ready myself for battle—my final battle—and suddenly Ambri is there, tugging at my shoulder.

"My esteemed lord, Ashtaroth," he says with a short bow. "Forgive Casziel, he's in a bad mood. Long night, no sleep. You know how it is.

I know how it is with those humans." He chuckles. "They really can wear you out in the bedroom. But he's better now, aren't you, Cas?"

I swivel my head to him incredulously. He shoots me an urgent look, then quickly turns his smile back to Ashtaroth.

"Awfully sorry about your snake, my lord, but Cas didn't mean it. Slip of the hand. Dreadful shame too, but it's back on the Other Side alive and well...er, perhaps not *well*. Or alive either, come to think of it."

"*Silence*," Ashtaroth roars. "Begone, Ambri." He turns his gaze to me. "It's obvious Casziel has unfinished business with me."

Unfinished business...

A twinge of a memory—a whiff of pipe smoke infiltrates the red haze of my rage but is quickly swallowed in the room's overpowering vapors.

Ambri bows again. "Yes, yes of course. I merely thought—"

I whirl on him. "*Go*," I snarl and give him a shove, afraid his wagging tongue will bring him Ashtaroth's wrath. He falls to his hands and knees, though I hadn't been as rough as that.

"My apologies," he says, rising and brushing off his red coat and backing to the shattered door. "I see where I'm not welcome. Shame to miss the fun, though. I'm sure it'll be a lovely sword fight. Not my favorite kind of sword fight, mind you..." He gives a little salute. "Right, then. Cheers."

When he's gone, I whirl back on Ashtaroth.

"Your time is running out," the demon lord muses, hefting his blade. "You will return to the Other Side and resume your servitude. If it means doing so on the end of my sword, so be it."

"So be it," I say and lunge fast, a beat of my wings giving me speed. My sword cleaves the air and he parries the blow, then pushes me back.

"Fool," he says, shocked—and pleased—by my ferocity. "But if this folly rekindles the fire you've been missing, then I welcome it."

And I'll welcome the look on his face when he delivers the killing blow and realizes it isn't sending me to the Other Side but to Oblivion.

With a cry, I attack again and the battle rages. He meets my every sword thrust, our blades singing. The curtains, the furniture...everything in the room suffers our fury and yet I come on.

We spill out into the tavern's common room, and I let my rage flow through me as it had the night I lost my wife. It gives me strength. Power. Ashtaroth begins to falter under my onslaught, but his arrogant smirk never wavers. For that I'm glad. He has no idea he's about to grant me my freedom.

Pain squeezes my heart with an iron fist.

Forgive me, my love. It's the only way.

"Yes, this is what I've been waiting for," Ashtaroth cries at our crossed swords. "My beautiful prince. The King of the South. Perhaps you'll reclaim your rightful place on your throne of blood…"

I shove him back while the other demons cower behind furniture or flee altogether. Eistibus watches from behind the bar as the storm of our battle destroys his pub.

Ashtaroth wards off another bone rattling blow from my sword, but I reverse my blade and it finally bites flesh on his shoulder. His eyes flare with rage. He thrusts a hand to me, speaks a word, and I'm blown backward to slam heavily against the wall.

"This is foolishness, Casziel," he says. "Come. Let us—"

Ashtaroth stops, listening. Then a smile I'll see forever in my nightmares blooms over his face. Delight lights up his eyes, and he turns to me with an expression of purest triumph.

"Ah. There she is," he says, like a little sigh.

Every muscle in my body goes rigid. "What…?"

But he's already dissipating before my eyes.

"No!" I scream and thrust my arms forward. "*Ma ki-ta!*"

The gale-force wind wrecks what's left of the tavern that is now empty, the stragglers feeling my fury.

I stare at the silent ruins.

"Lucy…"

24

"E TERNAL SLEEP?" MY tears dripped onto the page, blurring the words on Cas's letter. "No," I whispered. Then louder. "No. No."

I tore off my bed, put on a long T-shirt and sweatpants, and threw open the front door. Rain fell in torrents. Though it was only a few hours past noon, the sky was leaden and dark as if night were about to fall. Lightning crashed, and I turned my face into the storm.

"*Casziel!*" I screamed.

It was his true name. We were bonded. He had to return to me; he had no choice.

Nothing.

My tears mixed with rain on my cheeks. I inhaled deep to call again. To *command* him to come back to me.

"It won't work," said a low, smooth voice. "He's a bloody stubborn fool but powerful, nonetheless."

A little cry fell out of my mouth to see a beautiful man in a bloodred jacket of rich velvet leaning against the banister at the bottom of the stairs, a sword strapped to his slender waist. Black feather wings were folded tight, the rain streaking off them in silver droplets. His arms were crossed, casual, as if there wasn't a storm soaking him to the bone. Black eyes in a perfect face watched me.

"Who are you?"

"Ambri, at your service." He bowed low, his golden hair dripping. He straightened, studied me. "I can see why he loves you, following you throughout the centuries like he has. Truly, you are blinding."

"Where is he?"

"Gone to meet Oblivion."

The word had scared me down to my soul when I read it in Casziel's note and again when this demon spoke it.

"What is Oblivion?"

"Death for the dead."

"I thought demons couldn't be killed. They're immortal."

"All souls are immortal," Ambri said, "until they choose not to be. Oblivion can be had in a variety of ways. A demon slaying another demon while in his human form, for instance. Our mutual friend has gone to pick a fight with the only demon powerful enough to send him to Oblivion. If you wish to stop him, it's not Casziel you need to summon."

"Ashtaroth," I murmured.

"Indeed. But this is not child's play, dove. To save your beloved, Ashtaroth will require...an exchange."

But I already knew what Ashtaroth wanted for Casziel's freedom. I shivered in the cold rain, then set my jaw and ceased my teeth's chattering.

"How do I summon him? Saying his name won't be enough."

"Quite. You'll need to perform a true ritual."

Despair gnawed at me as the minutes slipped away with every falling rain drop. "How? I don't know what I need or what to do..." I stopped, thinking. "Ashtaroth's sign." The image of it was burned into my memory just as deeply as it was burned into Casziel's back.

"Clever girl. And this will help lock him into the sigil." Ambri rummaged into his jacket and withdrew a slender black candle. "I swiped it from the old man. You're welcome."

"But the rain...?"

He sniffed and tossed me the candle. "Black magic doesn't care about your rain. You're at the edge of the map, girl."

"Why are you helping me?"

He smirked. "It might very well be that I've *helped* you consign yourself to an eternity of suffering, the likes of which you cannot fathom."

"You're here for Cas. Because you love him too."

"Love is a strong word and not found in my vocabulary," Ambri said. "Or in any demon's, come to think of it. Rather goes against our principles, though I'll admit to a certain...*fondness* for him." He shrugged. "And if I were you, I'd want to have a say in my own fate. But try not to be too hard on him, dove. Casziel wants to protect you at all costs. Shield you—"

"From my own life," I said. "I don't want to be shielded. I want to..."

Live. I wanted to live my life, in all the pain and heartbreak and love and joy. I wanted to be the heroine of my own story. To not be rescued again and again by Casziel, if being rescued meant I was returned to my little life, safe and sound, while he suffered or ceased to be. He was worth saving too, even if he didn't believe it.

Ambri nodded, as if reading my thoughts. "Right, then. Well, I'm off. Take care. Try not to get yourself condemned to hell. It's not as fun as it sounds."

"Wait! Stay. Help me summon Ashtaroth."

"I've done all I can. Any more, and I'll be flogged with burning whips until the flesh is flayed from my body—normally an enjoyable experience... Besides, you don't need my help. I'm not strong enough."

"But I am?"

"Humans are infinitely more powerful than my kind." He leaned on the railing casually, as if we weren't in the midst of a downpour. "I'll let you in on a little trade secret: The only way we can defeat you is if you let us. Good luck, dove."

I watched, awestruck, as he dissipated into a cloud of shiny black beetles that took flight into the night and disappeared.

When Ambri had vanished, I hurried into my apartment and rummaged in my desk drawer for Dad's old Zippo. Before I could talk myself out of it, I went back outside into the deluge. The rain soaked through my clothes and left me shivering.

I searched the trash-strewn lot and found an old broom someone had thrown out. I cleared a large space in the dirt that was now mud—about eight feet in diameter—and closed my eyes. I recalled the brand burned into Casziel's back, every line, every swirl. Then I turned the broom upside down and used the end of the handle to recreate the pentagram with its lines and circles.

When it was finished, I tossed the broom aside, set Ambri's candle in the center, and lit it with the Zippo. There was no *earthly* reason why the candle flame should withstand the pouring rain, but it stood tall and calm in the storm.

I have to do the same. Be brave. Be brave...

I took a steadying breath to quell my rising fear. But there was nothing to decide. I had no clue what was going to happen next, but I had to do everything in my power to save Casziel. Because it wasn't too late. If I believed that, we were lost.

I stood at the foot of the pentagram and raised my arms to the sky.

"*Ashtaroth!*"

Nothing happened. I grit my teeth, ready to try again, when a vapor began to rise. The candle smoked unnaturally, and a foul stench rose with it. Snakes erupted out of the mud as if a pipe had burst underground. They slithered in writhing waves from the center of the pentagram to every corner of the lot, curling around my ankles.

It worked.

The plume turned into a cloud, the scent of rotting things growing almost overpowering. I fell back, my arm over my nose. Snakes hissed as I trampled them, and my heart tried to climb out of my chest at what I'd done—the evil energy I'd summoned that was literally writhing at my feet.

The cloud dissipated, and Ashtaroth was there.

At the wedding, he'd been wearing a human suit but now he towered over me in his terrible, demonic glory. Rainwater glistened off his black horns. His wings brought the night early, beating enough to keep his rotting body a few feet off the ground. An immense sword was in his hand, and he looked terrifyingly *happy*.

"I knew you'd call, my pet."

Terror wracked every part of me, but I recalled Ambri's words: *The only way we can defeat you is if you let us.*

I stood straight, chin up. "I summoned you. You have to do what I say."

He threw back his horned head and laughed. Booming, mocking laughter that rivaled the thunder.

"Ah, how beautifully innocent. *Lucy born of light.*" A sneer touched every word. "Very well. You've called me. Whatever shall you do with me?"

My throat felt as if I hadn't had water in years. I tasted a few raindrops and found my voice.

"Let Casziel go."

"Is that your command?"

"Y-yes."

Ashtaroth narrowed his eyes. "Done."

I blinked. "He's free?"

"Of course… For a price. You didn't very well believe I'd let him go so easy?"

"What do you want?"

"I've already made my terms clear."

Fear chewed at my insides. My voice wavered but I fought through the tears. "Okay. Let him go and…" I swallowed hard. "Take me instead. He's suffered enough."

"Girl," Ashtaroth said with a soul-curdling smile, "you don't know the meaning of the word." He held out his hand to me. "Come, my pet. Come…"

I realized then that Ashtaroth couldn't leave the pentagram. His outstretched hand was waiting for me to put mine in it. He couldn't take me, I had to surrender.

My soul recoiled but I could think of no other way. He'd already had Casziel for centuries. Maybe it was my turn…

I started to reach out trembling fingers when a raven darted in from the darkness. Casziel suddenly appeared beside me in his demonic form but dressed in his human clothes—black jeans, shirt, leather jacket. His skin was luminescent, his sword drawn. He put himself between me and Ashtaroth at the edge of the pentagram.

"Lucy," he breathed, agonized. "What are you doing?"

I touched his cheek. "Saving you."

"Saving…?" He shook his head, his expression aghast. "No. *No.* You have no idea what you're saying. I told you, you can't save me, Lucy. Nothing can."

"Love can," I said, hot tears spilling down my cold cheeks. "There's nothing more powerful. It can save you. I believe that with all my heart."

Casziel was shaking his head, and over his immense wings, I saw Ashtaroth, a triumphant sneer on his lips, raise his sword.

"Look out!" I cried.

222 | EMMA SCOTT

Cas shoved me to the ground and whirled, bringing his sword up just as Ashtaroth brought his down. Steel sang out against steel. Ashtaroth pressed hard—Casziel's sword dipped until it touched the ground—then Ashtaroth kicked his midsection, sending Cas crashing into the wooden stairs.

I cowered, my heels scrabbling against mud as Ashtaroth loomed over me.

"There is no end to your *husband's* lies," he said. "You *can* save him, sweet Lucy born of light." He reached for me again. "Come with me, pet, and I will release him—"

"*NO!*"

Behind me, Casziel morphed into his raven form. He streaked at Ashtaroth's face, wings flapping and talons slashing, tearing skin. His beak was like a knife as he punctured one of Ashtaroth's eyes. It popped like a ripe grape and dripped down his cheek.

Ashtaroth unleashed a scream of rage, and he gripped the bird in one hand. I heard the sickening crunch of bone, and then he flung the raven away. Casziel reformed on the ground beside me. His right wing was bent and broken, his right arm sickeningly misshapen and hanging limply at his side.

"Cas..." I cried. I rushed to him, kneeling in the mud. "Oh God..."

"Lucy..." he begged, his breath hitching with pain. "Please listen to me...Run. *Run.*"

I started to shake my head when there came a buzzing sound under the din of the storm. It grew louder and I turned to see a cloud of flies hovering behind us.

The cloudy mass became distinct and then Deber and Keeb were there in their demonic bodies. Deber smiled a ghastly smile through stringy gray hair and then stuck her tongue out at me. It was covered in flies. Keeb shuffled beside her sister in her shapeless gray dress, giggling obscenely. Their wings weren't black feathers but veined and clear.

"Our sweet boy," Deber cooed, cocking her head at Casziel slumped at my feet. "What a delight you've been."

"Yours?" I stared. "What do you mean?"

"Aye, he's ours. Like you," Deber said, and Keeb snickered behind her hair. "How else do you think we've managed to convince him how unworthy he is for all these years? He's so beautiful...beautifully *hopeless.*"

I felt sick at the torture Casziel endured for so long. My love for him grew fiercer when I didn't think that was possible.

He struggled to sit up. "Lucy, don't..."

I scrambled to my feet and pulled his sword out of his broken grip. I struggled to raise it with both hands—it weighed at least a hundred pounds—but I put myself between Cas and the twins.

The three demons laughed at my struggle, my wet hair streaming into my face, drenched to the bone and covered in mud.

"Pestilence," Ashtaroth said to Deber like a proud father. "Smiter." He inclined his horned head to Keeb. "Send Casziel back to the Other Side."

"No!" I cried. "No one touches him!"

"Fear not, pet," Ashtaroth said. "He can't very well stay here in that state. We'll sort it all out on the Other Side where he can heal—"

Movement behind me drew my attention.

A wickedly curved dagger had materialized in Keeb's hand. With a murderous shriek, she lunged at Casziel, intending to slice his throat. Sheer desperation gave me strength. I swung the heavy sword and cleaved Keeb's head off her neck. It flew to *splat* in the mud and her body collapsed with it. Both dissipated to flies and then nothing.

"Sister!"

Deber stared with black eyes where Keeb had been, then turned them on me, rage burning hot. With an inhuman shriek, she opened her mouth and a stream of flies surged out. I squeezed my eyes shut against the frenzied swarm and bit back a cry as Deber's fingernails raked across my cheeks, my arms.

With a grunt, I hefted Casziel's sword and blindly thrusted it forward. A heavy jerk shuddered up my arms and a cry tore from Deber. I peeked my eyes open. The demon was impaled on the blade, black blood gushing from where the sword pierced her midsection.

She glared at me with shock, then dissolved into a cloud of flies. They buzzed for a few seconds then disappeared too.

"Interesting," Ashtaroth mused. "Perhaps there is more to you, girl, after all."

I couldn't hold the sword anymore. It fell from my hands as I collapsed to the ground beside Casziel. He shook his head; black tears streaked his pale white cheeks. I curled my fingers around his good hand.

"I can make you...forget," he whispered. "All this terror. This nightmare. One word..."

"No. I don't want to forget you. I will *never* forget you." I bent my head and kissed him. "I love you. I have always loved you and I always will."

I started to rise, to go to Ashtaroth, but Cas took my arm with a shockingly strong grip, pulling me back to the muddy, snake-infested ground. He struggled to his feet, a grimace on his face, and gripped his sword in his weaker left hand.

He raised the blade to Ashtaroth. "*You...will...not...take...her.*"

Uncertainty and a twinge of fear at Casziel's tone flashed over Ashtaroth's face. Then he snarled. "This ends now. You will watch her willingly walk to her fate, the same way you watched her die in the bowels of your temple—helpless to stop it."

With a roar of rage, Cas lashed at Ashtaroth. The *clang* of steel rang out in the relentless rain. Casziel swung again in a deadly arc. Ashtaroth dodged and fell back, but Cas was relentless, even with a broken right arm and useless wing at his side. Another swing. Their blades clashed and the power in Cas's blow drove Ashtaroth back. Another. And another. It was all Ashtaroth could do to keep the silver frenzy of Casziel's sword at bay.

But it couldn't last. My heart was tearing in half, knowing every second was bringing Casziel closer to death. Worse than death—a return to the Other Side where he'd be enslaved to Ashtaroth for eternity.

Finally, with a thrashing of wings, Cas knocked Ashtaroth down at the edge of the pentagram, winded but unhurt.

Casziel turned to me. Even in his bloodless expression, even amid the dread blackness of his eyes, I saw and felt his love for me. It was pouring out of him like rain.

"You were right, Lucy," he said, his voice breaking. "Love saved me. Yours. It won't end with my death. I'll carry it with me..."

"Please," I cried, tears streaming. "Don't go..."

My words choked off in a scream as Ashtaroth rose up from behind. With one smooth stroke, he plunged his sword through Casziel's back. I watched, horror-struck, as the blade burst out of his chest.

Casziel's human chest.

In the split second before the blade touched him, Casziel had morphed into his human body.

Time seemed to freeze as Cas hung suspended off the sword, and then he slid to his knees. I caught him as he fell and cradled him against me. Red blood poured instead of black, staining Casziel's olive-toned skin. He turned his gaze up to me. Human eyes full of love. His bloodstained lips curled in a trembling smile. Somewhere distant was Ashtaroth's scream of defeat.

"No, Cas," I breathed. "No, don't... Oh, please, no..."

I put my hand over the gushing wound where the scar had been. Hot blood pumped under my palm. There was so much of it. Too much...

"No!" Ashtaroth cried and then put on a horrible, forced smile, reaching for me again. "Come, my pet. You don't have to stay here. Your grief...I can make it go away. I can show you how to use it. To take vengeance on a life so cruel. So unfair..."

"No." I stroked Cas's cheek as his chest hitched in horrifying spasms. I put my mouth to his ear, my tears streaming with the rain. "Listen to me. I saw everything. You couldn't have saved me. Do you hear me? It wasn't your fault. I'm grateful. So grateful to love you and be loved by you. I wouldn't trade one minute of it. Not for anything. Okay?"

Casziel was staring at the sky, his hiccupping breaths slowing. A tear brimmed in the corner of his eye and journeyed down his cheek. I kissed it, tasting the salt on my lips.

"Let go, baby," I whispered, my words choked by tears. "It's okay...to let go."

Ashtaroth loosed another roar, mad with fury. "She will know unending pain; I promise you, Casziel. I will send my servitors... Legions of them. You will go to your precious Oblivion knowing you have consigned her to infinite torment!"

He raised his sword, and I had a moment to wonder if Ambri had lied—that I was about to die. Then the lot was flooded with pure white light and the unmistakable whiff of pipe smoke.

Unfinished business...

Ashtaroth's agonized scream ripped the air. I squinted to see the light tear through the demon, ribbons of white flame burning through him and streaking on the ground like a fuse to destroy every writhing snake until there was nothing left. Ashtaroth's cry echoed through the ether. Then the light faded, leaving nothing. All was quiet, the rain pattering around me the only sound.

"He's gone," I told Casziel with a tearful laugh. "You're safe. You're—" My words choked off in a little cry. His eyes were staring, his body still. "Oh, Cas. No…"

I grasped at his bloodstained shirt, jostling him. His fixed gaze didn't move. I pressed my cheek to his chest and heard nothing. A low moan issued from somewhere deep inside me. From the bottom of my soul. For long moments, I just held him, rocking him in my arms, my tears soaking his shirt to mingle with the blood. I squeezed my eyes shut while the rain fell.

I don't know how long I'd been holding him when I heard gentle footfalls. The scent of pipe smoke grew stronger, sweet and familiar.

Slowly, I raised my head. "Daddy?"

The lot was empty, but Dad was there. I could feel him all around me.

"It's time to go, Lucy."

"No, I can't. Cas…"

I looked back down, Casziel was gone.

"No…" I clutched fistfuls of mud as the sobs wracked me, turning me inside out. "I thought I was ready. I'm not ready. I can't give him up again. Not yet. Please…"

The white light returned, this time less like fire and more like clouds or cotton. Soft and gentle and edged in pale blue. It wrapped me in a kind of peace I shouldn't have known, not when the grief for Casziel was still a piercing agony in my chest. The light didn't soothe the pain completely, but there was so much love in me, it suffused me until nothing was stronger.

Because nothing is.

The light grew brighter and brighter, forcing me to close my eyes again. As the air flooded with it, I saw a single black feather, stark in the white light. I grabbed it, clutched it tight, just as I was enveloped completely.

"Come on, pumpkin." Dad's voice was soft and warm and full of love. "Let's go home."

THE JOURNEY TO my apartment was slow and dreamlike. Every muscle ached, each step leaden. I trembled with cold, drenched with rain and covered with mud and blood. Casziel's blood. There was so much of it… The warm light and Dad's presence guided me to my bed where I clutched the black feather in my fist.

My head touched the pillow and I slept, and there were no dreams.

Hours later, I woke with a gasp and bolted upright, panic surging through me. The panic of having lost something precious…

Breathing hard, I glanced around. My T-shirt and sweatpants were clean and dry. The scratches and snakebites on my arms and legs were gone. Sunlight had broken through the storm, streaming into my place with silvery light.

"No." Anger, fear, and panic surged in me like a high tide. "No, it's not over. It was real. It was…"

I found the black feather under my pillow. I held it up to the light. Nearly a foot long, it had heat to it and smelled faintly of smoke and ash.

Grief wrapped around me like a tight band. Suffocating and merciless. Nothing felt real. My apartment was a set on a stage, the books and dishes and dead houseplant, all props. Only the feather—and who it had belonged to—was tangible.

A great sob rose in me, but I pushed it down and breathed like a woman in labor, waiting for the clenching pain to ease. It did but lurked, ready to tear me apart if I let it. I couldn't let it.

"Daddy?" I whispered.

Nothing.

My phone chimed a text from Jana.

RU OK? Missed you yesterday. Big stuff happening with our tennis star. Things moving quickly. Come in here and run this show, girl! <3

The idea of showering, dressing, taking the E train across town, and then facing everyone at work was the most ludicrous thing I'd ever imagined. But if I stayed home alone, flashes of Cas lying in my arms, bleeding—dying—would come for me. I'd be overwhelmed by living nightmares—demons with black eyes and slashing swords and Ashtaroth's outstretched hand, offering me a way out…

I texted, **Be there soon.**

Moving like a zombie, I headed out. At Ocean Alliance, the feeling of being on a movie set intensified. Jana hurried to me with a huge grin on her face that fell when she saw me.

"Woah, hey. Are you okay?"

"Fine."

"Lucy—"

"I don't want to talk about it," I said, my voice sounding unlike me—firm, strong, and leaving no room for argument. "Let's get to work."

Jana agreed but only because I didn't give her a choice. She sat with me, going over my research, now and then shooting me concerned glances that I ignored. Somehow, I made it through the day.

On our way out, Jana took my arm, stopping me.

"Listen, I don't know what happened. You don't have to tell me anything you don't want to tell me, but I need to know you're okay. Are you okay? Did something happen with Cas?"

His name was like an arrow into my heart. I managed a faint smile. "I can't talk about it yet, but you don't have to worry about me."

"Too late for that."

"I'll be okay. Promise."

Okay felt like a million miles away—a million lifetimes—but there was nothing Jana could do. It was unfair to burden her with the mountain of pain that wanted to pour out of me.

"See you tomorrow," I said and began the trek home.

Inside my place, I went directly to the black feather, safely stowed under my pillow. I'd wanted to bring it to work, carry it with me everywhere, but that was impossible. If I lost it...

I lost him.

The pain slugged me in the chest like a cannonball, but I pushed it down and made dinner that I didn't eat. I dressed in pajamas and held a book I didn't read. The next morning, I got up and did it all over again.

And the day after that, for three days. I was first to the office, last to leave; I hardly ate and stayed up until three in the morning attempting to read so that I'd fall asleep—exhausted—without allowing my mind time to replay the events of the last few weeks. But I was doing *just fine.* Everything was *back to normal.* There was *nothing wrong.*

Somewhere in the back of my mind, I knew it couldn't hold, but I was surviving. Even Deber and Keeb had nothing to say.

I've slain my demons...

I came home from work and my phone rang as I stepped in the door. Cole was one more vague text away from jumping on a plane, so I answered. Audio call, not FaceTime. If he saw my face, he *would* jump on a plane and ruin his final exams.

"Hey," I said.

"*Hi,*" he said pointedly.

"I know, I'm sorry. I've been...busy."

"We've both been busy plenty of times. This is different. What's going on, Luce? Please tell me."

Tears threatened but I blinked them back. What could I tell my best friend? That the love of my life—the love of my every lifetime—had been killed in a battle of demons in the empty lot behind my apartment? That there'd been flies and snakes and a candle that burned in the rain? That for a few precious hours, I'd found what I'd been missing and then it was ripped away?

I reached for the feather under my pillow and held it close, its soft tip brushing my chin. The heat of it and the ashy scent were fading. I closed my eyes.

"You were right," I managed. "Cas and I... You were right. It was him. Not Guy. Guy's in Sri Lanka but Cas had to...leave, like I told you. So...yeah. I'll be okay."

I was conscious I was rambling but hoped it all sounded like boy drama to Cole. I held my breath and let it out when the edge of concern in his tone softened slightly.

"Damn, Luce, I'm sorry. I thought he was the one."

"Yeah, thanks. Me too." I cleared my throat. "How about you? You sound tired. Still not sleeping?"

"Oh, the irony, I'm sleeping more but having crazy dreams... Anyway, doesn't matter. We break for summer in a few weeks. I'll come for a visit."

"No, let me come to you. I need to get out of this city."

"Even better! I can show you around, you can meet some people. It'll be great."

"Yep. Great."

"Lucy," Cole said. I braced myself. "You're my best friend. I'm not done worrying about you. I know there's more to the story with Cas than you've told me."

A flash of a sword bursting out of his chest racked me. I squeezed my eyes shut. "Uh huh."

"And I just want you to know that I'm here whenever you're ready to talk. Okay?"

"Okay. Thanks, Cole."

"Love you."

"Love you," I said and quickly hung up.

That night, I ate three bites of dinner and went to bed, staring at the words on the page of a book, not seeing them. I forced myself to keep going until my eyes closed and I slept.

My alarm went off the next morning, as usual. And, as usual, I reached under my pillow for the feather. My hand slid over smooth sheet. I tossed my pillow aside. There was nothing but a feather-shaped smudge of ash.

"No. No, no, no..."

I tore my bed apart, shook out the covers. Gone. The dam in me nearly broke, but I somehow managed to hold myself together. I dressed for work and headed for the door. In the middle of my place, purse in hand, I stopped. Edgar was still in his pot by the open window, utterly dead. His leaves were wilted and brown, falling off one by one. I'd watered him a couple times, but it was too late. He wasn't coming back.

THE SINNER | 231

I carried the plant to the kitchen, stepped on the pedal to open the trashcan, and tossed him in. The lid closed with a snap, and my bag dropped from my hand. I crumpled to the floor as the sobs shook me, breaking me down. I cried until my hands trembled and my stomach ached. Outside, the rain had returned–not a storm but a steady downpour. Inside, I cried my own deluge of tears and wondered if I'd ever get off the floor again.

But I did.

I dug deep and peeled myself off the floor. I dried my tears and went out. At the top of my stairs, I locked the door, then turned. My gasp was lost in the rain.

There was a dead body in the empty lot.

I froze, my insides constricting, my pulse slowing to a heavy clang. Not dead, my mind registered. I could see legs, moving slightly. Under the patter of rain, I heard a low moan.

I took a step down, then another.

Casziel was slowly pulling himself to sitting. He was dressed in all black—jeans, boots, leather jacket. He glanced around with a slightly bewildered look on his face. His beautiful, handsome face that I loved more than any other. His gaze landed on me, and he smiled.

"Lucy."

The deep tenor of his voice broke me from my stasis. I wanted to fly into his arms, the surge of joy so monumental and profound I could scarcely breathe. Or believe.

I shook my head, backing away. "No. No, this isn't… I saw you die. I held you while you died…"

"I know," he said gruffly. "I remember. But Lucy, I—"

"This isn't real. It's not real," I cried, slipping on a stair and sitting down hard. Tears started to pour again as my body struggled with a thousand different emotions. Hope flooded me while possibilities mixed with *impossibilities*. A demon was toying with me. Taking my worst pain and driving a new knife into the wound.

I covered my eyes. "Leave me alone. *Leave me alone!*"

"Lucy…"

Casziel's voice was agonized. I heard him climb the steps, felt him sit beside me. The scent of him—fresh rain and his own warmth— washed over me, clean and good.

"Lucy, it's me. I'm back. Somehow. They let me come back and now I'm here." I heard his ragged intake of breath, his voice rough with emotion. "Gods above, you are so beautiful. Look at me. Please look at me, Lucy. Look at me so I know it's not a dream."

I lowered my hands and opened my swollen eyes. His face was close to mine, his expression full of concern. And love. So much love.

"This is real?"

Cas nodded and started to speak, but I put my hand to his mouth, silencing him. He held still, his own eyes shining as I let my hands explore, holding his jaw, tracing his lips, his brows, the straight line of his nose. The aura of otherworldliness was gone, and he looked so very human—a freckle near his ear, a lock of damp hair falling over his forehead. Slowly, the solidity of him—the warmth of his skin under the cool rain—became undeniably real.

"Cas?" I whispered.

He nodded, tears standing out in his eyes. "Yes, beloved. It's me."

I finally let the truth sink in and reached for him, a ragged sob issuing from my throat. He gathered me into his arms, and we sat on the stairs in the rain, holding each other, his tears in my hair, my face pressed tight to his neck. We held each other softly, tentatively, then harder. He squeezed the sobs from me, and I clung to him, letting them pour out.

"What happened?" I asked eventually, pulling away to hold his face in my hands. "How are you here?"

He shook his head. "I don't know. It's kind of hazy. I was somewhere else, surrounded by white light. And I knew…" His voice choked. "I knew that light was forgiveness. And then I was here."

He's here.

"I can't believe it," I said, tears flooding my eyes all over again. "How much do you remember?"

"I remember us. And fighting Ashtaroth." He shook his head, his gaze distant. "I remember what I was. Something…not human. And I remember everything that happened while I was here but not the in-between." He nodded at the lot below. "Or what happened after I died down there."

"You don't remember the Other Side?"

His brows came together. "I used to know what that meant, didn't I? Not anymore. I don't think I'm supposed to remember. It's like a dream. I came awake in your backyard, and I think that's all I'm supposed to know for certain. That I've been given a second chance.

And that it wasn't love that condemned me. I loved you, but I hated myself for letting you die. That hate made me what I was."

"It wasn't your fault," I whispered, cupping his cheek. "It was never your fault."

"I finally understood that when I was dying in your arms. I heard you, Lucy. You said you were grateful, and I realized I was too." His voice cracked, and he looked away. "And that I..."

"What?" I asked softly.

"I never mourned them," he said. "My parents. My sister... I watched them die and buried the grief until Ashtaroth found it. I blamed him for turning me into what I'd been, but I did that." A trembling smile broke through his grimace. "She was so beautiful, my sister. Aria. Her name was Aria..."

I pulled him close. I kissed his jaw, his cheek, his temple. He raised rich brown eyes to me, so free of the pain that had lived in them when they'd been amber, that my heart broke at his beauty.

"Can I kiss you now?" he asked roughly. "Or if you want to start over...? Start slow?"

I shook my head. "I want you to kiss me. I want everything..."

He bent his head and pressed his lips to mine, hard yet sweet, with a small groan of relief stemming from his throat. I let out an answering cry, my own lips parting, and kissed him deeply. Surrendering to the moment, the completion. Four thousand years of lost love flowed back and forth between us, filling in all of our broken and empty places, making us whole at last.

We kissed and then simply held each other, my head against his chest, listening to the steady rhythm of his heart. I let my fingers trace his jaw, his neck, then down. There should've been a scar on his throat, but his olive-toned skin was smooth. I tugged the collar down a little.

"No scars," I said. "They're gone."

"But one." He pulled his shirt down, showing the silver dollar scar over his heart. "So that I never forget the gift I've been given. You, Lucy. I'm here because of you. You're my heroine. You saved me." He took my hand and put it over the scar. "You made me whole again."

Before I could speak, he kissed me again, and we went to bed. Our bodies fell into each other, and I drew him inside me, so beautifully perfect. He never stopped kissing me, so I couldn't tell him he saved me too. He pulled the walls down around my little life and showed me how wide and vast it truly was. How much I had in me and how much I had to give.

But we had time now. I didn't know how much—nothing was guaranteed. But I vowed to honor every day, every moment, with the love of my life.

This life and the next, and every lifetime to come.

EPILOGUE

I

One year later…

I UNLOCKED THE door to my little apartment and pushed it open. Moving boxes crowded the kitchen, though I didn't think we had enough stuff to warrant so many of them. I picked my way through the living room, bypassing more boxes, and hung my coat up in our tiny, over-stuffed closet.

I smiled and glanced at the clock. A little after four. Cas would be done with his classes soon. NYU's newest associate professor of Ancient Civilizations was also the youngest person to ever hold the post. The board of trustees had been ready to dismiss his application, having no résumé, no teaching experience, and no credentials of any kind. But whoever had given Cas back to me, had given us a little help, too. On that rainy morning, we found a wallet in his jeans pocket with a thousand dollars in cash and a social security card with his name on it.

"The money's from Ambri," he'd said, smiling fondly. "I was going to pay you back with it. And this…"

The social security card was his passport to this lifetime.

With my help, we put together a presentation that left NYU slack-jawed at his expertise. To explain his uncommon talent, he told them his family had taken great care to pass down the traditions of his heritage, generation after generation. It was a weak explanation at best, but while some archeologists and linguists could speak Sumerian, Cas was fluent. He unlocked doors to pronunciation and context that had been mysteries for thousands of years.

Now, major museums across the globe were sniffing out NYU's prodigy, calling on him to translate broken or faded tablets, identify and date artifacts, and generally fill in the missing pieces of Mesopotamian history with information no one could've possibly known…unless they'd lived it.

Outside, the November sky was leaden and gray. It was going to be cold tonight, the perfect night to cuddle up on the couch and watch *Schitt's Creek*, wrapped securely in Cas's arms. Then he'd take me to bed. We'd bring each other to one crashing orgasm after another, then lie tangled up together, whole and perfect.

I was at the window, watering Edgar Junior, when it came over me…that overwhelming feeling of being so impossibly happy, it was almost scary. Maybe it wasn't real. Maybe I'd wake up from this crazy dream to find it was no different than waking from the dreams of Japan or Russia. My bed would be empty, and that sense of incompletion would swoop in…

I heard Cas come in, muttering a curse at the boxes near the door.

"Hey," I called without turning, making my tone as light as possible. "How was your day? Did you—?"

My question dissolved into a soft moan as Cas slipped his arms around my waist and put his mouth to my neck. Pleasant shivers rippled through me as his teeth nipped, his tongue and lips migrating up to my ear.

"Did I miss you?" he finished. "Yes. Did I daydream about having you? Yes. Did I fantasize about taking you on my lectern in class, or on my desk in my office, or up against the wall in the hallway…?"

"That's a lot of places," I managed weakly, melting against him. "What's gotten into you?"

"The subject for today's lesson was sex and marriage rites an ancient Sumer," he said. "You have no idea how difficult it is to describe your own wedding night to a room full of college students without getting an erection."

I laughed, but it faded fast, and he felt my tension.

"What's wrong? I didn't actually give particulars of our night—"

"No, of course you didn't." I turned in the circle of his arms and stopped, arrested by how beautiful he was. How he looked at me with such love and want, the way I'd always dreamed of being looked at. It was all too perfect. Too good.

"You don't have to be with me," I blurted.

He blinked. "Sorry, what?"

"I-I don't know. I just...I need some air."

I went outside and sat on the top step of the stairs. I heard Cas follow me and quickly brushed away the tears of frustration that slid down my cheeks.

"Lucy. Talk to me."

"We were married four thousand years ago, but that doesn't mean you have to stick with me. Or be...obligated."

"Obligated," he said flatly. "But I am *obligated*. I'm obligated by how much I love you." He sat down beside me. "Where is this coming from?"

"Nothing. I don't know. My *inner demons* telling me this is too good to be true."

Cas muttered a curse and withdrew a small black box from his suit pocket. He turned it around and around in his hands. A little gasp fell from my lips.

"I should've given it to you months ago," he said. "Every day since I came back, I could've gotten down on my knees and asked if you'd be my wife."

"Why didn't you?" I asked softly.

He turned to me, his eyes heavy and full of love. "The same reason you came out here. 'Inner demons' telling me that it wouldn't be good enough. So I've been reading your romance novels for guidance. I wanted to make my proposal something special. To give you what they call a *grand gesture*."

A fresh rush of love swept through me at the idea of this man pouring through my romances, just like I had, looking for something he could give me. "Is that why you insisted on packing my books last? You've been reading them?"

"Yes, but I can't do what the billionaires do." An adorably grouchy scowl came over his face. "And how are there so many billionaires in the first place? Or British nobility? How many eligible dukes does the royal family have?"

I laughed. "You have to suspend disbelief in the name of love."

He scowled. "It's enough to make a poor professor feel inadequate."

"I don't need a grand gesture." I hid a smile in his shoulder. "But if you wanted to open the box, I wouldn't mind."

"Not yet. Your books taught me another phrase—the grovel." I started to laugh but he turned to me, so earnest and serious. "I must beg your forgiveness, Lucy."

"For what?"

"For so many things. Little wounds I've given you...and large ones. Ones that cut deep. For the time I told you to mind your fucking business in the department store. I couldn't stand the idea of you being worried about me. Already, your gentle heart cared for a bastard like me."

"Oh, Cas. You don't have to—"

"I do. I'm sorry I made you feel ashamed when you were dressed up to go to the singing bar, when in truth, I was stunned by your beauty."

"Really? I thought you hated all of it. The makeup, the dress..."

"No. The women in Larsa lined their eyes with kohl. You looked so much like Li'ili in that moment, I could scarcely breathe. But I did hate that red dress. Because you weren't wearing it for me." He brushed a lock of hair off my cheek. "But I liked your hair pulled away from your face so that I could see more of it. I never tire of looking at your face. I never will."

I could hardly see for the tears now. "Casziel..."

"And I'm sorry I didn't dance with you at the wedding. It should've been me, not Guy. I should never have put your hand in his. I should never have said those terrible things to you. I said them instead of what was in my heart, and that is that I'll love you forever. I *have* loved you forever, through every century, with every lifetime that's passed and every lifetime to come. There is only you. There will only ever be you. My love. My life." His jaw clenched. "And if you'll have me again...my wife."

He opened the box to reveal a gold ring with an oval of lapis lazuli, surrounded by tiny pale blue diamonds.

"Lapis is the sacred stone of our people," he said, taking the ring from the box. "The same color as your eyes."

My hand flew to my heart. "Cas...it's so beautiful."

"Not half as beautiful as you. In body and soul." He slipped the ring on my finger and pressed my hand to his lips. "Lucy Dennings…we were wed once before, but I'll never take your love for granted. It is the greatest gift I'll ever receive, and I'll spend this life making myself worthy of it, if you'll let me."

"Yes," I whispered. "Yes, Cas. Of course, I will."

His smile was breathtaking, and he kissed me softly, his mouth taking mine in tender touches, pouring his love into me. I could taste it, feel it, breathe it in until it filled me up and left no room for doubt. I rested my head against his chest while he held me, and we sat in the twilight, basking in the wholeness of us. The ring wasn't merely pretty, it felt like a seal to bind us together. A promise fulfilled, at long last.

"Will you miss it?" Cas asked after a while, nodding to the barren lot below us.

"A little. It's where I found you. Twice."

"You were so brave, Lucy. To see me as I was and take me into your home. To accept me."

I smiled. "It helped that you were naked."

He laughed a little. "I don't remember what happened on the Other Side, but I know I have a lot to make up for."

"Be one more good person in the world," I said. "That's all it needs."

"I think I can do that. I have you to show me how."

Cas kissed me again and the joy flowed through me freely. My beloved. My soulmate, and my happily ever after.

EPILOGUE

II

Two years later...

"**A**RE YOU SURE?" I asked, holding my wife's face in my hands.

"I'm sure," Lucy said, smiling gently. "If something is going to happen then it's going to happen. We can't let it stop you from this opportunity. It's huge, Cas. Once in a lifetime."

I shook my head. "The *opportunity* is nothing compared to you. If something went wrong and I wasn't there..."

"I'll be okay," she said, pulling my hands from her face and pressing a kiss to the tungsten and lapis wedding band on my left hand. "I insist. It's just a week."

A week was an eternity when your wife was nine weeks pregnant for the second time. Her doctor said everything looked good, but how could she know for sure? If we lost this one too...

"No," I said, the thought curling my stomach. "I can't leave you. The Cairo presentation will survive without me."

"The Cairo presentation *is* you."

I fumed. A trove of Sumerian artifacts had been discovered in the gulf region. They'd been transported to the National Museum in Cairo where they awaited me to date and identify them.

"It's a box full of rubble. It doesn't mean anything, but you...you are everything."

"And you are so sexy when you say things like that," Lucy said, kissing the scowl on my lips.

I started to protest but she cut me off.

"I feel fine. And you are brilliant. This is historic." Lucy wrapped her arms around my waist, resting her head against my chest. "It's going to be okay, Cas. Whatever happens, it's going to be okay."

I held her tight. "How do you know?"

"I don't. I just have to trust that our angels are watching."

"Lucy..."

"Go, or you'll miss your plane and I'll be late to my meeting." She kissed me again. Softly but with her own deep strength pouring in. "We can't put our lives on hold out of fear."

I nodded reluctantly. It had been a year and a half since our wedding, and I loved my wife more and more every day. Watching her suffer through a miscarriage had ripped my heart to shreds twice over—once for her and once for me. But she reminded me that we had to go through the hard stuff to make the good all the richer and that even the most precious things don't always stay as long as we like them too.

I kissed her a final time and dragged my rolling suitcase out the door of our Midtown apartment, leaving her at her desk by the window overlooking the Park. After the resounding success of their athletic shoe campaign, Lucy and Jana had opened their own company dedicated solely to sustainable apparel. I could not have been prouder of Lucy, working tirelessly to make real and lasting change for the good of the planet. She'd proven herself to be stronger and braver than I'd ever imagined, facing life's obstacles—and heartaches—with courage and love that never wavered. But each step away from her that morning felt like a betrayal. Or a horrible mistake.

Three hours later, I was waiting in line at airport security when a sense of urgency clenched my heart. I caught a whiff of pipe smoke in the sanitized airport air.

"Lucy..."

I shoved my way back through the line, fumbling for my phone while leaving a trail of curses and dirty looks behind me. I called her number. No answer.

"Fuck."

I was pacing in the Uber pick up area when a text came in from Jana—a string of panicked words that struck me like bullets.

Lucy's at the OBGYN. Something's happened. She was bleeding. I can't be there I'm upstate come quickly.

"Oh fuck, no," I breathed. "No, please not again."

The Uber came and I redirected the driver to Dr. D'Onofrio's office, the woman who had guided us through one agonizing loss already.

"Lucy Abisare," I told the woman at reception. "I'm her husband."

Her smile scraped at me like glass. "Oh yes, go right in. Exam room three."

I burst into the room and my heart ripped in half to see Lucy on the exam table. A paper sheet covered the lower half of her body, and one hand covered her eyes as she sobbed.

"Lucy." I rushed to her, took her free hand, and pressed the back of it to my lips. "Oh, my beloved. I'm so sorry. I'm so sorry."

She was shaking her head, hardly able to speak. "Two babies."

"I know," I said angrily, my own cheeks wet with tears. "I know and you're so brave. So goddamn brave."

"No, it's two babies," she managed through sobs. She uncovered her eyes to look at me, and I realized she wasn't grimacing in pain; she was smiling. "Cas...I thought they were going to tell me there were no babies but there are two babies."

I stared, my mouth ajar. "But...you were bleeding..."

"The doctor says it can happen. But I'm okay. They're okay."

I shook my head, disbelieving. "Are you sure?"

Lucy nodded and pressed her forehead to mine. "Two babies, Cas. I think they're the ones we lost... I think they came back."

"Oh my God." I couldn't stop my own tears from mingling with hers as I kissed her. "Twins. We're going to have twins?"

"Yes, indeed." Dr. D'Onofrio breezed into the room. "Congratulations, Cas." She gestured to the grainy black and white ultrasound on the wall monitor. "This is baby number one." She pointed out an indistinct blob in a little cavern of my wife's womb. "And this is baby number two."

A surge of joy tried to find me and hit a brick wall. "But Lucy...she's okay?"

Because fucking hell, I couldn't bear to watch her suffer again.

"I understand your concerns. We're going to be monitoring her very closely, especially given your history. But as far as I can see, everything looks good. Two strong solid heartbeats."

The doctor explained a little more, gave us instructions, and then left us alone. I clutched Lucy's hand, hardly daring to let her go.

"Jana called you," she said.

"She texted, but I was already on my way back. Someone told me to go back."

She smiled. "I'm so glad. I thought you were already on the plane."

"I think Grandpa made sure I wasn't."

Lucy laughed through tears, and I held her close, our foreheads pressed together.

"They came back," she whispered. "The two we lost; they came back. Don't you think?"

I frowned. She'd said that earlier and I'd missed it. "Two?"

Lucy nodded. "The first was in Larsa. Cas...I never told you. When I saw our last night, I knew we were going to have a baby. Li'ili—I—was pregnant."

I stared. "Why didn't you tell me?"

"I wanted to, so many times. But it seemed like it would hurt you for no reason. And then we had the miscarriage last year and I saw how you tried to be brave for me and take all the pain. But you were hurting too. And I couldn't do it to you again."

"You were trying to protect me."

She nodded. "I'm so sorry. I just...I didn't want to break your heart."

I shook my head, fighting tears. "We can't protect each other, Lucy. I learned that lesson the hard way. We can only be there for each other, through the good and the bad. Okay?"

"You're right. If you had missed this moment because I pushed you to get on the plane, I'd never have forgiven myself."

"It's okay," I said, kissing her forehead, her cheek, her lips. "I'm here. And I think you're right. They came back."

"A boy and a girl," Lucy said. "We're having one of each."

"You think so?"

"I feel it. I'd like to name the boy Garrett. After my father."

I almost told her it was tempting fate to give a name to these little flickering heartbeats, but that was fear speaking, and we weren't going to live in fear.

"And Aria for the girl," I said gruffly. "For my sister."

"Garrett and Aria." Lucy's smile was radiant. "Beautiful."

But she was beautiful, and my heart was filled with so much love, I could hardly contain it. And it came with a certainty that I felt in my bones. In my soul. We'd live again and again, sometimes pulled apart, maybe losing each other for a little while.

But we'd always find our way back to each other in the end.

EPILOGUE

III

One hundred and fifty-one years later...

"I THINK YOU should do it, Mom. It's been two years."

"You'd be okay with that?" I asked and tapped the implant in my temple to activate NeuroLink. I mentally asked for the air quality for New Los Angeles. The information scrolled across my vision, and I blinked it away. "Air-Q says it's going to be hazy today so bring your purifier."

"Yes, Mom," my daughter drawled, rolling her eyes. "And you're avoiding the subject."

I looked at my fifteen-year-old daughter, wise before her time. I'd always thought it was the divorce. It'd been rough on all of us, but once Giles and I finally agreed our marriage was over, I had room in my life for something besides anger and frustration. And our daughter saw it.

"I guess I thought it would be too hard for you to see me with someone other than your dad."

She put her arms around me from behind where I sat at the kitchen counter, blueprints for my next project hovering in front of us.

"What's hard is seeing you lonely and unhappy," she said. "You're too much of a hot commodity to be sitting at home alone, scrolling the entire Kindle romance library night after night."

"Not the *entire* library…"

She laughed and kissed my cheek. Outside the window, an empty car glided up to the curb.

"My ride's here."

"Have a good day at Demo."

"I will," she said, then made a shooing motion. "And you. Go."

I laughed. "Okay, okay. Maybe I'll go and get a coffee and see what happens."

"Ooooh, coffee. Sexy." She blew me a kiss and went out.

Through the window, I watched her go down the front walk. The batwing door of the electric car opened, and she climbed in. It glided away, taking her to Demonstration Complex #387, where she and her classmates would have to show that they could apply that week's data in physical space.

I initiated a conference call with my team of architects, their faces appearing on the screen in front of me, and we went over the plans for the new recycling center. It was the biggest one yet and yet not big enough. After high tides had swept Los Angeles into the ocean eighty years ago, it finally dawned on humanity that we were in serious trouble. Recycling plants began to pop up all over the world. Some said it was too little too late, but I didn't believe it. I believed in second chances.

Maybe even for myself.

When the meeting was over and the screens were shut down, I tapped my temple and called for a ride to the closest coffee shop to our housing complex. On the way over, I linked my order, and my cappuccino was waiting for me when I got there. I managed to find a table in the crowded café; the rest were occupied with people who looked like they were staring off into space, scrolling their Links.

Except for one man at the next table. He looked to be about my age, early forties. He kept himself in good shape—his dark clothes fit him well, and his black hair was thick and rich. Almost as striking, he had an actual book in his hand. Cutting down trees had been outlawed more than fifty years ago, but this was the real thing. He flipped real pages of words written on real paper. An antique. I was surprised he risked taking it out in public and nearly commented to that effect.

A little voice told me to keep my mouth shut, drink my coffee, and mind my own business. That this beautiful man didn't want me bothering him.

Those voices had been loudest in the worst months of my disintegrating marriage, telling me to stay, telling me that I was a failure if I put my happiness over the family unit. But when I stopped listening to them and filed for divorce, it felt as if a huge weight had been lifted. As if my life had been on pause and was now resuming.

I leaned over. "I'm sorry to bother you, but is that an actual book?"

The man looked up and the smile that broke over his face made my heart stutter. Light brown eyes met mine. They were soft with kindness yet sharply intelligent. He took in my suit, my face. Maybe it was just my imagination, but his gaze lingered on my own dark blue eyes, with a spark of something like recognition...

"It's real." He held up the book's cover. *From the Back of the Room: The Collected Poems of Weston Turner.*

"Oh wow, I love that poet," I said. "He's a favorite."

"Yeah? Mine too." The man extended a hand. "I'm Cyrus."

"Lilith."

"Pleased to meet you, Lily," Cyrus said, then gave himself a shake. "That's not what you said. I don't know where that came from. Pleased to meet you, Lilith."

We both realized at the same time he was still holding my hand.

He let go self-consciously. "Am I just batting a thousand or what?"

"You're doing all right," I said, grinning. An actual grin. I smiled for my daughter, for colleagues, at strangers to be polite, but it seemed like I hadn't *grinned* in years. "Have we met before? You seem awfully familiar."

"You read my mind," Cyrus said. "But I didn't want it to sound like a line. You might get up and walk away and I don't want you to get up and walk away."

"You're in luck," I said, my cheeks warming. "I don't want to get up and walk away either."

It's literally the last thing I want to do.

His answering smile was gorgeous, not only because he was a handsome man, but because of how personal it seemed. Intimate. As if he saved that kind of smile for private moments, warm mornings spent wrapped in bedsheets...

Oh my God, you really do need to get out more.

"I'd like to buy you a coffee," Cyrus said. "But you already have a coffee. So how about dinner? Is that too fast?"

"Oh, um..."

"It's too fast. Never mind."

"No, I'd love to have dinner with you," I said quickly, cringing at the naked eagerness in my voice. "But I have to check in with my daughter."

"Oh yeah? How old?"

"Aria is fifteen," I said and waited for the spark of interest in his eyes to fade. But he smiled wider.

"No kidding? My son Garrett is fourteen." Cyrus shifted in his seat. "I should check with him too, actually. Since when do the kids give the permission?"

"In my case, it's a side-effect of divorce."

"Same here. How long?"

"Two years ago. You?"

"A year." Cyrus held up his left hand and wiggled his fingers. "You can still see the tan line where the ring used to be."

I nodded. "I find myself touching my finger all the time, as if I were careless and lost mine somewhere. Then I remember and…" I shook my head with a small shrug. "But it was for the best."

"I'm sorry," Cyrus said, then thought for a moment. "But I'm also not sorry. Maybe it makes me a selfish ass, but I'm pretty damn glad you're not with someone else. It'll make our dinner so much less awkward."

I laughed out loud. "True. And I'm not sorry, either. About my divorce, I mean. It was hard but necessary. Giles, my ex, is a good man and a great father to our daughter. But I always felt like I was missing something. Always looking over my shoulder for who was walking through the door next. And that was so incredibly unfair to him." I glanced up, realizing how much I'd said. But Cyrus was listening. Nodding.

"I feel the same," he said. "I'll always love Kaylah—she's the mother of my kid. But I never felt…"

"Complete?"

"Yes. I never felt that way they say you're supposed to feel."

"Like how they do in the stories," I finished and tucked a lock of hair behind my ear. "And I'm glad you still have love for her. I think that says a lot about you."

He smiled ruefully. "Thanks, that's nice to hear. I've been feeling like a grade-A asshole. Like I failed at life."

"Me too," I said and suddenly felt shy. "We have a lot in common."

"We do," Cyrus said. "Poetry and failure."

I laughed again. "You know, I've laughed more in a handful of minutes with you than I have in years. Thank you for that."

"It's not by accident. I'm trying my best." He grinned. "I like your smile too much."

A soft moment fell, and I felt myself getting lost in Cyrus's eyes. The depth of them that was enticingly new and somehow ancient too.

"Well I guess we should exchange codes," he said.

"I think it's the thing to do, but I'm no expert. It's been a while."

"Same. But how about we try something else instead," he said. "Do you know the little Italian bistro on Trebek Boulevard?"

"That's a favorite."

His smile was almost perplexed. "Mine too. I'll link us some reservations for 8 o'clock." He slid the book across the table to me.

I stared. "Are you giving this to me?"

Cyrus's eyes widened with mock alarm. "My favorite Weston Turner? Never. No, take it and get reacquainted. Then give it back to me tonight at dinner and we'll compare our favorite poems." He smiled. "We can pretend we're in the olden days when people didn't download each other's history but got to know each other face-to-face. Does that sound all right?"

It sounds perfect.

"What if I don't show up?" I teased.

"Are you going to steal my book, Lily?"

"No, Cyrus," I said, and just saying his name sent a pleasurable shiver all through me. "I'll be there."

"I hope so," he said and rose reluctantly. "I'll see you tonight at eight."

"See you."

Cyrus left with a parting smile that took half my heart out the door with him.

Oh stop. Don't be so dramatic.

But I watched him go until there was no sign of him, then opened the book and flipped through the pages. Carefully. I couldn't believe Cyrus trusted such a valuable relic to a total stranger.

Because we're not strangers.

I flipped to a random poem called "Time Bends" and read, my heart thudding louder and harder with every word.

There's blood in my beer.
I drink it down
and wipe away tears.
Nothing makes the past gentle
Or easy to swallow.
The night comes like
a thunderclap.
Blackness drops like blindness.
Time bends.
It folds the years
and suddenly I'm there
on that dusty, bone-choked field.
It was two years ago.
It was yesterday.
It was last night.
Dreams become memories,
become now.
So what is real?
This moment,
this breath...
I close my eyes
and time travel
To the place where I died
The sand soaking up my blood
I wring it out,
drink it down.
It goes down hard,
grit in my throat,
a weight in my lap
I can't stand up
and walk away.
But I can be anywhere
Any when
I can kiss you for the first time
Again and again
All I have to do is
sleep.

I'd read the poem before—about Turner's time in the Army, serving in Syria many, many years ago. But now it seemed like it was talking straight to me. Lines jumped out, ripe with new meaning.

Dreams become memories,
become now.

I can kiss you for the first time
Again and again

I closed the book and held it to my heart. In a world of data and downloads, it felt solid and real. Cyrus felt real too in a way I couldn't explain. As if a piece of my dreams had taken shape and form, at long last...

The little voices in my head tried to talk me out of it.

A man that beautiful and perfect has to be a figment of your imagination. Maybe he's one of those new dating holograms...

The rest of the day crawled.

At eight o'clock, I stepped into the restaurant. Cyrus was already there at an intimate table for two. Instantly, my heart felt full and warm when it had no business feeling either. He stood up when he saw me, his face breaking into a devastatingly handsome smile of happiness and something like awe. I moved toward him as if drawn by an invisible white line tethering us together.

He took my hand and held it, his dark gaze roaming over me.

"There you are, Lily," he said softly. "It's about time."

But I wasn't late.

A strange joy—the feeling of something deep inside me falling into place—swept over me. My hand in his tightened and held on.

"I was about to say the same to you."

THE END

AUTHOR'S NOTE II

While a lot of this book is purely fictional, some unfortunate facts are all too real. This beautiful planet of ours needs our help if we're to keep it beautiful for this lifetime and every one of our lifetimes to come.

www.oceana.org

www.theoceancleanup.com

ACKNOWLEDGMENTS

A huge thank you to my Gal Friday, Melissa Panio-Petersen, still retaining her title as Most Thoughtful Person Ever. I thought of you many times as Lucy came to life on the page. She has a lot of your kindness and generous heart. Love you.

To my amazing husband, Bill, my partner in all things, who saw this book when it was a spark of an idea and wouldn't let me blow it out. Thank you, my love, for everything you put into it and everything you give to me every day as we journey through this lifetime together. All my love.

To my beta reader, Marissa D'Onofrio. You slogged through a version of this book that was a pale shadow of its true self, but your sweet encouragement and love for the rough collection of words helped see me through to the end. Thank you.

To Lori Jackson for hitting it out of the park in one try (and reminding me with your artistry why I'm an author and not a graphic designer). Thank you for bringing my sweet Casziel, in all his winged glory, to life.

To Mary Ann Martinez. Thank you for bringing Cole's drawings of Lucy to life and for sharing your incredible talent with me and this book.

To Nina and her team at Valentine PR. Thank you for sticking with me through the hard times, for granting me the space when I needed it, and for being there for me when I was ready. Love you!

To Teresa Reif. Your love and friendship through my hardest moments is really astonishing to me. Thank you for standing in the heart of my worst storms and holding my hand through them until they passed. All my love.

A very special thanks to James Barrett Morison and his Tumblr blog on the Sumerian language. Without this valuable resource, I wouldn't have been able to give Casziel his voice. (Although all mistakes and liberties taken are mine.)

Every demon in this book is "real" thanks to Theresa Bane and her Encyclopedia of Demons, from which I was able to cast this motley crew of infernal bad boys and girls. I'm grateful not only for her extensive research into the underworld, but for every new or crazy idea for the book that came with it.

To the members of the Entourage. I cannot convey how many times you give me the strength, love, and energy to keep going when I feel like I can't. I get so tired of posting about my hard times, not wanting to let you all down, and every single time you share your love with me and lift me right back up. Thank you for that. It means more than I can say.

And to Robin Hill. You truly never fail to amaze me with your generosity and friendship that I cherish so much. The time you give me, and the love and support, feel like a bottomless well. But I never want to take for granted all you do. You touch my heart every day. Love you.

And to the readers, bloggers, and members of this romance community. This book is for you. It's my entire heart on the page, it's my journey with Izzy, it's what grief can look like in dark moments, it's my father's despair and ultimate peace. It's me being as authentic as I can for you. Because you deserve no less. But it's also for *us*, the romance lovers who constantly find our genre maligned and belittled. Time and again, we are called to defend books that celebrate love in all its forms, and that, to me, is just plain crazy. This book is a testament to what I've survived and continue to survive, but it's also every bit my thank you to this romance community that has lifted me up time and again and who doesn't need to defend a thing. We know that the most powerful experiences in life are told in this genre better than any other.

And that love always wins.

SNEAK PEEK

The Muse (Ambri's story) coming soon.
Keep up to date on this release and all Emma Scott book news by
subscribing to her newsletter at www.emmascottwrites.com.

ALSO BY EMMA SCOTT

Duets
Full Tilt ◆ All In

Bring Down the Stars (Beautiful Hearts #1)
Long Live the Beautiful Hearts (Beautiful Hearts #2)

Series
How to Save a Life (Dreamcatcher #1)
Sugar & Gold (Dreamcatcher #2)

The Girl in the Love Song (Lost Boys #1)
When You Come Back to Me (Lost Boys #2)
The Last Piece of His Heart (Lost Boys #3)

RUSH (RUSH #1)
Endless Possibility (RUSH #1.5)

Standalones
Love Beyond Words ◆ Unbreakable ◆ The Butterfly Project
Forever Right Now ◆ In Harmony ◆ A Five-Minute Life
Someday, Someday

MM Romance
Someday, Someday
When You Come Back to Me (Lost Boys #2)

Novellas
One Good Man ◆ Love Game

ABOUT THE AUTHOR

Emma Scott is a *USA Today* and *Wall St. Journal* best-selling author whose books have been translated in six languages and featured in *Buzzfeed, Huffington Post, New York Daily News* and *USA Today's Happy Ever After*. She writes emotional, character-driven romances in which art and love intertwine to heal and love always wins. If you enjoy emotionally-charged stories that rip your heart out and put it back together again with diverse characters and kind-hearted heroes, you will enjoy her novels.

Made in the USA
Monee, IL
17 January 2022

89124608R00154